D0409171

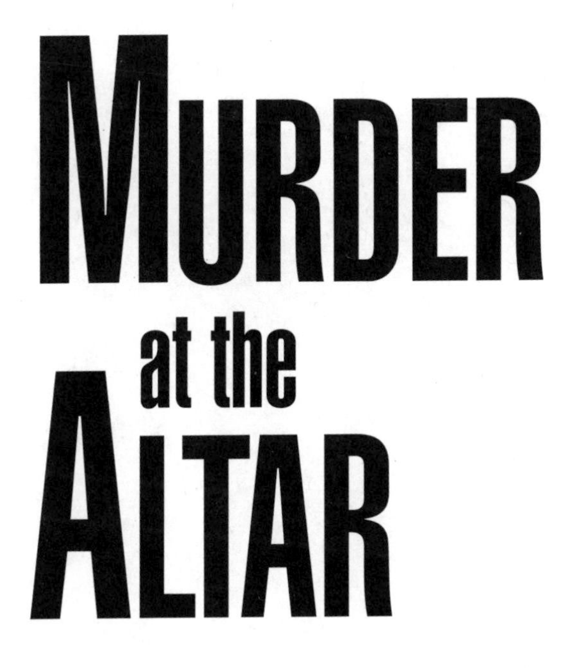
MURDER
at the
ALTAR

MURDER at the ALTAR

A Historical Novel

By Terry Phillips

Hye Books
Bakersfield, California
www.HyeBooks.com

"All human beings are born free and equal in dignity and rights. They are endowed with reason and conscience and should act towards one another in a spirit of brotherhood."
—United Nations Universal Declaration of Human Rights, Article 1

"Congress shall make no law respecting an establishment of religion, or prohibiting the free exercise thereof; or abridging the freedom of speech, or of the press; or the right of the people peaceably to assemble, and to petition the Government for a redress of grievances."
—United States Constitution, Bill of Rights, First Amendment

First printing 2008
Printed and bound in the United States of America.

For information, please contact Hye Books, P.O. Box 12492, Bakersfield, CA 93389.

Cover design by Chris Slattery
Page layout by Zand Gee
Print production by P.E.G. Solutions, Oakland, California.

Library of Congress Control Number: 2007937067
ISBN 1-892918-02-1

In memory of

my father, Gregory,

who always taught me

to tell the truth

CONTENTS

FOREWORD

Terry Phillips has written a mystery thriller that impels the reader to rush to the end. It is hard to stop until the final revelations. At the same time it is history, vital history for an Armenian community in America in the 1930s hardly two decades after the first genocide of the 20th century deprived this ancient people of its historical homeland and nearly annihilated its adult population. America was a refuge, but the most stable institution these new immigrants knew, the Armenian Church, was subject to internal dissensions resulting in a dramatic murder of its highest representative in the United States, an act committed in New York City in church during Christmas services and one that changed permanently the history of the Armenian Diaspora. Phillips brings it all to life after 75 years with details never before reported. By using the form of the novel, he has made what is a complicated affair very approachable, but perhaps controversial too. Great reading!

Dr. Dickran Kouymjian, Director
Center for Armenian Studies
California State University, Fresno

1

Then

Mateos Leylegian was not an especially violent man. Outside of his military service, he had never seriously harmed anyone, never broken any laws, never been arrested, and certainly never committed murder. No, this quiet little grocer had not been in real trouble his entire life. But all that was about to change.

On this Christmas Eve morning in 1933, the Armenian immigrant stood alone in the kitchen area of a tiny apartment at the rear of his grocery store on West Forty-ninth Street. It was in a particularly grimy section of New York City, close enough to the Hudson River that one could easily gaze at the New Jersey shoreline on the other side of the water. Yet, those who lived in this part of Midtown Manhattan did not enjoy a river view. Not in this neighborhood. And not from this apartment. And not this man. No, folks such as he didn't look up or out. They just looked down.

An old steam radiator sat in the corner hissing through smudged and cracked egg shell-colored paint. It heated the room to a stifling temperature. Nevertheless, Mateos was shivering. Fear and fatigue made him feel as if his head would burst, fall off his neck and tumble onto the floor. His sad, round, normally boyish face sagged from a lack of sleep. To look at him now, with uncharacteristically dark circles under his eyes and a strangely ashen complexion, you'd think he was much older than thirty-nine.

He had no appetite. An untouched slice of dark toast sat on the plate in front of him. Every time he considered taking a bite, his stomach muscles clenched tighter. Oh, he was hungry all right, but there was no way he could eat. He kept thinking about what had happened a week before.

More than one hundred members of the Armen Garo Club on Third Avenue got together that particular night to play cards, drink strong drinks and socialize. They called it a "tea party" – but everybody understood that it was much more than that.

Around midnight, a smaller group of men moved to a room in the back, locked the door and lowered the shades. The walls were decorated with pictures of military heroes. Prominently displayed was the tri-color flag of the last independent Armenian Republic. It consisted simply of three horizontal stripes: red for bloodshed, blue for the sky, and orange for the fertile land.

The group's leader strode to the front of the room with ceremonious gait. "You all know why we are here," he began in Armenian. "We are dedicated to the salvation of our motherland. We must protect and defend our nation, our culture, our flag."

A long, low cheer resonated throughout the room. The leader raised a glass of whiskey.

"To a free, independent, and united *Hayastan*," he toasted with dramatic flair, using the Armenian name for their nation.

"*Hayastan*!" repeated the group.

"To victory," continued the leader, nearly ready to drink.

"Victory!"

"And for traitors," he added ominously, "justice!"

"Justice!" repeated the group.

They drank. And then, one by one, each of the men swore to do what had to be done – to fulfill their destiny.

"*Jagadakir*!" the leader declared in Armenian. The term literally meant "written on the forehead."

Mateos took out a handkerchief and dabbed perspiration from his own forehead. The secrets he and his comrades shared that night would go with each of them to their graves. They had learned to keep confidences well. It was not only a matter of honor. It was a matter of survival. Lives depended on one's ability to keep secrets. Leylegian's own wife was killed during the Turkish massacres, quite possibly because someone had said too much. He would never make that mistake.

It was nearly half past seven in the morning now – plenty of time to get all the way uptown by subway, and plenty of time to get a good seat in church ahead of the expected crowd. Still, he worried. Because today, everything seemed to move at half-speed.

Slowly, shakily, he grabbed his coffee cup and gulped down the last swallow. He buttoned his woolen overcoat, put on his gray fedora, switched off the lights, and walked out the front door.

At the other end of town that morning, in the Washington Heights neighborhood, Nishan Siravakian was taking a shower when six men arrived at the front door. Siravakian's wife, Elise, answered.

"We're here to see Nishan," said one of them.

Being a good hostess and recognizing all but one of the visitors, she invited them in. "Please, sit down." Elise poured coffee and offered the men some of her delicious *pakhlava*. The layered pastry was her specialty.

A few moments later, Nishan walked into the dining room. "*Paree looys*," he said wishing them "good morning." Five of them responded in kind. The sixth – who bore a powerful resemblance to Siravakian – stood silently, cleaning his fingernails with the tip of a switchblade knife.

"Nishan, you must join us," said one of the men urgently. "We need you to come to Holy Cross Church."

Even though it was a block away from his home on West 188th Street, Siravakian couldn't understand why they would want to attend a service in this parish. He normally went to the downtown church on Twenty-seventh.

"Tourian is there today."

Ah, he thought, *now it's clear*. "OK, wait for me at the church. I'll meet you there," he said. Siravakian, a barber by trade, always dressed well. "Just give me a little while to get ready."

The men finished their coffee and pastries. The stranger who looked like Siravakian pocketed his knife.

"This is very good pastry, Missus," he said with a non-Armenian foreign accent. "Maybe you could give my wife the recipe and she could let you try her cannoli sometime."

Elise Siravakian smiled uneasily. Nishan showed the visitors to the front door.

"Listen, boys, when you go to that church, don't make any trouble."

"Don't worry, Mister Nishan," said the stranger." We just want to talk to him."

Then, he nudged one of the other fellows on the way out the door, and added, "*Ciao*."

In another Washington Heights apartment, Ara Gureghian had just finished getting ready for church. When it came to religion, the 28-year-old immigrant shoemaker was like a lot of Armenian men: They went to church on Sundays, but they didn't always go into church except on special occasions. Instead, they would stand outside, smoking, talking politics, and waiting for their womenfolk who were inside praying for them. But on this Sunday morning, Ara was thinking about the odd thing that happened the night before.

Across the street from his store, next to the Arax Restaurant was the Zarifian brothers' butcher shop. Around five o'clock, as Ara was closing up

for the evening, he looked through his front window and saw a clump of strangers on the opposite sidewalk. Never the shy type, he quickly locked the front door and crossed the avenue.

"Good evening," he said to the first unfamiliar face he encountered. The man ignored Ara, engrossed in quiet conversation with the other equally unfamiliar men. Gureghian reached out a friendly hand to touch the stranger's arm. He brushed Ara away with some force and a grunt.

"Beat it," interjected a second man in strongly accented English.

Ara was unfazed, recognizing Armenian tough guy wannabes when he saw them. Instead of leaving, he pushed past these bogus gangsters and into the store. Ara saw yet another unknown individual sitting at a grinding wheel, typically used by butchers to sharpen knives. Sparks flew as the stranger held a long-bladed, double-edged knife to the spinning stone.

Gureghian did know Dickran Candigian, the man behind the front counter.

"Give me a pound of coffee beans, Dick," he said to the grocer, while keeping one eye on the grinder. He was about to ask who the outsider was when the machine stopped spinning. Ara turned around. His eyes met those of the man working at the wheel. To Gureghian's surprise, the stranger gestured with a finger drawn across his throat.

Crazy, Ara thought to himself. Too tired to pursue the matter any further, he paid for his coffee beans and walked out the front door. The other strangers were no longer standing outside. Gureghian went home and gave it no further thought that night.

"Ara, come on. You'll be late." It was his mother, Nartouhi. She was going to church a bit later this morning but wanted her unmarried son to be there on time – while she was at home hoping for him to finally meet his future wife. That would only happen in church.

She straightened his tie. Even though the family had no money to speak of, Gureghian drove a nice car. The Hudson wasn't new anymore and it wasn't an expensive model, but always immaculately maintained. In the old country, young Ara was an apprentice to a phaeton carriage maker. When he landed in America ten years ago, all he wanted to do was design, build and drive cars. Now, at age 29, he was still trying to learn everything there was to know about them, inside and out.

"*Aghotk ureh intzee hamar,*" Ara's mother said, asking her son to say a prayer for her.

"OK, Momma." He kissed her on both cheeks, put up the collar on his black leather jacket, and set out into the frosty morning.

A few blocks away, Ohanes Andreassian and another man walked into the tiny Arax Restaurant on St. Nicholas Avenue. To call the Arax a restaurant is like calling your bathtub a swimming pool. At most, it might have been possible to squeeze a dozen patrons into the place at any given moment.

"Two coffees," ordered Andreassian as he and his companion sat down. A young German immigrant waitress quickly served them. Although they were the only customers in the place, both looked around nervously.

From the kitchen, Mike the cook recognized the voice of Ohanes in the other room. They had known each other some years before when both worked at another eatery downtown. The second man looked familiar, too, although Mike didn't know his name. He could hear fragments of conversation, mostly in Armenian.

"We have arranged everything. The traitor cannot escape," said one man.

"It will definitely happen this morning – about half an hour from now," the other answered.

"The wife brings the knife," said the first man in English, then quietly chuckled at his unintended rhyme.

Just then, Ohanes saw Mike looking at them through the kitchen window. He looked down at his cup, grimaced and then subtly gestured with his thumb toward the eavesdropper. Without finishing their coffees, the two men stood up, dropped some coins on the table and left.

2

Now

Everybody calls me Tommy. Well, almost everybody. My father always called me *moog* – the Armenian word for mouse. That might have been all right when I was a child, but it seems a little strange today. After all, this is 1975. I'm in my mid-60s and what some might call a "senior citizen." Personally, I like to think of myself as older, but not old.

Another name I have been known by is the one I used as a reporter: Thomas G. Peterson – Peterson being an anglicized version of my original family name, Petrossian. Did I mention that I once wrote for a newspaper? Anyway, an old editor suggested including the middle initial in my byline "to class it up."

I was born in New York City on the anniversary of the Great San Francisco Earthquake and Fire. According to a friend of mine, an expert on this subject, the City by the Bay was a victim of corrupt politicians and businessmen as much as of nature. I tell you all this because it helps explain my compulsive interest in conspiracies. I am convinced that the most important historical events are riddled with intrigue, manipulation, and hidden agendas. There is always more to every big story than we know – thus, my constant desire to discover what lies beneath the surface and reveal it. But I digress.

I am the only son of immigrant parents. My mother and father came to America from the country known as Armenia. Today, the place where they grew up is officially called Turkey. Of course, there is also an Armenian Republic, which became part of the Soviet Union in 1920. But when Mom and Dad lived in Asia Minor, it was ruled by the Ottoman Empire.

I should also say that, as a life-long bachelor, I am painfully aware of having produced no children – though not for lack of opportunity. And not for lack of practicing, either. In my wake, I must confess to having left a disturbing number of former girlfriends and one true love. Not that I'm proud of that. Quite the contrary. But by the time I understood the error of my ways, somehow it seemed too late – especially for that special woman whom I miss to this day. Alas, neither a wife nor offspring were in my destiny. Instead, I married the newspaper business and sired only stories.

One story changed my life – and the lives of Armenians all over America.

My passion for writing began in college, although I was truly initiated into the brotherhood of hacks when I went to work for the old New York Herald-Tribune. The Tribune was the Jimmy Cagney of newspapers: feisty, flamboyant, fast on its feet – and eternally dedicated to integrity.

At the height of the Trib's power and popularity, our paper was among New York City's top dailies – right alongside the Times, the Post, the Daily News, the Daily Mirror and the Sun – each competing to scoop the others, every one claiming to be the best in town. With all due modesty, I believe that we had the best writers and the best photographers. The police beat was a specialty, but we did a bang-up job with national and international news, too. Ours was a smarter angle, always giving the reader what would come to be known as a "different take."

Of course, it didn't hurt that the Reid family was willing to spend large sums of money to best their rival owners. For them, victory was never good enough unless it also included embarrassment for at least one of the other big rags. This spirit pervaded our newsroom, as I imagine was the case elsewhere. There were no rules limiting how far we could go to win this never-ending battle.

When The Trib folded in August of 1966, so did I. But that is another subject for another time.

For now, suffice it to know that I'm a retired reporter. Looking back, I guess I can't complain too much. Life has been good. And at the end of my career, I did what a lot of us New Yorkers do when we can't stand the cold or the rats or the high cost of living in Manhattan: I moved to Florida.

There's a condo off of Ocean Drive near Fifteenth Street in South Miami where I've been living for the past few years. I hesitate to call it home, but that is where I spend most of my time. It has a spectacular view of the water and is very convenient – close to shops, restaurants, the public library, and since I don't drive anymore, a bus stop. It's also remarkably quiet considering the crush of tourists.

My roommate provides good companionship and causes little trouble. He is a four-year old, jet black, short-haired cat named "Shadow." He's forever curling around my leg and purring at the slightest touch. Hardly a typical feline, he's not very finicky about food, either. I named him after the alter ego of my favorite old radio character – Lamont Cranston being an unsuitable moniker for a cat. Whenever I can't find something, I always ask my roomie because – wait for it – "the Shadow knows."

About a month ago, I was sitting in the dinette with my neighbor and fellow retiree, Ben Archibald. The native Floridian lost his wife many years ago but never got used to living alone. Consequently, Ben is a frequent visitor. We spend a lot of time together playing backgammon, shooting the breeze, and leering at the scantily clad young ladies who pass our complex on the way to the beach. (Hey, even aging widowers enjoy looking. No crime in that.)

This particular morning, Ben stopped by to borrow a fly swatter. (Who borrows a fly swatter?) He ended up staying for 30 minutes to tell me why the Hurricanes were a great team. I couldn't care less about Florida college football but it was raining today so there were no beach bunnies to ogle.

"Hey, how's the book coming along, Tommy?" Ben asked from out of nowhere. Like all ex-reporters, I told everyone I'd been working on a novel.

"Oh, I'm still sketching a few ideas," I lied.

"What's it about?"

I was stuck. There was no novel, of course. No ideas, no concepts, no notions. Nothing.

"It's about a guy who murders his nosy, fly swatter stealing neighbor." Ben let out a double-barreled shotgun of a laugh, grabbed the fly swatter and left.

Today's mail brought some sad news: An old friend passed away. Bedros Iskenderian had been a police officer when we lived in New York. His son wrote to let me know that "Izzy" (as I liked to call him) died peacefully in his sleep. I was planning to visit him next year for his 80th birthday. It was a grave reminder that life is short.

That got me to thinking about my own mortality. I lit my first and only cigarette of the morning. Gone were those days with two or three packs of unfiltered smokes. Doctor's orders. They went away with bottomless cups of coffee. Man, all this clean living would have killed me back then. Last year, a chest x-ray revealed a spot on my left lung. That led to a tentative diagnosis of cancer. Suffice to say that I'm living on borrowed time.

Izzy and I spent a lot of time together following the Archbishop's assassination. That story certainly had a huge impact on my life, so why not write a book about it? Maybe this was exactly what I had been looking for.

As I sat in front of the typewriter, Shadow slinked his way onto my lap. I rubbed his head with my left hand, rapped the keys with my right.

Where to begin, I wondered. *Where to begin*?

I figured that it would be easy, that this story would write itself. After nearly a quarter hour of staring at the sheet of paper in the machine, nothing happened. No matter how long I looked at that first damned blank page, the words refused to appear magically. So, as in my days of journalism, I stopped waiting for inspiration and just banged out what I knew. As the keys began clattering through the ribbon, Shadow sprang to the floor and settled down to sulk. Meanwhile, I wrote these beginning sentences:

> **This story was compelling to cover. Having said that, I never meant to get so personally involved. I only wanted what I always want – a good story. Well, maybe a great story. OK, I'll admit it: I wanted a Pulitzer Prize-winning story.**

I stopped typing and angrily slapped the page with the back of my hand. This was not going anywhere, I thought. There were plenty of facts in my head, but no story and too many gaps. Too many years had passed. I was, to say the least, discouraged. Clearly, I would need to go back to the place where it all happened. I asked Ben to take care of Shadow for a short while and rummaged through my closet for the warmer clothes I needed to pack.

3

Then

On this Christmas Eve morning, Tom Peterson was just another 23-year-old working stiff, going to church, looking for a little physical and spiritual comfort in the middle of a Depression-era winter. Franklin D. Roosevelt was in the White House, and after thirteen years of Prohibition, booze was legal once more. Happy days were, indeed, here again.

Tom strode briskly along St. Nicholas Avenue, past the familiar landmarks of Washington Heights: the Jewish deli, the Armenian shoemaker's shop, the Greek candy store, the Chinese laundry. As he lit up a cigarette and rounded the corner onto West 187th Street toward Holy Cross Church, the reporter noticed an unusually large number of people in front of the smoky brick building, waiting to go inside. While it was Christmas Eve in America, Armenians celebrated the birth of Jesus on January 6. So for them, today was just another Sunday. The main difference here was that the one conducting this high mass would be their Archbishop.

One man stood on the sidewalk handing out circulars to publicize the upcoming New Year's Eve party. This middle-aged chap wore a light-colored hat and warm, woolen, double-breasted overcoat – clearly well-dressed for the weather and the occasion. Nevertheless, he kept nervously stomping his black dress shoes on the slushy wet concrete, trying to fend off the chill. Tom did not know this other man, but he would later recognize him in a courtroom as Ohanes Andreassian who, minutes before, had sat nervously in the Arax Restaurant with another man.

Peterson worked his way up the front steps, past the crowd, and glanced back at the street. The remnants of an earlier snowfall hushed the sounds of those few automobiles that passed by. The window ledges all around were prettily coated in the fluffy white stuff, adding a festive, seasonal touch.

Tom took one last drag on his cigarette, then dropped the butt and stomped it out before going inside. He edged his way through the tiny, crowded vestibule, noticing that the door off to his left was slightly open. It led to the priest's office which the clergy and choir members were using this morning as a dressing room. On ordinary Sundays, the celebrants would get dressed in the vestry next to the altar and begin the Divine

Liturgy from there. But on special occasions (such as when an archbishop was officiating), a commencing procession would begin from the rear of the church. Thus, preparations were being made in this office today.

Tom peered inside and saw Ghevont Tourian. The Archbishop was hard to miss. The 54-year old clergyman was well over six feet tall and built like an Olympic wrestler. He had a massive head, topped with an abundance of coarse, jet-black hair, and complemented by a showy salt-and-pepper goatee. Even sitting down, he was huge.

Tourian had taken a vow of poverty, but it didn't seem to prevent him from being well-fed...very well-fed. Lavish and colorful vestments stretched around his more than bountiful girth. He looked physically suited to command. He certainly commanded attention. If he hadn't entered the priesthood, this fellow would likely have risen to at least the rank of captain in the military, or possibly would have become a captain of industry. But Tourian had religion in his blood.

Just as he did every Sunday morning, the big man was holding a bejeweled gold cross – a family heirloom. The item was more than a keepsake; it was a connection to his religious roots and a physical source of solace. Some people carry a rabbit's foot. Others keep photos in a wallet. Tourian had this cross.

Two deacons adjusted the Archbishop's glittering green, gold and purple garments made of fine silk and satin, intricately embroidered. Around his neck hung heavy, diamond- and jewel-encrusted gold chains. He closed his eyes and pressed that cross against his forehead, trying to clear his mind of the secular unrest that divided his flock. As Prelate of the Armenian Church in North and South America, Tourian stood in the middle of a most passionate religious and political controversy. It turned on the question of national independence for that little country which, a dozen years earlier, had become part of the Soviet Union.

The self-rule dispute had enflamed the passions of the Armenian community, but Tourian was trying to keep the Church out of this debate. He hoped to diffuse the highly charged emotions that sparked all around him. Regardless of his best intentions, the Archbishop had received some especially hateful criticism in recent months. He was even physically assaulted for his political views. The last attack happened in Massachusetts exactly two weeks before.

Tourian had celebrated mass at Holy Trinity church on Shawmut Avenue in Boston. That community was very supportive of the Archbishop. If his enemies were going to try anything, that might be a likely place.

The church board had been so concerned about the Archbishop's safety on that particular Sunday that they posted a trustee at the end of every pew during services to make sure no one could get out of his seat while Tourian was in the sanctuary.

Before the Divine Liturgy began, Tourian turned to his friend, Krikor Israelian, a member of the parish council. "Do you suppose we could have some *lahmajoon* for lunch?" he asked, referring to his favorite dish, a sort of spicy, cheeseless meat pizza.

"Of course, *Serpazan Hyr*," Israelian replied, addressing the Archbishop with his formal Armenian title. Krikor then quickly passed the request to his wife, Puregh, who left the church immediately, along with her mother, to go home and start cooking.

The origin of this dish is in dispute. Most Middle Eastern nations include it in their cuisine. Among Armenians, the best *lahmajoon* was reputedly made best by those from the city of Aintab in southern Turkey – the Israelians' hometown. It ordinarily required many hours of preparation.

After church services ended, Krikor brought the Archbishop to his house in nearby Medford where, miraculously, freshly-made *lahmajoon* awaited them.

In typically patriarchal manner, meals were handled entirely by the women. That, of course, included cleaning up afterwards. Meanwhile, the menfolk moved into the living room. Krikor sat next to the Archbishop and put his two-year-old son on the cleric's knee. Tourian tousled the boy's blond hair.

"You know that they're going to kill me," he said calmly.

Israelian vigorously protested. "We would never let that happen to you," he said, emphasizing that the trustees had taken extra precautions to prevent any harm.

"Just the same," insisted Tourian, "they're going to kill me." Then he turned to face his host and added, "Don't forget me."

A fortnight later, the parish trustees of Holy Cross Church in New York were equally concerned about Tourian's safety. They also decided to be very careful, and persuaded the police department to post a patrolman at the church entrance.

Armenians came from all parts of the Tri-State area to attend the December 24th service. Not much of a churchgoer himself, Peterson hadn't planned to be there. But it was Christmas Eve and he really didn't have anything better to do today. He wandered inside to wait for the start of the ritual *Badarak* service. The chapel was jammed. With well over 200 appropriately pious people, pressed shoulder-to-shoulder, hip-to-hip, there was barely breathing room inside.

Tommy had a theory about crowds: The more people there are in a given area, he reasoned, the less likely any individual is to be recognized. It's analogous to the old "can't see the forest for the trees" idea. With such a full house this morning, even some of the regular, dues-paying Holy Cross members were probably unaware that there were many strangers among them.

The reporter really didn't like large gatherings. In fact, he didn't like being around other people very much at all. That was a bit odd since his chosen profession required him to mingle with the masses rather regularly. So, he was already beginning to get a little fidgety. Peterson decided to slide into the right-hand bench nearest the front door, against the wall and be able to slip away if the spirit so moved him.

Suddenly, before he could duck out, the organ bellowed out a magnificent chord that signaled the ceremony was about to begin. It was too late to escape.

The seated congregants came to their feet. At the head of the procession was Mr. Minassian who bore the *pourvar*, a jingling and smoking incense burner. It emitted those sweetly pungent fumes which, in sufficient

quantity, could choke even the worst heathens into becoming believers. Minassian walked backwards, slowly waving the *pourvar* back and forth, and leading the solemn pageant into the sanctuary down the center aisle of the church.

Following him walked the church's pastor, Bishop Hovsep Garabedian. Next were fourteen members of the church choir, marching in pairs. Each carried a flickering candle with rivulets of wax dripping down the side of a silver holder. They sang out a hymn reserved for announcing the entrance of high church officials.

And then, majestically dominating the scene, marched Tourian. Slightly behind him came the two deacons, Sarkis Demurjian and George Kasangian, each holding a broomstick-length pole atop which was a round, ornate silver fan with a dozen small, rattling bells.

One more man trailed the group, but he obviously didn't belong – was not part of the ceremony. Unlike the others, he was drably dressed in an old brown suit. Peterson recognized this heavyset, hardened individual who wore a suspicious look on his face and a loaded .22 revolver bulging out from under his jacket. Khosroff Gorgodian was the Archbishop's bodyguard. At the urging of close friends, Tourian had hired the armed undercover agent to provide his personal security.

Gorgodian, a rug mender by trade, was known more for his bluster and sheer strength than good judgment. He had accompanied Tourian from his residence at the Hotel Seville earlier that morning and stayed with the cleric until this very moment. Now Gorgodian tagged along with the entourage only as far as the entrance to the sanctuary, and stopped just a few feet away from Tom. The bodyguard remained standing inside the vestibule, assuming that his protective services wouldn't be required beyond that point.

The music grew ever louder as the choir and organ competed to see whose vibrating crescendos would dominate the room.

Advancing toward the altar, Tourian turned from side to side, blessing the congregation. As he reached the fifth row of pews from the back, he raised his pastoral staff and cross. At that moment, Peterson was astonished to see a blur of at least half a dozen men bounding out of their seats and into the aisle. This was not a usual part of the ceremony. They sidestepped the acolytes and approached the Archbishop. One deacon tried to stop them, but he was brusquely shoved aside.

Tourian turned toward the two closest men, believing that they wanted a blessing. The pair smiled and bowed, and the Archbishop offered the cross for them to kiss. But before their lips reached the holy symbol, an explosion of shouts shattered the sacred ceremony. In an instant, Tourian was surrounded by a mob of men. Although the Archbishop towered above them, the phalanx prevented most in the congregation from seeing what would happen next.

Instinctively, Tom pushed his way closer. From where he stood, Peterson had trouble seeing the faces of those encircling the cleric – and probably wouldn't have recognized them even if he had seen clearly. Nevertheless, the reporter thought he spotted one stocky, dark-eyed man grabbing Tourian's hand, dropping heavily to his knees in front of the Archbishop, and blocking Tourian from moving forward. Another attacker seemed to pin back the victim's arms. Peterson noticed a third man hit the prelate in the head, knocking off his white miter, while several more held back would-be defenders.

Somewhere within this swarm, the assassin-in-chief brusquely brought out the butcher's knife hidden inside his coat and thrust its blade deep into the Archbishop's belly. In a flash, the double-edged, razor-sharp steel sliced through Tourian's outer robe and past the undergarments, penetrating vital organs. Without being fully withdrawn, the knife plunged again into the clergyman's bleeding body, this time with fatal effect.

At first, the Archbishop seemed nearly unaware that he had been stabbed. Several seconds later, he felt a sharp, searing sensation in his flank and started to choke. Tourian's face reflected the trauma as his eyes widened and his lips involuntarily drew back and down.

The Archbishop leaned forward onto his staff, causing it to creak and bend under his 220-pound frame. He let out a quiet but agonized moan. A white-haired woman in the adjacent pew caught the anguished look in the cleric's eye and began to scream. It was the first clear vocal indication that a crime was being committed. One by one, the choir members stopped singing. The organist stopped playing. The procession scattered topsy-turvy. Except for some sounds of scuffling, the whole place became oddly silent.

At that moment, Tom Peterson was no longer simply an Armenian-American worshipper in church on a Sunday morning. Suddenly, he snapped into journalism mode. His first priority was to cover this breaking story. The other normal concerns would have to wait.

But he was also a human being. Too much happened too quickly to comprehend in any meaningful way. It was difficult to know which way to look, what to see, how to prioritize. Peterson, the street-smart New York City crime reporter, was temporarily paralyzed in a state of disbelief and sensory overload – like everyone else.

Just as in a nightmare, Tom opened his mouth to yell, but could make no sound.

Just as in a nightmare, these few moments seemed to last forever.

Just as in a nightmare, the horrifying images would keep replaying in his head at slow-motion speed for a long time afterwards.

The man who was leading the celebrants, walking backwards with the incense burner toward the altar – Nishan Minassian – had momentarily looked over his shoulder to check their path. Hearing the commotion, he turned back and noticed the skirmish now in front of him. Minassian handed the censer to one of the choir girls and pressed forward toward the Archbishop.

Tourian had now collapsed to the red carpeting. The next day, the New York Times would report that he "fell full length in the aisle, with his head toward the altar, and his face turned toward a large picture of the Crucifixion, which hung on the east wall of the church." Even in this hideous tragedy, The Times found a poetic embellishment.

One of the deacons, Sarkis Demurjian, helped the Archbishop to his feet, not yet aware of how the cleric had been hurt. Despite Tom's momentary immobility, by now he had gotten close enough to see Tourian's lips whisper, "I am wounded."

The next to react was one of the choir boys in the procession. Ten-year-old Kalouste Keosayian was a tough little kid. He swung his candle at one of those who had approached the Archbishop, giving the guy a solid thump in the head.

Tom was locked in a semi-trance state, continuing to take in fleeting fragments of this tumult. The man holding the butcher's knife released his grip on the weapon and on a white handkerchief wrapped around its handle. The glinting blade fell heavily to the floor. The white cloth caught on the man's sleeve, seeming to defy the laws of time and space; apparently fluttering mid-air, futilely offering hope of peace; then surrendered to gravity and inevitability, breaking the spell when it landed.

The scene now erupted into total pandemonium. Congregants excitedly poured out of the pews and into the center aisle, the only exit path. Simultaneously, the choir was trying to escape from the aisle into the pews. Several people cried out, "The knife!"

Mr. Minassian spotted the murder weapon at the feet of one man being beaten by several other parishioners. That man was Mateos Leylegian.

The censer bearer picked up the knife and took it to the altar. He placed the bloody blade on the organ bench, then returned to the fracas.

Meanwhile, Tourian's bodyguard blinked himself into action, drew his pistol and commanded, "Give me room!" to those who blocked his path. He became a one-man platoon, fiercely thrusting his way into the thick of this chaos.

As he pushed down the center aisle, Gorgodian came face to face with the assailant Osgan Yarganian. This man saw the gun and tried to get out of the way. The bodyguard assumed this fleeing figure was one of the Archbishop's attackers, grabbed him by the hair and threw him to the floor.

"Don't move!" Gorgodian ordered. But Yarganian had already regained his feet and fled out the door.

Right behind him, Martin Mozian came running. Again, Gorgodian grabbed a clump of hair – this time with both hands – and forced him down. Unlike Yarganian before him, Mozian did not immediately get back up.

Gorgodian now encountered a third man, Juan Gonzales Tchalikian. This suspect did not respond to Gorgodian's threats, and was moving too fast and too erratically to grab. So, the bodyguard swung his revolver like a club and bashed Tchalikian on the head. Undeterred, Tchalikian also kept running and got away.

By now, Demurjian and the others from the procession were slowly helping the Archbishop to walk down the aisle toward the front door. Gorgodian finally got through to them and put his hand around Tourian's head.

"What's wrong?" asked the bodyguard.

"They hit me on my side," whispered the cleric.

As the fog in his mind cleared, Peterson was torn over what to do next. He decided to follow the Archbishop. Step by step, Demurjian and Gorgodian slowly half-walked and half-carried Tourian back to the priest's office. They carefully placed the big man onto an overstuffed sofa.

Standing in the doorway, Tom watched the deacon put Tourian's feet up on the couch. It was at this moment, seeing the Prelate's blood-soaked trousers, that Sarkis first realized what had happened inside the church. The Archbishop's breathing was now hard and heavy as he struggled to retain the last traces of his existence. Demurjian couldn't take anymore of this trauma. He dashed out of the room, out of the church and toward the street.

Meanwhile, Bishop Garabedian had pressed past the reporter. Seeing the Archbishop's now-limp body, he halfheartedly tried to comfort his superior.

"*Serpazan Hyr*?" he said weakly, addressing the Archbishop.

Peterson heard the deacon cry from outside, "Doctor, doctor, doctor, doctor, doctor!" However, Sarkis had not been the first to summon help. For an instant later, a neighborhood physician appeared with his medical bag in hand. Demurjian directed "Doc" Housepian to the wounded cleric.

The doctor arrived at Tourian's side and confirmed what the others already knew. After checking for a pulse, he shook his head. There was nothing to be done. The knife had inflicted injuries too extensive to treat. His life was irretrievable. He was gone.

Hearing a mounting ruckus in the sanctuary, Peterson was drawn back to the nave. It was the first time Tom could remember hearing curse words spoken inside this or any church.

Demurjian, who had run back inside, was a man possessed. He leaped at one of those strangers he remembered as having attacked Tourian.

"You, you!" he shouted, flailing fists and accusations. "You, you!"

Other members of the congregation exchanged blows. Most of the punches were landing on one man laying in the aisle – Mateos Leylegian.

Gorgodian was back in the church now and attempted to take charge. "Stand aside!" he shouted at full voice. His authoritative tone caused an abrupt parting of people who moved away like marionettes. Scores of parishioners fled toward the entrance. In a futile and nearly ludicrous effort to get to the murderers, Gorgodian again drew his pistol and began waiving it in the air, intimidating the crowd. The sight of his gun caused people to stop running and retreat from the door, possibly averting even greater frenzy.

Titus Zarookian, chairman of the board of trustees, tried to calm the crowd. "Don't be afraid," he called out in Armenian. "It's Mr. Gorgodian, the Archbishop's bodyguard."

Peterson had seen enough. He decided to walk out of the church before the cops got there. He knew better than to hang around, let alone insinuate himself into the crowd. Not only might he get arrested for obstruction, there was a good chance that the detectives would consider him a witness – and keep him from getting back to his office in time to meet tonight's deadline.

The reporter ran a half block to the grocery store on St. Nicholas Avenue and grabbed the pay phone to call his newspaper. It wouldn't do to get scooped on a big story he had exclusively – at least so far. But that was about to change, too. When the citywide communiqué went out, police monitors at every newspaper in town came to life. In less than half an hour, Tom would have a lot of company.

At the very moment of Tourian's murder, Nishan Siravakian was strolling up Audubon Avenue – oblivious to the calamity unfolding a few hundred feet away. When he reached 187th Street, he encountered a Jewish friend and his wife.

"Good morning, Nish. How are you today?"

Before Siravakian could answer, a woman's scream from down the street pierced the brisk air.

"What the hell?"

They raced to the corner in time to see parishioners pouring out of the church just as others were still arriving.

Nine-year old Anahid Boyajian and her younger brother, Leo, approached Holy Cross with their grandmother several minutes after the Archbishop's murder. Seeing all the turmoil, the old woman acted instinctively.

"Come quickly," she said, tugging her grandchildren back toward their apartment on Audubon Avenue.

Another Sunday school child, eight-year old Arousyag Amanatian, had been delayed by her younger cousin, Haig Ashjian, who was having trouble finding his hat. He heard his mother's admonition.

"Haig," called Nevart Ashjian as she saw her son heading bare-headed toward the door. "Never go outside without a hat," she reminded him. Her rule applied from the first day of October to the very end of April – a habit he would maintain well into adulthood.

As the cousins finally got to church, a teacher and several of the grief-stricken parishioners were already shooing other youngsters away.

"They killed the Archbishop," one of the adults sobbed. "Go home, go home."

In fact, most of the community children had been shielded from the morning's gruesome event. The Sunday school building was separate from the church itself. So, while unspeakable acts were taking place in the sanctuary, the youngsters and their teachers were too far away to know what was happening.

As the Boyajians reached the corner, little Anahid turned around and saw a man in a dark, pin-striped suit running toward them. He would later be identified in court as one of the Archbishop's accused killers, Defendant Number Eight, Mihran Zadigian. Not far behind was Antranik Desteian a church trustee. When he caught up with Zadigian, Desteian began to thump him on the head with his cane. The trustee struck with such force that the walking stick broke into three pieces.

Nishan Siravakian finally got to the church entrance.

"What's going on?" he asked.

"They killed him!" yelled one man who was knocked about by several others running outside. Nishan was also badly jostled in the commotion and steadied himself on the building's brickwork façade.

"That's the one!" cried another man pointing to the barber.

"What?"

"Him!"

"He did it!"

"Who?"

"It was Nishan!"

"No, no. Wait!"

Siravakian's friends extracted him from the chaotic scene and walked away, unaware of why several congregants thought he had killed the Archbishop.

Meanwhile, the N.Y.P.D. patrolman who had been standing guard outside in front of the church responded to the commotion indoors. Officer Charles Ueberlacker of the 34th Precinct's Wadsworth Avenue station bolted through the door to confront bedlam inside. As he tried to push his way through the throng, the officer lost his footing and fell to the floor.

"Hey, you wops!" he called out, using the only ethnic slur he could think of. "Let me through. I'm the police!"

Ueberlacker scrambled to get upright. He reached the spot where several parishioners were still hitting Leylegian.

"Satan!" cried one woman in Armenian as she spat upon them. "Damn you to hell!" yelled another. From all sides, congregants punched and kicked him.

"All right, OK, that's enough," said Ueberlacker. The hearty patrolman pushed away the furious church members and grabbed the detainee, who was now too weak to resist after his pummeling.

Khosroff Gorgodian tried to redeem himself.

"This is the one," said the Archbishop's bodyguard.

Ueberlacker shook his head. "Nice work," he muttered sarcastically, then shook his head again.

"Bodyguard," said one of the women nearby. She pronounced this word in three distinct syllables. It was the worst possible slur she could think of.

Another parishioner ran up to the policeman. "Officer, somebody has called the police station," he said breathlessly. "They're sending help."

"Good."

Ueberlacker decided to assert a little more authority before reinforcements (and, no doubt, superior officers) arrived. He took a deep breath.

"All right, nobody is to leave here," he announced, all the while holding his prisoner. "You are all witnesses to a crime."

He looked at the dark red pool of blood on the floor. It was almost exactly the same color as the carpet. Blood had also splashed onto the pews. The officer began to drag his prisoner past that spot where Tourian was killed. But intuition told him that something was missing.

"Where's the knife?" he demanded.

Immediately, everyone started looking at each other, then at their feet.

"There," said young Kalouste pointing toward the front of the chapel, twenty feet away from where the killing took place.

"On the altar?" responded Ueberlacker incredulously. The boy started toward the knife. "No! Don't touch it. Don't touch anything until the other police officers get here."

The patrolman took Leylegian out of the sanctuary and into the vestry. He shoved Mateos into a corner, opposite the Archbishop's lifeless body.

"Stay right there!" he commanded.

"Officer, officer!" cried a parishioner, gesturing urgently out the front door. "There is another one!"

Ueberlacker dashed outside and arrested a second man who was across the street. Other parishioners pointed at him and shouted, "Murderer!"

The patrolman brought Nishan Tuktikian into the church and stood guard, awaiting reinforcements.

The next policeman to arrive was Officer Julius Jacobson who was driving nearby when he heard the dispatcher drone, "Calling all cars, calling all cars in the vicinity of West 187th Street between Audubon and St. Nicholas. Report to Holy Cross Church. Possible homicide."

The patrolman was met at the front door by Nishan Minassian. "I want to show you the knife," said the censer bearer. Jacobson did not yet know what had happened, but was happy to deal with a cooperative citizen. The two walked into the sanctuary where Mr. Minassian pointed to the murder weapon.

"They killed him with that," said Nishan, pointing shakily at the knife. The officer gingerly picked up the weapon using the white handkerchief lying next to it.

Since the policeman had taken charge inside the church, Gorgodian pocketed his revolver and dashed outside to try capturing some of the other conspirators. When he reached the sidewalk, the bodyguard felt a hand on his arm. Gorgodian turned around and saw Ohanes Andreassian.

"Watch out," said Andreassian. "You are going to be next."

"What do you mean?"

"That is all I am going to tell you," he replied.

Before Gorgodian could ask anything else, he felt someone fishing for the pistol in his back pocket. The bodyguard brushed away that hand, grabbed the gun himself and headed back inside the church just as the sound of police sirens blared down the block.

Four more radio cars arrived from Emergency Squad Number 8 at Wadsworth Station. They roared to a halt. Out of the lead vehicle emerged N.Y.P.D. Detective Lt. James Donnelly. Just like a celebrity's grand arrival, Donnelly drew all eyes. Streaming sunlight illuminated his full head of red hair. The lieutenant was accompanied by several other detectives and a splay of uniformed cops. They pressed through the front door and into the church.

"All right, all right, everyone just calm down now," loudly declared Donnelly with his noticeable Irish brogue. Then, for what seemed like a full minute, he stood at the entrance and silently surveyed the entire scene. Hands in his overcoat pockets, he took in every detail.

Ueberlacker greeted his superior. He quickly ushered the lieutenant into the vestry and recounted what he knew: two suspects were in custody but there was talk of several more conspirators who got away. The lieutenant nodded grimly.

"Billy." Detective William O'Shea was instantly at Donnelly's side. He pointed at the accused killers. "Get those two gentlemen into a paddy wagon."

"Yes, sir."

"The body goes there, too. And witnesses – all of them. Those that speak English and those that don't." To no one in particular, Donnelly asked, "Where's the murder weapon?"

Right on cue, Officer Jacobson walked in carrying the butcher's knife which he had recovered from the altar. He handed it to Detective Frank Gowrie who, in turn, gave the weapon to his superior officer. Lt. Donnelly carefully examined it without even the slightest touch. It was a rather new-looking knife with an eight-inch blade and a wooden handle. The lieutenant noticed that the droplets of blood on the cutting edges were still wet and spotted rather than smeared.

"*Trying to avoid fingerprints, they were*," Donnelly thought to himself, pointing at the handkerchief. The policeman saw no symbolism in this white cloth, only evidence.

"Fine. Billy, take this, too." O'Shea handled it cautiously, almost tenderly.

Again to himself, Donnelly thought, "*Chrissakes. What kind of people murder a priest in a church?*" He shook his head and muttered, "Fuckin' animals."

A number of parishioners had gathered outside, and were gradually managing to overcome the shock as they stood under an unseasonably sunny sky. Among them was the shoemaker, Ara Gureghian. He was trying to make sense of the tumult around him. Ara noticed one man approach a parked car across the street and urgently tell its occupants to drive away.

Many people in the growing crowd outside were crying. Every single face was either flushed or wet or both. With handkerchiefs and with bare hands, they wiped tears and anger from their faces.

Through the cacophony, Gureghian tried to discern other snippets of conversation. He heard several people saying that the Archbishop's death was a blessing.

"He was nothing but trouble for us," declared one man in Armenian.

"He was stupid," said another.

"Shut up, you!" replied a third in the same language.

"That's no way to speak about our dead Archbishop," added a fourth man.

The pairs began to shove and scuffle. But then, like an act of divine intervention, a sudden gust of wind came up and blew dust into the eyes of the would-be brawlers, momentarily distracting them from their argument. They were quickly separated by other parishioners.

"Why are you back so soon?" asked Elise Siravakian when her husband walked in the front door.

"Sit down, dear." Nishan told his wife what had happened. "Now I know why they wanted me to go with them."

"Thank God you didn't," she said after learning about the tragedy.

The two sat in the kitchen and stared at the floor for several long minutes. Neither knew what to think, let alone what to say. Finally, Nishan looked up at his wife, with a sudden questioning expression.

"By the way," he asked haltingly, "who— who was that other man up here this morning?"

"What other man?"

"You know, the *odar*," he said, using the Armenian word for foreigner.

"They told me he was an Italian friend from Chicago."

The barber blinked at his wife. "Italian?"

She nodded. "From Chicago." A shiver went through her body.

"Italian from Chicago?" Siravakian shook his head. *That doesn't make any sense*, he thought. As Nishan loosened his tie and removed his suit jacket, his face suddenly blanched. "I don't feel so good," he said. "I'm going to get undressed. I'm going back to bed."

Elise wiped a single tear from her cheek, and then covered her mouth. This

Italian from Chicago bore an uncanny resemblance to her husband. *Meeyah*, she whispered to herself. It was an old country expression, roughly equivalent to the Yiddish *oy vey* but with a greater sense of doom.

It took several days for news of Ghevont Tourian's death to reach his folks in the old country. His aunt decided not to tell the Archbishop's mother who had been quite ill with a cancer. It was generally feared that the shock of hearing about the cleric's slaying might kill her, too. So, the relatives conspired to keep up the illusion of a living son. Her mail and newspapers were carefully censored. Visitors were warned to say nothing about what had happened. In her presence, they would hide their grief. From time to time, they invented, and then read to her his letters from America. Since she was bed-ridden, there was no risk of strangers on the street accidentally disclosing the fact of his murder.

When family members went out, they would change into black mourning clothes, and then put on normal garments when they returned – always away from his mother's sight. Mrs. Tourian would never know the awful truth about her son's assassination. But even in this faraway land, the impact of Archbishop Tourian's life and death continued long after his passing.

4

Now

The Silver Meteor pulled out of Amtrak's Miami station at 7:25 a.m. I never did like to fly, and ever since wrenching my back in an auto accident a few years ago, I considered the rails friendlier than the "friendly skies" – despite what the advertisements said. I found train travel to be much more relaxing and much more civilized, even if not always cheaper.

I had settled into my sleeper compartment and waited for the car attendant to come by. He showed up before we cleared the city limits. Charlie wore a snappy uniform and had the demeanor of one who had been born into his job.

"Good morning, sir," he said leaning lightly against the door jamb. "May I check your ticket please?"

I handed him the red, white and mostly blue envelope.

"New York City. You must be heading home, Mr. Peterson," he speculated. "Nobody from Florida goes to New York in the middle of winter."

"I'm going to look for ghosts," I replied.

"Oh really?" He played along. "Well, you be careful now."

Charlie handed back my ticket, then quickly gave me brief instructions on how to use the various facilities. This private Viewliner was quite a splurge, but I couldn't see myself sitting in a single seat for 36 hours.

"I'll come by to take your meal reservations later on. Would you like a newspaper, sir?" he asked, offering me a variety of dailies.

I took the New York Times and sat down. With more than a day's journey ahead, I figured I'd have plenty of time to collect my thoughts. I had never stopped wondering about the Tourian murder. *Did the police arrest the real killer? Who was really responsible for the Archbishop's death?* Maybe my re-investigation could lay those doubts to rest.

I had written hundreds of stories over the years. But none had any real impact. I always felt a desire to accomplish something of duration. Maybe this book would give me the satisfaction I lacked. It was a good reason to take this trip.

I brought along a medium-sized notebook which I fully intended to turn into a travel journal. But instead of writing, I immediately found myself glued to the window watching the East Coast roll by. Our first long stop – lasting about 20 minutes – wouldn't be until late afternoon in Jacksonville. I gradually became accustomed to the constant clack-clack soundtrack accompanying the *cinema vérité* passing before my eyes. The scenery was mostly a mix of houses, flat lands, and orange groves.

Once we were out of Florida, I was taken aback by reminders that it was Christmas time. Entire neighborhoods seemed to have lights on their houses. Some folks put up decorations in Miami, but it never really felt like Christmas to me there. For a brief moment, I recalled the oncologist's recent warning that this might be my last Christmas. With so little time left, he said, I should make each day count. That was another good reason for this trip.

I took my meals in the dining car, mostly to begin acclimating myself to being around lots of other people again. My life had become quite solitary these past few years and I knew that the crush of seven million New Yorkers would be a bit of a shock. So, I deliberately put myself among strangers. That's the way single diners are seated on a train – with strangers. It was all very polite, very 19th century. Gentlemen stood for ladies and would have tipped our hats if we were wearing them. The staff dressed in very starched, very white uniforms and positively oozed courtesy. Besides all that, the food was superb.

I slept from Fayetteville, North Carolina until we pulled into Baltimore the next morning. Once again, the views kept me captivated, chugging now through Delaware, Pennsylvania and New Jersey. Just after 7 p.m., as we moved beyond Newark, I finally glimpsed the fiercely illuminated Manhattan skyline. I was home.

With my overstuffed suitcase in hand, I galumphed up the endless stairs from the platform at Penn Station and emerged at last into a cold, clear New York evening. I pulled my overcoat from the outer pocket of my valise.

Being in the center of the universe once more was a shock to me; in many ways, the City was merely a replica of the one from my youth. I intended to ease back into the Big Apple. Instead, my eyes and ears were assaulted by the intense sensory bombardment of this incomparable metropolis.

The worst of it, I suppose, was the noise. I had forgotten just how loud everything is here. No wonder they call it "the city that never sleeps." Who can sleep with all that screeching and honking and whining and wailing?

And yet, when I lived in New York, I would miss the clamor when it wasn't there. From time to time, I used to go out of town for a weekend in the country or at the shore. I remember how hard it would be to sleep at night – too damned quiet. I also longed for the urban energy I had left behind.

There was a certain comfort from the physical vibrations of all those people and vehicles and buildings. I guess that during the more than half century I spent here, I just got used to the sounds of the city. Despite the cumulative effect of all those decibels, my hearing is still excellent. Unlike many of my generation who labor to understand what others say, my ears have not suffered noticeably from age, nor from exposure to sirens or gunshots or what have you. Would that I could say the same for the rest of me.

I debated whether to walk to my nearby hotel or take a cab. As I strolled onto the sidewalk, I was reminded that New Yorkers don't stroll. Even on the weekend, it was constant rush hour. Pushing and shoving was just another way of saying, "Get the hell out of my way or I'll kill you."

My luggage and I took refuge in the first Yellow Cab that stopped. To my surprise, the driver said nothing. (I had forgotten that "Where to, Mac?" is only asked in the movies.)

"Hotel Wolcott," I ordered at last, trying to sound as nonchalant as possible.

The lethargic man behind the wheel gave me a long look. Now, he had something to say. "That's a few blocks from here, you know."

I nodded toward the sizeable Samsonite suitcase and shrugged my shoulders.

"Say, what will it cost me to go up to Washington Heights later on?"

"During the day, about ten bucks. At night, maybe your life."

Everybody's a comedian.

This was no longer the New York City I first remembered. In those pre-Depression-era rough and tumble days, the police really owned the streets. Six decades later, this was now New York City in economic crisis. Cops were being laid off. Garbage was piling up. The words "municipal bankruptcy" were on every wag's lips. Welcome home, sucker.

Never mind, I thought. It's just a visit. I'll be here for only a few days, do a little research, grab a bag of bagels from H&H, then get on the train and back to my little Miami condo. No problem.

I needed to come up with a course of action. It seemed strange that I would have to think about this at all. Back then, I operated on instinct. I knew the five boroughs like Babe Ruth once knew the stitches on a baseball sailing over the outfield wall at Yankee Stadium.

But that was then and I was now out of practice. I needed to reflect a bit. I also needed to watch my pennies. Even when I was salaried and wrote for the Tribune, expense accounts were practically non-existent. This trip was entirely on me. And New York City was not cheap.

I checked into my hotel. One of the reasons I chose the Wolcott (apart from the fact that it coincidentally shared a name with one of my favorite raconteurs) is that it was centrally located. Another is that it was nice but not too pricey. Still another is that the assistant manager was married to my sister's youngest daughter, so the staff probably wouldn't take advantage of me just because I was an old man from out of town.

This hotel had a beautifully ornate lobby belying its reasonable prices. With the high ceilings, imposing columns and gold leaf, I felt as if I had walked into a French palace. It even smelled swanky. I handed my credit card to the reservation clerk. The young woman behind the desk recognized the name. It's good to have connections.

"Hello, Mr. Peterson." She didn't need to say that she knew my nephew and I was grateful for her subtlety. "Welcome to the Wolcott."

We went through the perfunctory check-in process, but before riding the elevator up to my room, I asked the clerk for advice about using the subway to get around tomorrow. After all, it had been a few years and things do change.

"Where are you going, Mr. Peterson?"

"West 187th Street," I told her.

She studied my face and reasonably nice attire and asked, "You going up there by yourself, sir?"

"Yeah, I used to live in that neighborhood when I was a kid."

That stopped her. She looked at me with a mixture of surprise and sympathy. Then she added, "Oh yeah, I guess it was different way back then." (I hated that phrase.)

She suggested that the subway might be a bit complicated for me and that I would be more comfortable in a taxi.

Did I really look that frail? I wondered, *or had the old neighborhood really changed so much?* Rather than belabor the matter, I switched subjects.

"Any good shows on Broadway tonight?" I asked.

"Do the Yankees play ball in the Bronx?" she asked good-naturedly, and reached for a copy of today's Times on the desk.

I could see that this young woman was sizing me up to determine whether I'd be more interested in a musical revival, straight drama or perhaps something avant-garde off-Broadway. I knew that, this being a Saturday night, the most popular performances would be sold out.

"Let me save you some trouble," I offered. "How about that new Hal Prince musical – you know, the one that opened earlier this year? Where is that playing?"

Now she was really surprised. *No such thing as a former New Yorker*, I thought proudly to myself. The clerk quickly scanned the list, unsure of the name. I was way ahead of her. Having spotted the title, *On the Twentieth Century*, I helpfully put my finger on it.

"Oh, right," she chuckled. "That's a good one," the young woman quipped, making no effort to cover her lack of theater savvy. Then again, it wasn't her job. After all, she was not the concierge. The Wolcott didn't have one.

I turned the newspaper around.

"St. James Theatre, 246 West Forty-fourth Street," I read aloud. "Thanks a lot, miss."

Before she had a chance to ask if she could call the theater for me, I was on my way to the elevators. I decided to skip the theater and go to bed early. Anyway, it was probably too late to make the curtain; I would have hated to miss the overture, too; and besides, I needed a good night's sleep.

First thing the next morning, I got dressed for church. The Wolcott was on a side street, so I had to walk a block to catch a taxi.

Before going up to Washington Heights, I wanted to see an old friend – the Herald Tribune. I knew the Trib building was still there, although I suspected that she wouldn't really be the same. It was a lot like revisiting a childhood school: one vaguely expects to see familiar faces on campus, even though those fellow students have long since grown up and moved on.

As the cab rounded the corner from Eighth Avenue onto 41st Street, I was pleased to see the memorable structure standing in its same spot. Granted, it now housed an array of anonymous offices. Nevertheless, the shades of presses past surely haunted this high-rise. For an instant, I closed my eyes and saw them come alive again – actually heard the clatter of linotype in my mind's ear.

I joined the New York Herald Tribune staff about five years before Archbishop Tourian's murder. As I look back on my vainglorious career, I am painfully aware of two things. First, I'm a damn fine writer who never felt fully appreciated – let alone adequately compensated. Oh, I made a decent living at a great paper, but my ego was never quite gratified. The other is that maybe I picked the wrong line of work altogether. It was definitely not my first choice.

While earning a bachelor's degree in history at Columbia University, I had planned to teach. But one of my extracurricular activities was writing for our student newspaper, the Columbia Spectator. An article I did about crimes committed against immigrants won a Scholastic Press Association award and the attention of every big newspaper in town.

So, my career was chosen for me. I accepted an offer from the Tribune because that paper promised to let me continue writing smart stories about dumb crimes. I was not the first Columbia man to go to work for that periodical. Bennett Cerf, who was ten years my elder, also got a job at the Trib after graduation. But for reasons which remain mysterious to me, he was fired after a brief stint as a reporter there. Poor Bennett. All he did with his life was to become one of the most successful book publishers in the world – and something of a celebrity as a panelist on the CBS television game show, "What's My Line?"

I must confess to a certain vanity about my work which I had truly hoped to satisfy with one little accolade: the Pulitzer Prize. Alas, it was not to be.

From my earliest days on the job, I knew I had made the right choice. My work was absorbing and my writing was top-notch (if I do say so myself). There was a series on the numbers rackets, several juicy pieces about bribery and one story – an exposé of rich lawyers stealing money from their poor clients – which deserved an award (I note with all due modesty). But over the years, I watched my colleagues and competitors beat me.

Never mind, I told myself. I was undeterred. The Tourian murder was definitely Pulitzer material. But instead, the judges of journalism honored Royce Brier of the San Francisco Chronicle for his account of the lynching of two kidnappers in San Jose, California. True, it was a good story. John Holmes and Thomas Thurmond had been arrested for grabbing up a local merchant's son. On November 26, 1933, a crowd of angry citizens broke into the city jail, dragged the suspects to a park across the street and hanged them from a pair of oak trees. Mob justice in the Old West was alive and well. Still…more deserving of praise than my splendid prose? Please. I protest.

The next year, I would turn out dozens of dazzling pieces on the Tourian murder trial as well as some lengthy backgrounders about the Armenian community. Meanwhile, a colleague at the Tribune, William H. Taylor, was destined to win my prize for his series of articles on international yacht races. Bill and I had become pals over the years. But after the way he lorded winning of that award over me, I would never speak to him again.

With my back to what had been the paper's main entrance, I reopened my eyes, surveyed the street and tried to remember what was here those many years ago. Hadn't there been a little coffee shop across the way? And next to it, a tailor? And I'm sure there used to be a theater on the corner.

Standing here reminded me that I was a long way from the scene of the crime. If not for the fact that I happened to be in church that morning, I never would have gotten so much as a sidebar on the story. Washington Heights was one hundred forty-six blocks from here.

"You OK, buddy?" The taxi driver had a concerned look on his face. I had asked him to wait for me, not knowing how long I'd linger.

"Yes, I'm fine." I shook off my daydreaming and got back into the cab. "Let's go up to 187th Street." I didn't feel like riding underground this morning.

5

Then

In this summer of 1894, Karnig Tourian picked a fat, ripe apricot from a tree in his neighbor's back yard. In the waning hours of this perfect Saturday afternoon, the boy's fancy turned to his favorite hobby – eating apricots. Karnig's neighbors were away for the weekend, so the teenager took advantage of their absence, and presumed an open invitation to enjoy these fine fruits growing in the adjoining garden.

The Tourian family lived near Constantinople in Scutari. The ancient Greeks had named this town Chrysopolis, meaning "City of Gold." Sitting on the Asian side of the Bosporus Straits, it served as a British army base during the Crimean War and achieved distinction for the military hospital where Florence Nightingale worked.

This was not exactly a rich country anymore. Centuries before, Armenia was a powerful, independent kingdom. Now, this land (and nearly all of historic Armenia), was ruled by Turks. Nevertheless, Armenian people had been only slightly assimilated. Armenian students who had studied in Europe returned home with ideas of Western democracy. These led to the creation of an Armenian national constitution which permitted them some political autonomy within the Ottoman system.

But by the end of the 19th century, Scutari was just another suburb of the Ottoman capital. Christian Armenians were treated as second-class citizens in this largely Muslim country. That oppressive status spurred the birth of several political groups which shared the eventual goal of greater independence. Their tactics ranged from gradual reform to total revolution. The counter-reaction from Turkey was increased oppression, massacres and general efforts to silence the rebels.

Karnig held the perfectly shaped fruit up to his considerable nose, savoring the midsummer scent before gently separating it into two nearly identical halves. A dark brown pit stared up at him from the left half. He twisted it out and flicked it away, leaving the cot's virgin center fully exposed. Then, as he had done so many times before, the 15-year old boy lovingly contemplated this edible embodiment of passion and poetry with all the enthusiasm he could apply to something so mundane as food.

"Are you going to eat that or just stare at it?" Armen Poochigian was Karnig's best friend, but even he was growing impatient with this miniature drama.

"I don't want to rush," Tourian answered in the defensive. "Anyway, this one is really great. Look." He held it out toward Armen who rolled his eyes slightly. The boy knew that whatever reaction he made (including silence) would provoke a sermon. And he got one.

"Ask any Armenian to name his favorite fruit," Karnig began. "Go ahead, just ask. The answer will always be the same – apricots."

Tourian pretended to speak like a scholar. "Whether they're fresh or dried or candied; in jams, pies or cookies; even drunk as brandy, the most excellent of all fruits is the apricot."

Armen kept quiet, staring at his feet and hoping now for his pal to finish this speech. But Karnig continued.

"Just pronouncing the word, *dzeeran*, causes one's mouth to salivate a bit, preparing the mouth to welcome this delightful visitor."

This was over the top even for Karnig.

"Have I gone too far?" he asked to no one at all. "Perhaps. But like all Armenians, I love apricots!" And with a flourish, he devoured the fruit in his hand and punctuated the performance with an ear-to-ear grin.

The adolescence of Karnig Tourian did not dwell on typical obsessions with sex or sports or other "silliness," as he put it. The already-too-mature lad was way beyond those natural urges of his puberty. He focused instead on literature, beauty, philosophy, and to a certain extent (judging by his expansive waistline), gastronomy. Still, he was a gourmet rather than a gourmand.

"So, are we going to spend all day eating apricots?" Armen asked.

Tourian shot him a startled look. "What else did you have in mind?"

His friend let out a high-pitched giggling whinny, turned scarlet from laughing so hard, and then clapped Karnig on the back. At once, the two boys took off running in figure eights and oblong circles through the small grove of various fruit trees. Although Tourian was larger and heavier, he managed to keep up. The plump teenager was somewhat of a physical anomaly. Most of his peers, like Armen, were slight of build and somewhat underweight. Perhaps that is why he and his younger brother and sister survived, while three other siblings did not.

For such a stout kid, Karnig was surprisingly agile. The bigger boy dashed back to the apricot tree and climbed onto the thick, lower branch. This game served as entertainment for them. Armen watched his pal admiringly. It wasn't only his physical strength and stamina that made Karnig impressive. He was one of the lucky ones, born into a relatively affluent family.

The leaves of this massive apricot tree fluttered around Karnig's legs as he repositioned himself to reach the highest branches. Just as the boy was about to pick another one, his self-indulgence was interrupted by a familiar voice.

"Karnig!" His mother called from their house. A flash of guilt momentarily surged through him. "Come on, dear," she implored in her native Armenian – the language that Lord Byron had recommended that everyone use for speaking to God. "Karnig-jan," she repeated, adding the suffix of endearment. "Time for dinner."

Mrs. Tourian raised her son alone, his father having succumbed to pneumonia nearly ten years before. Being a good provider, he planned for his own demise and left them with enough money from his thriving import business to live rather comfortably. In former times, the family would probably have been considered among the nobility. Today, they were merely well-to-do, well-educated, well-respected fellow subjects with quasi-celebrity status.

In public, Armenians resentfully spoke Turkish; occasionally dressed like Turks, ate like Turks, sang like Turks and danced like Turks; but steadfastly refused to think like Turks. At home, of course, they still completely conformed to the culture of their own ancestors, often finding ways, large and small, to resist the loss of their identity. They still practiced their religion (an ancient version of Christianity) openly and freely. All their children learned to read and write in that distinctive, curvy alphabet. All the elders (grandparents, godparents, uncles and aunts) also taught children Armenian folk songs and fairy tales.

As a child, Karnig attended Holy Cross Church which, coincidentally, bore the same name as one which he would someday visit in America – his last church. While Tourian studied at the elite Berberian School, he showed great interest in reading about religion. So, the family decided that the boy should follow in his ancestors' legendary footsteps.

Karnig's Uncle Yeghishé, for example, was a rising clergyman who would someday become the Armenian Patriarch in Jerusalem. Another relative, Cousin Bedros, had attained quite some renown as one of Armenia's best-loved poets before dying tragically of tuberculosis at the age of 21, in the arms of Karnig's father. His demise is as storied as any in literature. It is said that as he drew his last breaths, Bedros whispered his final poem. It began:

> "When Death's pale angel stands before my face, with smile unfathomable, stern and chill, and when my sorrows with my soul exhale, know yet, my friends, that I am living still."

The elder Tourian took down each word as Bedros continued to recite. Then, with his last ounce of strength, the dying poet murmured these lines:

> "But when my grave forgotten shall remain in some dim nook, neglected and passed by, when from the world my memory fades away, that is the time when I indeed shall die!"

The entire poem was published under the title, "My Death."

Bedros left the family with one other legacy: their name. The Tourians were descendants of iron craftsmen. The original family was Zimbayan, from the Turkish word *zimba* for a punching tool used in their trade. But the poet persuaded his relatives to adopt the Armenian version – hence, Tourian.

Unknown to all of them, young Karnig had a heavier fate. He was headed for a unique place in the history of Armenians, destined to become, for some, one of his people's most honored men – and for others, one of the most hated. But for now, it was time to go home, time to eat dinner, time to continue his education, and time to prepare for his very special future.

The very same year that Tourian was growing up in Scutari, another Armenian family welcomed their new son in the village of Havav about 500 miles away. Mateos Leylegian was born on May 28, 1894. Though not as well off as the Tourians, the Leylegian clan traced its roots from central Anatolia back to the Tabriz area of northwest Persia.

In the early 1700s, persistent famine and Afghan invasions drove many Armenians from that region, and among them, the Leylegian brothers. Along the way they separated, each hoping to find a better future. Mateos's predecessor settled in Havav, not far from the city of Palu, Turkey.

Destiny produced one more native son in Havav. Almost exactly 12 months after the birth of Mateos, Nishan Tuktikian came into the world. He grew up a bit more rough and tumble than Mateos, but the two boys became playmates and best friends.

One distinctive feature of this ancient village was that its population was one hundred percent Armenian. Another distinction was the nearby 12th century St. Mary's monastery. It was officially named *Kaghtsrahayiats Soorp Asdvadzadzin*, or the Holy Mother of God, and served as a clandestine meeting place – particularly for members of the Armenian Revolutionary Federation. Those members included the Leylegian and Tuktikian families.

The villages surrounding Havav were inhabited primarily by Kurdish people who were, by and large, herders. On the other hand, most Armenians in that area were agrarian people. The Leylegian family had a particular affinity for the soil, a real knack for growing things. But they could not overcome the forces of nature. Central Armenia was hit by drought during the infancy of Mateos and Nishan. It devastated the region's agricultural economy.

By 1895, things had gotten so bad that neighboring villagers were raiding each other's goods. Turks used the word *talan* to describe this province-wide pillaging. Some people were killed, especially those who got in the way of looters. But it was not the sort of government-organized genocide that was coming in the early twentieth century. Rather, these raids were run by warlords. And the Kurds did not specifically target Armenians in these attacks. They were more broadly anti-Christian in nature. The fighting tended to be internecine, born out of personal desperation rather than against any particular religious or ethnic group.

Nevertheless, Havav was badly damaged during these assaults. Schools were destroyed. One church was left in ruins. The village's very existence was threatened. So, many Armenians decided to arm themselves. They started to gather illicit weapons, using the monastery as a secret arsenal. In 1908, the Sultan was deposed. A group of western-educated Turks took over the government, giving Armenians hope for peace and stability.

Then came 1915. Instead of protecting their Armenian minority, this new government of "Young Turks" ordered their relocation, deportation and eventual slaughter. On April 24, the wholesale slaughter began: Women, children, priests and the elderly were slain in their homes and in their churches and on the streets.

In May of that year, the Turks massacred most of the villagers in Havav.

By then, Mateos and Nishan had already left for America. They went to the New World in 1913 and settled in Providence, Rhode Island. However, upon learning of the tragedies in their homeland, the pair returned overseas to join in the Armenian Legion of the French Army. They were sent to Cilicia, serving under French command, and battled against Turks for Armenia's liberation during World War One.

The Armenian Legion was disbanded in 1920, and both returned to their former jobs in Rhode Island. A decade later, they resettled in New York City.

After two years of study under his cousin, Archbishop Yeghishé Tourian, at Armash Seminary, Karnig stood at the altar. It was the dawn of a new century. He was about to take his first steps as an ordained celibate priest. Following the traditions of the Armenian Apostolic Church, the new clergyman would receive a new first name. From that day forward, Karnig became known as Ghevont.

Many non-Armenians or *odars* have difficulty replicating some sounds in the Armenian language. One of these is the diphthong, *gh* (which sounds close to the Parisian French *r*). So, it was no surprise that Ghevont Tourian's first name would be mispronounced. Even among Armenians, Tourian's first name was problematic. Those who lived in the Russian (and later Soviet) empire erroneously called him Levon or Leon. That misnomer would follow him all the way to the New World.

It even affected his descendants. The Archbishop's brother had a grandson, also named Ghevont. He, too, was born in Constantinople (by then called "Istanbul") and later moved to Greece where he opened a little tourist shop, sold souvenirs and told stories about his famous ancestor. His Armenian friends would teasingly call him *dzoh* (meaning "kid") which the Greeks misheard as "Joe." Thus, the namesake and last male descendant of Archbishop Ghevont (né Karnig) Tourian became the merchant-philosopher, Joe Tourian.

In May of 1931, Ghevont Tourian found himself sailing across the Atlantic Ocean onboard the White Star liner, *Britannic*, a sister ship of the ill-fated *Titanic*. As the Archbishop steamed toward America, he contemplated his difficult journey since entering the priesthood.

> Tourian thought about the time in 1913, when he was summoned to the Holy See in Etchmiadzin, Armenia. The head of the Apostolic Church there elevated the celibate priest to the rank of bishop, and then sent him back to Turkey. But in the months which followed, it became increasingly unsafe for

Armenians to remain in that country. All across Anatolia, Armenians were about to be murdered, tortured and deported.

Ghevont's own brother, Haroutiun, was killed. So was the husband of his sister, Satenik. Acting on a premonition, Tourian rescued his remaining relatives. He took them to Bulgaria where, with the help of local townsfolk, they survived starvation, war, massacres, and various other calamities of the collapsing Ottoman Empire. The Turkish government ordered his arrest, but Bulgarian Tsar Ferdinand intervened and provided special quarters near the royal palace until the war ended.

Despite limited communications, reports of the 1915 horrors spread rapidly. When they ended, an estimated one and one half million Armenians were dead. This act of ethnic cleansing was the Ottoman Empire's final solution to their perceived problem. By removing revolutionaries who might conspire with the country's enemies, Turkey would be left for Turks. All this happened in the midst of the Great War, the war to end all wars, so who would notice? None would dare call it a crime against humanity, let alone "genocide" – a word which did not exist then. The government was simply dealing with a troublesome minority while at the same time guaranteeing national security.

Tourian recalled that in 1920, he returned to Turkey and became Prelate of Smyrna. Even after the Muslim Ottoman Empire conquered Byzantium, this former Greek port still had a vibrant Christian community, including a large number of Armenians. At this moment, the Archbishop was the most prominent Armenian government representative there. Sitting with majestic nobility in a high-backed velvet chair befitting his office, he actually looked like a king. But it was only appearance.

Two years later, catastrophe struck that port city. Turks had regained control over the occupying Greek Army and were forcing foreigners to flee. There was total panic. Residents in Smyrna's Armenian quarters had hopes of being rescued by an array of international naval vessels in the harbor. But it became clear that there was no rescue force coming. They were captives in their own homes.

And then, Smyrna was set on fire – by whom, it is not clear. Nevertheless, whatever possibilities for refuge had existed were quickly being consumed by flames. As Smyrna burned, Tourian followed the throng to the coast. Thousands leapt into the sea. Western ships moved in to protect their varying national interests. Only a few even tried saving any refugees. Among those swimming for their lives in the Mediterranean was the plump figure of an Armenian clergyman.

Ghevont Tourian was rescued by a British ship. He reached safety in Athens where he served as prelate until 1926. Next, he moved to Manchester, England where he learned to speak English and published many of his sermons. Seven years later, the Mother Church dispatched him to the United States.

When the *Britannic* reached New York, Tourian was greeted by a reception committee at the pier. "I am looking forward to my stay in America," he told a New York Times reporter, "and hope that I shall be able to further the friendly relations that exist between the people of Armenia and the Government of the United States."

Yes, this assignment was clearly very important to him. Little did he know that it would be his last.

6

Now

It took the taxi about twenty minutes to get from the old Tribune building to Washington Heights. I had the driver drop me off in front of a little bodega on St. Nicholas Avenue. It felt strangely good being here again. Stepping out of the car and onto the sidewalk, I looked around half expecting to see something familiar. But, of course, the neighborhood was not quite recognizable.

Washington Heights is officially demarcated by 155th Street and Fairview Avenue, running between the Harlem River and the Hudson. The boundaries of this quarter haven't changed in a hundred years.

I closed my eyes for a few moments and tried to remember the day of Tourian's murder. Here in the relative tranquility of an early Sunday morning, it was easier to imagine myself back in 1933. Then as now, this was an enclave of newcomers who could get by without speaking a word of English. But there used to be many nationalities living here: Greeks, Armenians, Hungarians, Romanians, Jews, Germans, you name it – a veritable ethnic goulash. It felt more like home to me then. Today, it was decidedly Latino – mostly Dominican. I was visibly, palpably an outsider. The few old European immigrants who remained seemed increasingly isolated in the midst of a new dominant culture.

This had been a vibrant neighborhood back then. Although the Depression had made life harder for everyone, the Heights was a very desirable place to live. With all the trolleys, buses and subway trains coming through here, it was easy and convenient to get to jobs and shopping. Uptown apartments were comparatively affordable, yet without the crowded hustle and bustle of downtown. It was as close to suburban life as Manhattan had to offer.

After a bit of reverie, I felt a hand on my arm. A slight shiver went through me as I opened my eyes.

"Are you all right, sir?" It was a police officer.

"Uh, yeah." I was a bit bewildered. "Why do you ask?"

The cop was young enough to be my son but feigned that professional maturity of one beyond his 30-something years. "Well, you've been standing here with your eyes closed for a long time."

I blushed. "Sorry, I was just thinking." I really must have seemed a bit out of place, a time traveler of sorts.

The policeman stared at me with a nearly imperceptible grin. He continued holding my arm, as if worried that I might fall if he let me go. Maybe he thought I was senile, standing out here in the frosty morning.

"I'm fine," I insisted, pulling away. "Really."

He released me and ceremonially touched a finger tip to the brim of his hat. "Have a good day, sir."

I quickly walked along 187th Street to Holy Cross Church. It was a beautiful morning – a cold, clear day just as it had been back on December 24, 1933. This day, as on that fateful one half a lifetime ago, I walked up the icy front steps leading to the entrance. I noticed the same sort of little zigzag cracks in the concrete steps. In much the same way, I took off my hat and gloves, blew warm breath onto my cupped hands, and rubbed them rapidly together in an effort to chase away the perpetual chill. Turning around and looking back toward the street from the front door, I also saw the same empty lot on the corner; heard the same clatter of cars bouncing in and out of deepening pot holes; smelled the same scent of urban snow mixed with the vague yet repugnant odor of too many people in too little space.

There were a few more differences, too. This church had been remodeled in 1953. On the outside, the structure was surrounded by a black, wrought-iron fence. It hadn't taken long for the paint to peel, nor for some local graffiti artists to spray on their distinctive but (at least to me) indecipherable tags. The interior was a bit more spacious. In addition to the center aisle, now there were two on the sides. One more difference: this church had a tomb in it.

I pushed open the front door and walked in.

"Good morning," I smiled and nodded to the woman standing behind a small, lace-covered table. There was a box of candles and a brass tray with a few dollar bills laying in it.

"Good morning," she said warmly, as if recognizing me. But, of course, she did not. I glanced at my watch.

"What time does the service start?" I asked.

"Ten o'clock," she said with a slight foreign accent. "Are you from out of town?"

I was not anxious to explain my presence, but I anticipated her curiosity.

"Miami," I answered, withholding the rest of the story.

"Oh," she replied. It was one of those long *oh*'s, the kind of *oh* that implies admiration and wonderment along with deep curiosity, and which promises many questions.

"Welcome," she added.

I put a dollar in the tray, took a candle and ducked any further interrogation. Walking through a second set of doors, I entered the sanctuary. Even though it was Sunday morning, the place was practically empty. A small, sand-filled alcove on the left held half a dozen burning candles. I lit mine from one of these and pressed it into place among the others.

I took a seat near the back and waited for the service to begin. Holy Cross was very much like every other Armenian Apostolic church in America. Just after 10 a.m., the priest and his deacons started going through the ancient ceremony. I kept losing my concentration. I couldn't take my eyes off a white marble slab embedded in the floor to the right of the altar.

My thoughts drifted back to the Archbishop's last autumn on earth.

"Where is Ghevont Tourian?"

That was the question everyone asked on September 3, 1933. Delegates to the annual general assembly of the Armenian Apostolic Church wondered where their prelate was.

"Ladies and gentlemen, your attention please." The chairman tried to bring the meeting to order. "Brothers and sisters, we need quiet. Take your seats."

"Where is he?" asked one delegate.

"*Oor eh*?" repeated another in Armenian.

And only a few weeks ago, the Archbishop was assaulted at a picnic in Massachusetts. In the past several days, rumors were circulating about Tourian's health, some even speculating that he had fled the country.

"People, please!" The chairman banged his gavel. "We are going to begin." Finally, delegates took their seats in the hall at St. Gregory the Illuminator's Church on Twenty-seventh Street.

The priests from each of the parishes in Manhattan stood together and recited an invocation. Then, the chairman returned to the podium.

"Dear believers, our Archbishop is not feeling well today." The delegates began to murmur again, provoking the chairman to raise his hands. "He will be unable to join us, but he sends his regrets and his blessings to you all."

One by one, delegates sympathetic to the pro-independence *Tashnag* party stood up and spoke harshly about the prelate's absence. The chairman allowed them to speak without interruption. After three-quarters of an hour, a delegate from New Jersey asked to be recognized.

"Yes, brother?"

"Mr. Chairman, how long must we suffer silently to these insults? I demand that we put a stop to political speeches and get on with church business." That led a dozen men to stand and shout personal slurs at the delegate at the podium. The chairman tried again to regain order.

"I move that we vote to remove Tourian," called one voice from the audience.

But the delegate at the podium refused to yield. "We will not listen to any more vile remarks from those people. My fellow delegates, let us leave this place at once!"

The auditorium erupted into a deafening match of accusations. The pro-Tourian delegates walked out en masse and reconvened a short while later at the Hotel Martinique. That group claimed to be the official assembly and deemed the other delegates to be renegades.

Meanwhile, the generally anti-Tourian faction remained at the church hall and voted to demand the Archbishop's resignation. They voted to have a committee draft a letter to be sent to Armenia, asking the Mother Church to recall Tourian.

In effect, that was the day the Armenian Apostolic Church split in America.

After the liturgy ended and the handful of congregants left, I was drawn to that corner and stared at the inscription on the sepulcher, carved in that familiar foreign alphabet. I stood, hypnotized by the words. Shamefully, I had forgotten how to read my mother's native language. And yet, although I could not understand these words, they had a powerful effect on me.

"May I help you?"

The question snapped me around. It was the new priest. He looked at me with a mixture of kindness and deference. People can be so polite to us old folks.

"I'm sorry, I just wanted to see the tomb," I explained.

"*Ghevont Arkebiskobos Tourian, Arachnort Amerigah Hayots, Dzenyal 1 Jan. 1879, Nahadagyal 24 Dec. 1933* – Archbishop Ghevont Tourian, Prelate of Armenians in America. Born on Jan. 1, 1879. Martyred on Dec. 24, 1933," he translated. "Do you know the story?"

Now it was my turn to be kind. "I was here that day." I extended a hand. "Tommy Peterson. Uh, Petrossian," I added to clarify the ethnic connection. "My family lived in the neighborhood back then."

The priest shook my hand enthusiastically and smiled.

"I'm Father Stepan," he said. "Here, let me show you something." He slid open a wooden closet door behind Archbishop Tourian's tomb. Hanging inside were some blue and white choir robes. From atop the shelf, he removed a flimsy cardboard box and set it down on a nearby table. He brushed off the dust, opened the top and revealed the contents. To my astonishment, it held the blood-stained, knife-slashed, coroner-marked vestments that had been worn by the murdered clergyman. I reached out and touched the silk cloth. I felt a sort of electric tingle and closed my eyes. That took me right back.

7

Then

Juan Gonzales Tchalikian ran from Holy Cross Church, clutching the back of his head. The slain Archbishop's bodyguard, Khosroff Gorgodian, had hit Tchalikian so hard with the butt of his revolver that it chipped off a piece of his skull. The Panamanian-born Armenian was in extreme pain. As he staggered down 187th Street toward St. Nicholas, the young man began to panic. Blood had splattered onto his white shirt and he began to think maybe he was seriously wounded.

"Hey, come in here," said a man pulling him into the Arax Restaurant. He was horrified to see the injury. "Let's get you cleaned up."

The good Samaritan washed Tchalikian's head and put a makeshift bandage on him. He helped him take off the stained shirt and gave him a fresh one.

"Where's your hat?"

"Hat? I don't have a hat."

"In this weather? Boy, you better take care of yourself."

The man helped Juan back outside and stopped a taxi.

"Come on, let's go."

The two climbed into the cab and headed uptown.

The rainstorm which blew through Manhattan that week brought with it the kind of frigid temperature that prompts many New Yorkers to grudgingly appreciate the West Coast. It was the kind of weather that makes you swear you'll never come back if you move across the country; the kind of weather that makes you willing to do just about anything to get warm.

That's what was going through Jim Donnelly's mind on this Christmas Eve morning in 1933. Although it was quite sunny outside that morning, the detective's bureau at the Wadsworth Avenue Station remained cold and damp. One of these days, he thought, I'm getting out of this god-awful place. They must have crime in California.

"Lieutenant?" His reverie was broken.

"Hmmm?"

It was Bill O'Shea, the detective third-grade who was doing everything possible to please his superior officers these days. Billy was bucking for a gold shield.

"We have a couple dozen Armenians downstairs, sir."

"OK."

"Assistant District Attorney Cohn is setting up to do the interviews, but some of those witnesses only want to talk to you."

Ah, the price of fame. Ever since Donnelly rescued a neighborhood child who had fallen off a subway platform, the good citizens of New York City thought he was J. Edgar Hoover, Dick Tracy and Superman rolled into one. "That's fine, Billy. I'll be right there."

O'Shea headed toward the door. "Oh, and one other thing, sir," he said.

"Yeah?"

"How do you want us to handle the press on this one?"

The lieutenant took a deep breath. The 18-year veteran of New York's finest was loath to deal with reporters. Unlike many of his peers, Donnelly had never mastered the fine art of media relations. His idea of good press was keeping his name out of the papers. And that rarely happened on big stories.

"I'll let you—"

But before he could finish his sentence, Donnelly was staring at the smiling face of Tom Peterson.

"Hey, lieutenant, looks like you caught a good one," the reporter began while unbuttoning his light grey overcoat with one hand and tipping back his matching fedora with the other.

"Not now, Tommy." Donnelly wanted to put a stop to this conversation as quickly as possible. He started to stand.

"What do you make of the Russian connection?"

Now, that was an unexpected question. Newspapers had page one stories about Russia and the Soviet Union every day. The reporter knew that Donnelly would have to pay attention. The policeman sat back down.

"OK, let's hear it."

Tom took a deep breath. He was going to give Donnelly a little history lesson. Although no one – not even this detective – wanted to hear too much about the background of a case, Peterson knew that what lay behind the Armenian conflict would be central to solving the Archbishop's murder.

"How far back do you want me to start," he asked genuinely.

Donnelly wearily rubbed his face with a meaty paw. "Oh, Mother of

God…"

Tom drew another breath, rocked back and forth on his heels and re-buttoned his overcoat.

"Let's go have a cup of coffee," he suggested.

Donnelly looked at his pocket watch, sighed heavily and turned to his underling.

"Billy, I'll be back in twenty minutes."

"Hey, George," Tom called as he walked into Spiro's Restaurant.

He might have preferred the automat a few blocks away. The coffee was better and the food was fresher. But Donnelly was buying so who was the reporter to complain? This was one of the best coffee shops in the neighborhood – and just a block away from Wadsworth Avenue stationhouse. Run by two Greek brothers (neither named Spiro), it was a sort of safe haven for politicians, policemen and other powerful people – a place where everyone was anonymous and where every conversation was off the record. In short, it was a perfect spot for journalistic background briefings. Usually, it was the reporters who got briefed here. This time, however, the tables were turned.

"How are you, Tommy?" replied the man behind the counter. "Long time no see."

"I'm still recuperating from that last blue plate special I had here," he joked.

"There's nothin' wrong with my food!" George retorted with a thick Greek accent, raising his voice in mock anger. "You make any problem here, I gonna call a cop."

Lt. Donnelly was on Tommy's heels and joined the banter. "What's the trouble, lads?"

"Oh, no problem, officer," answered the Greek. He laughed and waved a small meat cleaver in the air. "I take care every thin'."

The two men moved toward a back table.

"Coffee please, George," Peterson said.

"Two coffees, comin' up."

They removed their overcoats and sat down.

"So, let's hear about these Russians." Donnelly cut right to the chase.

Tom took a pack of Chesterfields from his shirt pocket (preferring the milder taste), tapped out a cigarette, slipped it between his lips and lit up. He narrowed his eyes and studied this policeman for a moment.

"You ever hear of a guy named Talaat Pasha?"

Donnelly shrugged, already slightly bored.

"Turkish Interior Minister back in 1915 – gave orders to get rid of a little, uh, *problem*," he said sarcastically. "See, there used to be a couple million Armenians living in Turkey. The Turks managed to kill or deport most of them."

"Turkey, huh?" the lieutenant asked.

"They wanted to eliminate these people from their homeland. Many of the folks in the church on 187th Street are survivors of that catastrophe. Some just barely escaped," he explained.

"So, what's all this got to do with the Russians?" Donnelly was becoming impatient.

"Well, one reason the Turks wanted to wipe out the Armenians is because they were afraid the Armenians would help Russia beat Turkey during the war. See, the Russians and the Armenians are both Christians."

Donnelly seemed perplexed. "I thought the Ruskies were atheists."

At that moment, George's brother, Gregory, arrived with two cups of coffee.

"No, that's just the Bolsheviks – the Communists," said the waiter. "Most Russians are Orthodox Christians – just like us Greeks."

The lieutenant burned his mouth on a gulp of the steaming coffee. "Jesus Christ!"

"Amen, brother," said Gregory and crossed himself as he walked away from our table.

Peterson smirked at the waiter's dry humor. Donnelly turned back to face the reporter. "All right, professor, let's get back to our lesson. What's the beef?"

Tom smiled. His student was hooked. "Russia gave protection to the Armenians who survived those Turkish horrors. After the war, Armenia was an independent country for a couple years. But then the Red Army marched in and now they're part of the Soviet Union."

"Yeah, well I give the Reds about two or three years before their people all starve or they start another revolution," added Donnelly. "So?"

"So, there are a lot of Armenians who don't want to wait two or three more years," he explained. "These mugs want their independence back. And their friends here are trying to start the revolution now."

Donnelly rubbed his square chin, soaking it all in. You couldn't blame him for being uninformed about the details of Russian politics, let alone the intricacies of this Armenian intrigue. After all, the United States had only established diplomatic relations with the U.S.S.R. a month before.

"OK, fine, so who's behind this revolution, boy-o?" he asked.

"That's the question of the hour." Tom glanced around in mock furtive style, and then continued in a near-whisper. "I'll tell you what I think."

Hours had passed since the Archbishop's assassination. The anniversary clock on the mantel chimed twice. But in this relatively large, third-floor walkup on the Lower East Side, time had crawled to a near standstill. Four men sat around the dining room table. The one who had conducted the meeting at the Third Street club a week before looked across at his younger brother who nervously tapped his fingers on the table.

"Would you stop that?" the leader said. "You're making me crazy with that tap, tap, tap!"

The younger man paused, then resumed his tapping. "Where are they?" he asked again.

The leader took an apple from the fruit bowl and began to slice it with an old hunting knife. He shoved the cut fruit into his mouth from the blade's edge. The brother stood, paced around the room, then sat back down.

"*Oosh eh*," he declared in Armenian fingering his pocket watch.

"It's not late. You're nervous. Here, have some fruit." The older man speared a slice and presented it to his brother. The other reached for it, then thought better of the offer and stood up again. He returned the watch to his pocket and began to pace once more.

Another man tried to calm the young man. "Brother, please sit down. You can't–"

A key turning in the latch announced the arrival of two more Armenians. The door flew open and they burst in, sweating heavily through their wool suits.

"He's dead," shouted the first man to come through the door, loosening his neck tie. "The bastard is dead."

The leader slammed his palm on the table. "Good! May he rot in hell!"

"Where are the others?" asked another.

"They're on their way."

The leader's brother stood up again, walked to the kitchen and opened the ice box. "Don't you have any milk?" he called from the other room.

"Milk?!" asked the leader derisively. "Let's drink *raki*."

This infamous Anatolian liqueur had a potent and immediate effect. It loosened the tongue and facilitated every mood, from heartbreak to boredom to jubilance – a drink for all occasions. Today was no exception.

"No, my stomach is killing me."

"It's good for you. Be a man."

The leader went to the kitchen and took a bottle of the clear beverage from the first shelf of the cabinet next to the sink. He grabbed a handful of small glasses from the next shelf, unscrewed the bottle cap and poured. The clear licorice-flavored drink turned milky white when mixed with water. They would drink it straight, however.

"To free Armenia!" they toasted and drained their glasses. They repeated this routine until the bottle was empty.

"So, tell us everything."

"It went like clockwork. He walked toward us, nice and slow. Then it happened. Everybody moved at once. Then the knife went in and out, in and out – just like a German sewing machine."

"Don't you mean Italian sewing machine?" said the second man.

The leader punched him hard in the arm. "Shush!" he said harshly.

The other grimaced, realizing his blunder. The storyteller continued. "Anyway, that big pig came down – boom!" He laughed energetically and clapped his hands together. "And there was blood everywhere."

The leader's brother sat morosely.

"What's wrong?"

"Did you say that his blood went everywhere?" He stared at the shoes of the other men, and then at his own. "I wonder if—"

"Shut up!" The leader slugged his brother in the shoulder. "Shut up, you!"

The younger brother grabbed a napkin and started to wipe the other men's shoes.

"No!" the leader shouted. "Stop it. Everything is fine. No blood, no shoes, no problem."

The leader lowered his voice to a whisper.

"Now, we wait for the others. They will be here tonight. Just relax, everybody. Relax."

8

Now

Father Stepan put away the slain Archbishop's vestments, and then led me to the pew nearest the altar.

"So, how may I help you?" he asked inviting me to sit down next to him. Even young priests in New York City have a habit of going straight to the dessert.

OK, no chitchat. I quickly summarized my plans to write a book. The clergyman listened patiently, nodding and exuding supportive interest. Then, to my amazement, his warm welcome instantly turned to ice. Father Stepan was on his feet and backing up.

"Well, I wish I could be of help. I'm sorry." He turned toward the altar and briskly walked away.

I sat there, like an idiot – mouth wide open, arms limp in my lap. I shook my head, trying to clear the buzzing noise from my ears, but which was actually inside my brain. It was the sound of astonishment.

Then, before the priest exited the sanctuary, I rose and found my voice.

"Father Stepan!" The shout was a bit angrier than I had intended, but the yell did succeed in stopping him. He turned back toward me and cocked his head to one side. I walked toward him, not wanting to lose my momentum.

"What are you afraid of?" I asked, continuing to close the gap between us. He took one step backward, then rested a hand on the side wall of the altar.

"Please, this is a house of God." He seemed on the verge of tears.

"This is a murder scene," I insisted.

He shook his head. "A long time ago."

"And the person responsible might still be free and unpunished." I clenched my jaw and my fists, starting to lose my temper. I felt the flush in my cheeks. "How can you walk away from this?"

We stood face to face again. He took a deep breath.

"It is God's will." He put a hand on my shoulder. "Please, leave it in God's hands." And in an instant, he was gone.

I stood in the middle of this church, absolutely baffled.

"What the hell was that," I muttered. My somewhat rhetorical question was answered by a man at the entrance.

"What did you expect?" he asked me. I turned around, trying to identify the speaker.

"Excuse me?" I squinted and held up my hand to block the stark winter sunlight streaming through the slightly open doors.

"People are still afraid here," he continued with a calming voice. The man walked slowly toward me, allowing the doors to shut behind him; now he was no longer a shadow. "They're still trying to heal their wounds." It took a moment for my eyes to readjust. The man looked to be about my own age, yet there was a certain youthfulness about him. He was very stocky, very bald.

"And you are?" I fished.

"Bob Moradian," he said, extending a hand. We shook.

"I'm—"

"Yes, Mr. Peterson, I know who you are." He smiled. "We all know who you are."

"*It's true*," I thought. An out-of-towner like me is bound to attract attention in a community as tightly knit as Armenians. Even New York City can feel like a small town, I suppose. It's amazing how often we run into the same few people in a metropolis of millions. But that shouldn't be shocking; the fact is that most of us spend the majority of our time within a few miles of our home or workplace.

I waited for Moradian to talk again. He obliged me.

"Mr. Peterson, the murder of Archbishop Tourian drove a knife into the heart of this entire community. No matter which side of the political fence, everyone was wounded." He sounded like a professor lecturing a freshman.

"Forgive me, Mr. Moradian—"

"Actually, it's *Doctor* Moradian. But please, call me Bob."

"Doctor?"

"Well, I'm semi-retired now. A psychiatrist."

Uh oh. I never did like shrinks.

"Well, Doctor—" I tried to hide my disdain with an air of false fawning, but he saw right through me.

"Bob." He flashed another warm smile.

"Bob, would you say this community – what's left of it – is suffering some sort of psychological trauma?"

"Undoubtedly," he said, welcoming the question. "Our people survived the massacres, dispersion, terrible economic troubles, and then this. It's enough to make the mind crack."

I rubbed my jaw thoughtfully. Here, finally, was someone with a logical view of Tourian's assassination.

"So, Doc—I'm sorry, Bob, shouldn't these folks want closure?" I was looking for some personal justification.

"Of course."

"And wouldn't they get that by knowing, finally, who ordered Tourian's killing?"

"Theoretically, yes. But you can't expect them to voluntarily go through that pain again."

My newsman's dilemma: How much grief is the truth worth? That was the eternal moral struggle of journalists, and those we serve hate us for it. Oh well.

"Unfortunately, it is my professional obligation to put them through that pain," I said defensively. I admit it was rather self-serving, but the only card I had to play here.

"In that sense, we are very much alike," he observed.

Oh great, I thought sardonically. *I have something in common with a shrink*.

"Anyway, you must be true to yourself, Mr. Peterson."

"Tommy."

"OK, what are you doing for lunch, Tommy?" The good doctor still directed our conversation. Before I could answer, he told me that his wife made the best *dolma* on either side of the Hudson. Her recipe was unique since it was made with onions rather than the typically stuffed grape or cabbage leaves. And anyway, their home was just on the other side of the George Washington Bridge…

Ten minutes later, we were in his car and heading across the river. The Moradian family lived in Englewood, New Jersey. It was a little town in the shadow of New York City but seemingly unaffected by the high energy of Manhattan. Many Armenians moved to suburbs like this one. A few stayed in the city and married non-Armenians. Either way, the old neighborhood in Washington Heights simply melted away.

On the other hand, Englewood felt as if it retained the slower pace of a much earlier decade. Residents still cut their lawns with hand mowers. Children still jumped rope and played hop scotch. Even Bob's car was at least 15 years old. But to me it looked nearly new.

As we walked into the house, the wonderful smell of Armenian cooking carried me back to my childhood.

"Margaret," he called, "we have company."

Mrs. Moradian greeted me with classic unbridled hospitality, and subtly showed Bob the affectionate irritation that comes from lack of spousal warning.

"Dear, this is Tommy Peterson."

"Petrossian," I added for ethnic clarity, extending a hand. "Nice to meet you, Mrs. Moradian.

"Oh please, call me Margaret." She warmly shook my hand and pulled me into the dining room. "My husband always forgets to let me know we're having lunch guests. That's why I always make more than enough."

For the next hour, the Moradians made me feel right at home. Margaret served some of my favorite appetizers. The best was *kheyma* – a combination of cracked wheat (called "*bulgar*") and uncooked, triple ground, very lean beef, garnished with parsley and served on lavosh bread. It's the Armenian version of steak tartar. As if that weren't enough, she laid out a plate of string cheese and some finely sliced, cured meat called *basturma*.

In addition to our hostess's famous stuffed onion *dolma*, this informal meal included a side dish of delicious *kufta* – a meatless patty filled with *bulgar*, chopped onions, and a variety of spices that happily remain a delicious mystery to me. We also had rice pilaf and a very nice green salad. It was all topped off by rice pudding for dessert and something which no one at this table would have dared to call "Turkish coffee."

In addition to her wonderful cooking, Margaret was a fabulous conversationalist. I've often had the impression that Armenian housewives would make great journalists. It's amazing what information they can extract. While his bride got me to talk about my book research, Bob leaned back in his chair. I repeated what I had said to Father Stepan before the priest's abortive exit and added a few other details.

"This is all so horrible, Tommy." Margaret stood up and started to clear the table. "I wonder if we'll ever get over it," she added before walking into the kitchen.

Bob leaned toward me and whispered, "She's a very sensitive woman."

"But it's all so hypocritical," I said. "I mean, even the clergy seem to be complicit."

Moradian raised an eyebrow. "What do you mean?"

"Well, they seem to be hiding something."

"Maybe they're just trying to protect the community from further pain."

I thought about that for a moment and had a sip of the heady but not-too-sweet Port wine my host had just served.

"Could be," I said, nodding. "Then again, I have to wonder if there isn't something else going on here."

Bob leaned back into his psychiatrist mode. "Go on."

"I've attended church on and off my whole life. But there are some things I just never understood or agreed with." The wine had lubricated my tongue. "For example, how can a priest bless soldiers going off to fight in a war? And how can the clergy pray for kings or dictators who oppress their own people?"

"Maybe they do it for survival." He stood up. "Come on, Tommy, I want to show you something." We walked down the hallway and into his study. The room was overflowing with books and papers. I was feeling a bit tipsy from the wine and steadied myself against a tall filing cabinet.

Moradian grabbed a bound report from the middle of one stack.

"This is a collection of personal interviews done with survivors," he said.

"Of the genocide?"

"Of the assassination."

I was puzzled. "Well, except for the Archbishop, wasn't everyone a 'survivor'?"

"Exactly," he said with a Cheshire cat smile.

Bob opened the report and began to read: "The most shocking experience I've ever had in my life. I was in shock. You couldn't even say why did this happen. It was so horrible, so sudden. I sat there for three or four hours outside the church. I mean it was doubly shocking as I sat across the street for three hours until the city people came and took the huge body away. I must say it took me almost ten years to get over that shock. Why in the church? Why did they destroy this man?"

He stopped, then turned the page and continued reading: "To this day, when I think of him I get chills. It is very hard to understand. I ask the eternal why."

The psychiatrist looked at me. "This is a woman who witnessed the assassination, speaking many years later. She must have used the word 'shock' ten times in the first five minutes."

I nodded. Moradian read on: "Weeks after the incident, I felt ashamed because the Armenian name was always in the newspaper as a criminal. It was repeated so much in the newspaper that I had a bad feeling." He stopped again.

"Shock and shame," I said. "A bad combination."

"And here's one more word – guilt." He turned to another page in the report: "The assassination was something awful that had happened and as an Armenian we felt guilty. We felt guilty because he was a highly respected bishop whom we loved."

I was dumbfounded. *No wonder he said the community didn't want to relive this experience*, I thought.

"But here's the clincher," he added. Bob turned a few more pages and read again: "I sometimes think we Armenians are not good enough to each other. We do not treat each other as well as we should and I think this might have been the extreme. I think the fact that we have been persecuted, the fact that we have been subjected to genocide and holocaust did something to us as humans. It left its mark upon us and I feel when the external threat of atrocities was removed, we somehow turned these feelings toward one another."

Moradian closed the report and dropped it on his desk. I let out a long, low whistle. The doctor put a hand on my shoulder.

"This murder did more than affect people's feelings. It destroyed families."

"Yes, I remember. Brothers and sisters stopped talking to each other," I said. The alcohol had made me quite emotional. I sniffed back tears. "Friends were torn apart."

"It divided our people right down the center and made enemies out of close relatives."

"You know, Bob—"

Before I could finish my sentence, Margaret walked into the room.

"Tommy, I just got off the phone with a woman who wants to meet you," she said sounding slightly conspiratorial.

"I didn't hear the phone ring," said her husband. Neither did I.

Mrs. Moradian ignored him. "She's also quite interested in the Archbishop's death."

That sobered me up and got my full attention. "Oh?"

"Yes. Her name is Professor Anna Rosen." Margaret grew increasingly enthusiastic. "She's staying in Manhattan," she added. You really should see her."

"Maybe she and I can get together this evening."

"That sounds like a nice plan," Bob grinned.

He had no idea.

9

Then

On the streets of Brooklyn, there existed many direct links with the Old Country. One of them was a 37-year-old New York City policeman name Bedros Iskenderian. This Armenian immigrant had joined the force in 1925. Tall, husky and balding, he was quiet by nature but a formidable chap who could get tough when he had to. His fellow officers called him Pete. But to Tom Peterson, he was always Izzy.

After Tom gave Lt. Donnelly his history lesson the morning of Tourian's murder, the reporter had a little studying to do himself. Naturally, he was going to see the only Armenian cop he knew. Izzy had been pounding a beat on Coney Island when he heard about the assassination. As Donnelly and Peterson returned from Spiro's, Bedros was walking into the 34th Precinct. Oddly enough, the patrolman was wearing civilian clothes.

"Izzy, you're just the man I wanted to see," Tom began.

"No time, Tommy," Iskenderian replied as he kept moving.

"And who might you be, asked Donnelly as he planted himself in front of the younger cop.

"Officer Bedros Iskenderian from the six-seven," he said flashing shield number 3407 inside his lapel.

"Brooklyn? Don't you fellas wear uniforms down there anymore?"

"I've just been promoted to detective and assigned a case here in the 18th Division—"

"An Armenian cop?" interrupted Donnelly. "Saints preserve us. Well, whatever it is you're working on, drop it. I need your help with a homicide."

"The Tourian murder," Izzy said matter-of-factly. "That's what I'm doing."

Donnelly paused, open-mouthed. *I've got to keep an eye on that goddamn foreigner*, he thought, but instead said flatly, "Good."

"The brass called me in," Izzy added.

Nice of them to let me know, Donnelly said to himself and understood that this was no time to pull rank. But he couldn't help himself. The lieutenant put a hand on Izzy's shoulder. "Why don't you wait here a minute while I go see the boss about this."

"We don't have time," Bedros said, pushing Donnelly's hand away as he kept moving. The lieutenant bristled slightly and put a firm grasp on the younger cop's arm. Peterson walked around them and headed toward the stairs.

"And where do you think you're going?" he asked.

"I thought I'd stick around and watch you two arrest each other."

Outnumbered, Donnelly rolled his eyes. "Jesus, Mary and Joseph," he mumbled.

All three went upstairs to the detective bureau. As they walked in, the phone on Donnelly's desk was ringing.

"Doesn't anybody else work here?" he asked of no one in particular. No one in particular was in the room to answer.

"Donnelly," he said into the mouthpiece as he unhooked the phone's receiver. Someone on the other end was speaking loudly enough for us all to hear unintelligible tinny squeaks coming through the earpiece. "Shit," he mumbled. "OK, I'll take care of it." More tinny squeaking. "Yeah, he's here. Hold on."

Donnelly offered the phone to Izzy.

"It's downtown."

Iskenderian took the call. "Yes, sir?"

Judging from the younger officer's facial expression, one could only assume that this was not going to be a short conversation. The lieutenant was being big-footed. It seems the bosses had already decided that this case needed an ethnic connection. That was Izzy. Officially, Donnelly would remain the primary investigator, but the day-to-day responsibility was being handed to the young Armenian. And that was a lucky thing for Tom, because it increased his chances of staying inside.

A few blocks away, Ara Gureghian was back home comforting his mother, Nartouhi. She had been sobbing throughout the morning, unable to believe the horrible news. Her son sat there watching this old woman grieve, unable to protect her from the pain. He remembered a time when she had rescued him.

It was one late summer day in 1927. Ara was working in his shop when a tall, somewhat hefty man walked in carrying a small wooden crate.

"I'm looking for the proprietor," said the visitor who wore a tight-fitting suit. The man sniffed and spoke quickly as he looked around.

"That's me."

"Who handles your lighting?" The question struck Gureghian as very odd.

"What do you mean?"

"Your lighting. Your lamps," he said. "They're old. Who replaces them?"

"Uh, my landlady does."

Ara put down the pair of boots he had been working on and now looked the visitor square in the face. The gentleman set the crate on Ara's countertop and opened it. Inside was a rather showy light fixture. The man lifted this polished brass contraption halfway out of its container.

"What do you think? Beautiful, eh?"

Ara wasn't sure if he should be angry or amused. He half laughed and half grunted. "I don't need that," he said dismissively.

"But it's not expensive," insisted the other.

"I already told you, my landlady – she takes care of that."

The visitor now had the lamp all the way out of the box. "Look, you don't need to pay for it," he said on the sly. "I'll just leave it with you for 60 days. Then you let me know you don't want it and I'll come back and get it," he said rapidly. "No charge."

By now, Ara's impatience was showing. The shoemaker had already turned back to his work, unaware that the visitor was hanging the lamp.

"I'll just leave it with you," the salesman said. "What's your name?"

Gureghian still looked the other way. "Ara."

"And your last name?"

The shoemaker pronounced it with full Armenian accent to befuddle the salesman.

"I can't understand that," said the man, taking a sheet of paper and folding it several times. "Here, just write it down for me."

Ara now just wanted this fellow to leave, and so he scrawled his signature at the bottom of the blank page. The man quickly attached the light fixture and was out the door.

A few days later, the landlady walked into the store and noticed the new lamp. Ara told her the story.

"Well, I already bought new ones for you" she said sounding rather hurt.

"It's no problem," replied Gureghian. "We'll just put this away." And with that, he took down the brass fixture and stuck it into a cardboard box behind the counter.

Several months later, two burly men walked into Ara's shoemaker shop. One flashed a badge. "Ara Gureghian?"

"Yes?"

"We're from the sheriff's department."

"OK. So?"

"So, we're here to collect for the lamp you bought and never paid for."

"Bought nothing," Ara answered jerking a thumb at the floor. "It's been sitting in that box there, waiting for guy who left it."

While Ara talked to the first man, the second cop moved toward the cash register and began to wrap his arms around it. Now Gureghian was furious. He grabbed a large hammer.

"Get away from my register," he ordered loudly.

The first cop pulled out a revolver. "Put down that hammer."

"You can shoot me," said Ara, "but not before I kill him."

Hearing the commotion, Gureghian's mother rushed in. "What's going on?" Nartouhi demanded.

"It's nothing, Momma, nothing." Then in Armenian, Ara quickly explained the situation.

The old woman turned to the man with the gun. "Please, sir," she began softly, "don't do that. How much would it take for you to leave my son alone?"

"He owes us $60." Mrs. Gureghian opened her purse, counted out three $20 bills and handed them over. In an instant, the two cops were gone. Ara slumped slightly.

"Momma, Momma," he began, knowing she had just paid out almost a month's salary.

"Calm down, Ara. Everything is ok. You go in the back. I brought you a sandwich."

Flustered, there was nothing more to do. Ara gave in to his mother's wishes and tried to put the matter behind him.

Several weeks passed and the young shoemaker said nothing about what had happened. He tried to maintain an upbeat attitude. But a persistent scowl belied his jovial words.

Giancarlo Mancini was the neighborhood iceman and a good friend of Ara Gureghian. One afternoon, the second-generation Italian stopped by the shoemaker's shop.

"Hey, Sheik!" called Giancarlo. Ara picked up the nickname because of his resemblance to Rudolph Valentino's character in the movie by that same name.

Gureghian nodded with a slight smile.

"Why so glum, chum?" Ara told him the story of the swindle and his mother's payoff. Mancini's face turned dark red. His eyes narrowed. "Tell me, Ara, was that guy a Jew?"

Ara shrugged. "Well, he had a big nose."

"Yeah, I know that Jew bastard." Mancini paced the floor for a minute, and then stopped. "Here's what we're gonna do, Ara. Tomorrow morning at six o'clock, before I start my rounds, you're gonna come with me."

Gureghian was puzzled. "What are you talking about?"

"I want you to meet a friend of mine. He's gonna take care of this."

Ara was beginning to see the light. "Oh, I don't know, Gianni."

The Italian put his hand on Gureghian's arm. "Ara, you trust me?"

"Sure," he answered directly.

"OK, I'll see you here tomorrow morning."

At 6 a.m. on the dot, Mancini met Ara in front of the shoemaker's store. The two walked to the 181st Street subway station and rode the Number One train down to Little Italy. They walked a few more blocks to a small pastry shop. A sign in the window indicated it was closed. Giancarlo knocked once, paused, knocked twice more and waited. A moment later, they heard someone walking inside and then unlatching the door. It opened just enough for the two to enter.

Ara and Giancarlo made their way through the dim room, past the counter, past the baking area and into what looked like a sizeable dining room. Four or five young men stood near the bar, talking quietly among themselves. Seated at a highly polished dark wood table was a stout gentleman whose name Ara would never learn. Two more men wearing dark, well-tailored suits sat to his left side.

Mancini approached this stern figure and kissed his hand. They spoke softly in Italian. Then Giancarlo gestured for Ara to approach.

"Uncle, this is my friend, Ara Gureghian. He's the one I told you about."

The older man nodded. "Hello, Aro," he said slightly mispronouncing Gureghian's first name. "Gureghian," he said almost to himself. "Armenian?"

"Yes, sir."

"Giancarlo tells me you are *tagliente come pugnale*. Sharp, like—" He turned to Giancarlo. "*Pugnale, come se dice*?"

"*Pugnale*? It means knife."

"Knife? No, no." Then it came to him. "Dagger! *Si*, you're sharp, like a dagger."

Ara half smiled at what he believed to be a compliment. The older man smiled back, then turned deadly serious all of a sudden.

"And you have a problem with this *bastardo*, this *assassino di Cristo*–" he searched for the right term "—this thief?" he asked.

Gureghian stood motionless, lowered his head slightly, not fully nodding, but enough to allow for a sense of agreement. The *capo* rubbed his mustachioed upper lip while sizing up the situation in front of him.

"Don't worry, Aro. I take care for you this," he said emotionlessly. "Giancarlo, he explain everything." The unidentified boss then gestured toward Ara with an open hand, as if giving him permission to leave. Before they left, Mancini moved closer to his uncle and the two spoke a few more whispered sentences in Italian.

On the way back to the shoemaker's shop, Giancarlo told Ara that a pair of men would show up there in a very fast car late the next afternoon. Gureghian was to accompany them and follow their instructions precisely and without hesitation.

"I don't know about this, Gianni." Ara was having second thoughts.

"It's ok, Ara. "No one is gonna get hurt. They're just gonna teach him a lesson."

Ara didn't say much to anyone for the rest of the day. Around five o'clock the next afternoon, as promised, a new Lincoln sedan arrived. Gureghian stood frozen for several minutes, then finally took off his leather apron, walked outside and locked the front door.

The driver and passenger both wore dark suits. The young man on the right rolled down his window.

"Are you Gureghian?"

"Yeah."

"Sheik?"

"Yeah."

"Get in."

Ara opened the back door and sat down.

"Where are we going?"

"Don't worry about it," said the driver as the Lincoln sped away. About fifteen minutes later, they were parked near a modest apartment building just across town. The passenger turned around and noticed that Ara was shaking.

"Hey, listen," he said. "There's no need to be nervous. We're not going to kill this guy. Nobody's going to get hurt. We're just going to talk to him."

"That's right," agreed the driver.

"Are you going to get my money back?" asked Ara.

"No," answered the passenger. "That's gone. You consider it a lesson. Let's go."

As they got out of the car, Ara was surprised by how short the other two men were. This was hardly the image he had of hoodlums. They walked to the front entrance and went inside.

"Now, we'll take the elevator up to the fourth floor," said the driver, "but we're going to walk back down. Got it?"

Ara nodded. As they got to the top floor, the driver reached up and unscrewed the only light bulb illuminating that landing. He gestured for Ara to stand in the now-darkened alcove.

"By the way, do you have a handkerchief?" asked the other man.

Gureghian took one out of his pocket and held it out. The man pushed it back.

"You hold onto that. Stand right over here and don't move," he ordered. "When you see this guy, all you do is drop that handkerchief. Don't do nothin' else and don't say nothin'."

The driver went to the public telephone in front of the elevator doors, pretending to speak with someone. Meanwhile, his partner stayed in the shadows with Gureghian. And they waited – and waited – for two hours. During that time, more than a dozen people had arrived and gone into their respective apartments. It had grown quite dark and Ara was beginning to think this guy was never going to show up. Just then, he heard the elevator motor whine. The doors clattered open. Out stepped their man. He carried a large briefcase in one hand and a wooden box in the other. Ara dropped his handkerchief.

At that moment, the driver hung up the pay phone, took an unlit cigarette from behind his left ear and walked up to his target. "Excuse me, mister," he began politely, holding out the cigarette. "Do you have a match?"

Feeling unthreatened by this relatively small fellow, the man put down his briefcase as well as the wooden box, and then put both hands into his pants pockets searching for a match. Seeing his victim immobilized, the driver simultaneously punched the taller man in his solar plexus and raised a knee into his crotch. The salesman doubled over. That was the cue for the other thug standing next to Ara. He now sprang from the shadows and threw his full force on the victim's back. The victim now fell to the floor, crying out in agony. Both attackers continued kicking and punching the prostrate man.

"This is what you get for cheating innocent people," said one breathlessly.

"Don't you ever pull this shit again," wheezed the other.

The racket drew attention from almost every resident on the floor. Apartment doors flew open and closed just as quickly. No one dared interfere. Besides, no one could call the police since the only available telephone was, at least temporarily, inaccessible. Eventually, the beating stopped. Ara was stunned by what he witnessed, regained his senses. Remembering the instructions, Gureghian scrambled toward the stairs.

"Hey, slow down." One of the thugs grabbed Ara by the arm. "Pick up your handkerchief." Ara did was he was told and again hurried down the stairs.

"Take it easy," said the other man. "You don't want to fall."

The three men deliberately descended to the ground floor. As they were exiting the building, the sound of sirens pierced the air. Once again, Ara felt anxious. But the two ruffians maintained their relaxed demeanor.

"Relax, pal. You ain't done nothin' wrong," said the driver. As he calmly accelerated away, a police car roared up to the building.

"That ain't got nothin' to do with us," agreed the other man.

Fifteen minutes later, they delivered Gureghian to his shoe shop. Ara's hands were shaking so much that he could almost not fit his key into the lock.

Early the next morning, Giancarlo Mancini came to visit Ara. "Hey, Sheik, how're you doing?"

"I didn't sleep at all last night."

The iceman smiled at his friend. "That son of a bitch will never bother you or any other poor immigrant again."

Ara was still disheartened.

"Ara, would you like to thank the man who arranged this?"

Gureghian thought for a moment, and then nodded.

"Come on, let's go."

About half an hour later, they were back at the pastry shop in Little Italy. Once inside, Ara walked up to his anonymous benefactor.

"Hello, Aro." The older gentleman was seated in the same spot – as if he had never moved. "Is everything ok with you now?"

Ara nodded, still uncomfortable speaking directly to this evidently powerful and dangerous man. Gureghian started to reach for his wallet.

"No!" Giancarlo was alarmed by his friend's impetuous act.

"But I wanted to thank him."

"So, just say 'thank you' to him," advised Mancini.

Ara took the advice. "Thank you, sir."

The older gentleman nodded his approval. "Aro, if you ever need anything, you come to me. And maybe someday, if I ever need something, I come to you. Giancarlo tells me you are an excellent shoemaker. I remember that."

The favor was never repaid.

The Archbishop lay dead, and Gureghian wistfully remembered what the Italian *capo* had called him: "*tagliente come pugnale* – sharp like a dagger." But as Ara watched his mother crying, he wished that he were as powerful as the Mafioso in the pastry shop. Or the two little hoods. Or even his own mother. The shoemaker would have liked to mete out justice personally to the Archbishop's assassins. But his religion would never allow that, and anyway he might not have had the physical strength or emotional courage to do what needed to be done.

Instead, Ara vowed to be a good American and tell the police what he knew.

10

Now

Standing in front of me this evening was the first woman I had ever loved. Anna Rosen looked just as beautiful to me now as she did when I first met her all those years before. Anna's last name was Kludjian back then. That was a lifetime ago. In the intervening years, she had two children, one recently married. And she had been a widow for quite a while.

Although we grew up in the same neighborhood, the difference in our ages made intimate socializing improbable for a long time. This was especially true because of our common Armenian roots, with all the family expectations and obligations.

I had already gone to work for the Trib when she was still in high school. We ran into each other shortly after her 21st birthday. A mutual friend invited each of us to a party that summer, and one thing led to another. It was the grand passion to end all grand passions. To this day, I can't explain why we didn't stay together and live happily ever after together. Oh, right – maybe it was because she moved to California with her parents that September. Yeah, that might have had something to do with it. But I digress.

I met Anna in the lobby of an apartment building in Greenwich Village, where her cousin lived. This evening, Anna's onyx-colored hair had lightened a little and there was a hint of rouge enhancing the natural blush in those perfect cheeks I remember so fondly. Her lissome body and dark, dark eyes still dazzled me. She was not one iota less sexy.

"Let's go get a bite to eat," she suggested.

We walked in the drizzle to a cafe, just two blocks away. It was remarkably uncrowded.

I was still a bit disoriented, stunned by the appearance of this lovely lady who had meant so much to me. A million questions flooded my brain. Why was Anna back in New York? How had she found me? Did she still feel as I felt? Was I wearing matching socks? Before I could get any answers, she smiled that smile that first caught my eye.

"I still can't believe it," I finally babbled. "Look at you."

"Look at you," she answered. "I like that moustache. When did you grow it?"

"When I was twelve." That got the laugh I hoped for. Anna was usually stingy with her laughs, so I considered it my mission in life to provoke her. "Actually, it was just a few years after you, uh—"

"After I left." That was a mood killer.

"I'm sorry. I didn't mean—"

She took my hand. "That's ok, Tom."

All right, so I lied. Not everybody calls me Tommy. With Anna, it was always Tom. Or sometimes Thomas. Or occasionally Tom-Tom. She had a way with words. But I always only called her Anna.

"Has it really been thirty years?" I asked.

"Thirty-one years," she said. "And three months."

"Right. But there was your high school reunion," I recalled.

She shook her head. "I didn't go. You and I talked on the phone, but that was shortly after my Walter died."

"Oh, right." I started to apologize.

"It's ok. You sent beautiful flowers and a lovely card." It was as if she were consoling me.

"I'm so sorry I couldn't make his funeral." I tugged at my left ear trying to remember.

She remembered for me. "The Kennedy assassination was the same week. Your paper wouldn't let you leave."

"Right. Right." All these years later, I still regretted that tragic coincidence. But as a newsman and a slave to events, there was simply no way to leave that story.

We sat there, alternately staring our largely uneaten food and at each other. The kid in me wanted to leap over the table and ravish her right there. The "senior citizen" controlled himself and instead asked about her kids. She talked about their school, their neighbors, their lives in California. And then, without my asking, she cleared up the mystery of her presence here.

Anna became a widow fifteen years ago, and for the first time in her life, had to think about how she would support herself and her children. Walter Rosen had left the family with some insurance money, but that would not have been enough. So, Anna went back to school, became a psychologist and opened a small family counseling practice. It was perfect for her and I thoroughly enjoyed hearing the details.

I also enjoyed learning that this encounter was more than a coincidence. Anna had kept in touch with the Moradians over the years. Coincidentally, she had flown to New York a few days ago to attend a professional conference. It was Margaret who had called her today, who told her about my visit, and who conspired with her for us to meet again. Margaret also told her about my renewed interest in the Tourian murder.

"But that was so long ago," Anna said pragmatically. "What can you possibly find out now that you didn't know then?"

"I need to try, Anna."

"I think that's what I've always loved about you, Tom-Tom," she said with a twinkle in her eyes. "You never give up."

Rather than taking the hint, I continued talking. "Something about it is still bothering me."

She gazed at me with a puzzled expression on her face. "I thought all this was settled in court back then."

"Well," I began, "technically, I suppose it was."

"But?"

"But I always thought the whole thing was too simplistic." The waitress came by to see if we wanted more drinks. Anna took my hand.

"Let's continue this conversation back at home."

We went back to the apartment building on Sullivan Street. Her cousin was out of town, so we had the place to ourselves. While Anna busied herself making coffee, I sat on the living room couch and thought out loud.

"There were a lot of threats against the Archbishop, but no one every really tried to kill him before that morning. They certainly had easier opportunities to do it and get away with it," I mused. "I wonder if those guys actually even had the guts to murder him themselves."

Anna brought out two cups of coffee and a plate of chocolate chip cookies. She put them on the coffee table and sat very close to me. I absentmindedly stirred in several spoonfuls of sugar.

"Go on, Sherlock."

I raised an eyebrow. "Are you trying to distract me?"

She grinned, then switched to mock seriousness. "Oh, no. Please, continue."

I was about to open my mouth when she interrupted.

"Wait." Then she took my face in her hands and kissed me. "There. I've been wanting to do that all evening."

11

The conflict among Armenians in America came to a boiling point at the 1933 Chicago Century of Progress International Exposition. Days were allotted to various nationalities. July 1 was set aside as Armenian Day. The organizing committee invited Archbishop Tourian as guest of honor. He was scheduled to speak at the Armenian exhibit around noon.

By 9:30 that morning, nearly five thousand people had already arrived at the Court of the Hall of Science.

Shortly before the Archbishop was due to appear, a choral group began to perform on stage. Suddenly, a woman marched in carrying a large tri-color flag. The *yerakouyn* with red, blue and orange horizontal stripes was the banner of the now-defunct Armenian Republic. The flag bearer was followed by about twenty men, women and children who carried smaller similar banners. This little patriotic parade strode onto the platform and the large standard was planted there.

The audience reacted with a mixture of raucous cheers and boos. A few days before, organizers of the Armenian Day events had feared such a reaction and explicitly prohibited use of the old republican flag. They immediately called in Major Felix Streyckmans, Chairman of the Committee on Nationalities.

"We can't proceed with the ceremonies if that flag remains on the platform," Sam Donian told the Major when he arrived. "You can see how upset the people are by this."

Streyckmans conferred with those who had brought the tri-color. They agreed to remove it from the platform, brought it down from the stage and set it on the floor – in front of the stage. Again, many in the audience began to complain.

At that moment, the Prelate arrived. He was shocked to see the flag of the former Armenian Republic prominently displayed in the hall.

The Major conferred with Tourian.

"I can't speak under this banner," said the Archbishop. "It would mean that I am taking a political side and supporting those who follow this revolutionary party." He explained that it would cause dissent in the United

States and might lead to reprisals against Armenians living in the U.S.S.R. Displaying those colors clearly constituted an affront to Soviet authority, he said. "They must take down that flag."

Several people in the audience sitting close to the stage strained to hear this discussion. "What did he say?" asked one Armenian man.

"I think he said something about that rag," replied another. This rumored insult quickly spread through the room.

"Well, what do you suggest?" the Major asked Tourian.

The Archbishop thought a moment. "This is an American meeting," he said. "Let's have only an American flag here. That way we can avoid all the difficulties and keep the Church out of this controversy."

Streyckmans promptly agreed. He returned to those with the tri-color and explained Tourian's plan.

"No! We want to keep our *yerakouyn* here," replied one man referring to the tri-color flag.

The Major brushed him aside, walked onto the stage and took the microphone.

"Ladies and gentlemen, your attention please." The room quieted to a low buzz. He briefly told the crowd what the Armenian committee and the Prelate proposed. Streyckmans explained that the program would not continue unless the banner were removed and an American flag put in its place. He then asked the audience to vote. Hands went up on both sides. The Major did a quick count.

"By my estimate, it is clear. About ninety percent of you agree to replace that flag with the stars and stripes." The room got loud again as members of the audience began to argue among themselves, both in English and Armenian. The cacophony grated on Streyckmans who was astonished by this unseemly reaction. "Now what?" he asked to no one in particular.

One man who wanted to keep the controversial banner in place told the Major that many people in the audience didn't understand English.

"All right, well let's do this once more in their native language." Streyckmans asked for a translator. A man from California approached the stage and repeated the Archbishop's proposal, this time in Armenian. Again, there was a vote. Again, the audience seemed overwhelming in support of the compromise.

"That's it," said the Major decisively. "We have a settlement. The tri-color is out, the American flag is in."

The moment this final election result was announced, someone picked up a folding chair and swung it at a plainclothes police officer – who just happened to be the head of security for the Exposition. At that point, all hell broke loose as visitors ran for the exits, bumping into tables and knocking over chairs. A nearby contingent of policemen rushed in and began to separate the various combatants. Lawmen detained nine people who seemed to be the most violent. One quick-witted officer rolled up the tri-color flag and laid it on the platform – an ironic (if unintentional) compromise.

To further diffuse the fracas, Streychmans asked someone to sing the American national anthem. The chanteuse, Madame Rose Zulalian, stepped up to the microphone and sang out. It took the noted contralto only a few bars from the "Star Spangled Banner" to bring the remaining audience members to attention.

To those who were present, this explosive confrontation had seemed to last an eternity. But the fighting ended almost as suddenly as it had begun. A few minutes later, the police released those who had been held at the rear of the hall, with no formal charges filed. The Armenian Day program continued without further incident; nevertheless, this melee hung heavily over the rest of that afternoon and evening and was the topic of conversation and newspaper editorials for months afterwards.

12

I can be really dense sometimes. This was not one of those times.

Anna leaned her head against my chest as I continued with my theories about why Archbishop Tourian was assassinated, about who might have been responsible, and about the possibility that the real killer was never found. She looked at me and smiled. After what must have seemed like many minutes, I finally reached for her hand. She let me take it to my lips.

"I was beginning to think you didn't feel that way anymore," she whispered.

"Are you kidding?"

We kissed fervently for many minutes. Then, without saying a word, we both stood up and Anna led me into her bedroom.

Despite all the intervening years since we last held each other like this, it was if time had stood still. In some ways, the real passage of time enhanced our lovemaking. Tonight, we felt no sense of urgency. As we rediscovered each other, our passion was unhurried. In this dreamlike moment, there was no need to turn back the clock. This was perfection.

After we got dressed, Anna was the one to bring up the Tourian case again.

"But what about all the witnesses?" she asked.

"The whole thing happened so fast," I said. "No one got a good look at what happened – not even me."

There was a long silence. For the first time in nearly forty years, I had just admitted being a witness to the assassination.

"You were there?" she asked, astonished. "I never knew."

"No one knew," I confessed quietly. "Not even Izzy.

"But why?"

"I couldn't very well be a witness and a news reporter."

Anna nodded slowly, then left the bedroom for several minutes. She returned carrying a thick, dark brown envelope. It was marked only by a string of seemingly random numbers.

"Thomas, I am going to show you something," she said, straightening the brass brad.

"What—" She held up her hand to stop me.

"I think you need to read these." She removed the half-dozen sheets of paper and handed them to me.

On these slightly yellowed, lined pages, obviously torn from a spiral notebook, were the neatly handwritten words of someone who seemed intimately connected with the Tourian murder. It was dated January 11, 1934. As I read the words, my eyes got wider.

> *My dear pal, keep to yourself all that I am going to write you about. I was very thankful to you and to the Whitinsville committee for entertaining me for three days in right good fashion. We had a glorious time with the comrades drinking for the "soul" of that rotting carcass of that dog. Next it will be the others' turn.*
>
> *From your place I came to Boston. The same thing here. From Boston I went to New York. But my heart was broken to pieces. The Committee and some women comrades of the Red Cross entertained me in right good fashion. They were all in great rejoicing. We decided to go and see the boys on their way to court from jail. Tourian's dogs fell on them and gave them a good beating. I wanted to put my knife through a few of them, but V. Aharonian would not let me do, saying they would be out in a few days, and then one by one they would rot like dogs like Tourian.*

My mouth fell open. The name "Aharonian" was vaguely familiar to me, but I didn't know why. I continued reading.

> *The Committee and our lady comrades said that they have bribed the lawyer and the judge, also some of the cops. Everything is OK. With money, you can do anything. Money is all-powerful. Plenty of money, plenty of men to do the killing. Everything is OK.*

General Sebooh is here. He sends you much love. They will be there next Sunday for a very important meeting. Money is going to be raised and they will want "killers," too. Long live Armenian Revolutionary Federation. Long live our commanders, all our killers. Down with Tourian dogs.

Regards,
Sincere Dagger

I read several more pages, then looked up at Anna. Her eyes were slightly watery as she nodded, slowly.

"How did you get these?" I asked.

"They were given to me by a former client who is now deceased. Ethically, I can't tell you anything about that person. But since the letter was written by someone else to a third party, my client's identity wouldn't help you anyway."

I frowned. "I see. So, then what does it mean?"

Anna took my hand. "Tom, I just wanted you to realize that I also understand there was a lot more to this than what we knew."

I nodded and she smiled that smile.

13

Then

While Bedros "Pete" Iskenderian was on the phone, Tom Peterson sat in Lt. Donnelly's office, continuing his lecture on Armenian politics. They were joined by Assistant District Attorney Joseph Cohn. The prosecutor happened to be on call this weekend, and caught the Tourian case. A.D.A. Cohn had come in to interview witnesses and to meet those who had already been arrested.

As Peterson started to explain his conspiracy theory of partisan control over religion, Izzy walked in. Having finished his phone calls, he quickly briefed Cohn and Donnelly on progress with the investigation. There would probably be more arrests today or tomorrow after wearing out some tire rubber and shoe leather.

"I'll check in with you later this afternoon, Loo," Pete said to the lieutenant, and then headed out the door with Tom tagging along.

"Keep a light on for us, honey," Peterson added for fun. Donnelly didn't have time to argue with the reporter who dashed out the door right behind Iskenderian.

"Pete and Peterson," mumbled the lieutenant. "The Armenians have taken over."

The few unmarked cars assigned to the Wadsworth Avenue detectives were kept behind the station house. Pete found a clean Ford with a full tank of gas.

"Tommy, let's take a ride." He tossed the keys to Peterson. "You drive."

He knew the reporter was better behind the wheel. It also left Iskenderian free to observe. Things were a bit less strict in those days.

"Where to, guv'nor?" Tom asked in mock British chauffeur fashion.

"Let's go downtown."

"We gonna see a show?"

"We're gonna put on a show."

Pete had quite a show in mind, too. They were headed for the Armen Garo Social and Reading Club at 366 Third Avenue. The club also served as local headquarters for the Armenian Revolutionary Federation or *Tashnag* party.

The organization had been founded in 1890 by various pro-independence groups who got together to liberate Armenia from the Turkish Ottoman Empire.

For the next several decades, the Turkish government punished these political activists and those who sympathized with their cause. This persecution culminated with the massacre of one and a half million Armenians in 1915. Turkish control continued until the end of the World War in 1918, while Russians held onto their half until the Bolshevik Revolution. In 1919, the *Tashnags* created a nascent independent Armenian Republic, but it lasted scarcely two years. Armenia again found itself split between Turks on one side and the Soviet Union on the other.

The ARF was once more a political party without territory to govern. Its new domain was the Diaspora, as Armenians scattered throughout Europe, the Middle East and America. At that point, the story led to vibrant, passionate and at times fierce disputes over the fate of the Armenian nation. One side believed they should leave well-enough alone. Yes, half of their motherland – including the city of Etchmiadzin, Holy See of the Armenian Apostolic Church – was now under the thumb of Soviet dictators. But at least they weren't being slaughtered by Turks there.

On the other side was the view that there could be no rest until Armenia was free from foreign oppression, whether Muslims in Turkey or communists in Soviet Russia. Moreover, argued some in the *Tashnag* party, the Armenian Church was complicit by accepting the yoke of the Kremlin.

This morning, unknown to Tom, Iskenderian had arranged for some serious backup – a squadron of uniformed and plainclothes cops waiting around the corner. When Pete and Tom arrived, twenty-five boys in blue and a half dozen detectives were ready to burst into the club.

But as if in anticipation of an assault, the entrance was sealed tighter than a jar of your grandmother's plum preserves.

"Maybe they're closed," offered Tom. "It is Christmas Eve, you know."

"Not for them it isn't," said Pete with a grin.

He forcefully applied a single beefy shoulder and the front door gave way. The club consisted largely of a library, a reception room and a hall. An army of New York's finest flowed inside, weapons drawn, grabbing up everyone in sight and threatening to plug anyone who moved. This was a classic raid, but without the bootleg liquor.

While the uniforms were keeping club members busy, Tom and Iskenderian moved into the ARF office. There, they found file cabinets, book cases, desks and chairs, as well as Armenian- and English-language newspapers strewn everywhere. On one wall was a placard of the party emblem: a fist holding the staff of a red banner, crisscrossed by a pen, a shovel and a dagger.

"You know, Izzy, I always wondered about that sign," said Tom, looking at the poster. "My grandfather said it was very symbolic."

"Well, according to my grandfather, the pen represents writing," said Pete. "The shovel is for the earth."

"And that knife?"

The policeman chuckled. "You figure it out."

Lt. Donnelly began to wonder if this case was too big for him. Two hours had passed since Archbishop Tourian's murder and it was already obvious that this was not a simple homicide. The case involved an international conspiracy with evidence dating back to the last century (at least) and with suspects possibly linked to Turkey, Armenia or even the Kremlin. He might as well be chasing Mata Hari! Well, as his mentor, Assistant Chief Inspector John J. Sullivan, always said, *Start with what you know, boy-o.*

"Billy!" yelled Donnelly. No need to raise his voice. Bill O'Shea was never far.

"Yes, Lieutenant?"

"What do we have so far on this priest killing?"

"Archbishop."

"What? Oh yeah, right. I know – he was an archbishop." It was only noon and Donnelly was already reaching for the bicarbonate of soda. He rubbed his belly and winced at the pain. "Just tell me where things stand so far."

"Sorry, Lieutenant." O'Shea opened his notebook. Meticulously accurate in keeping records, he would have made a better accountant than a cop. "We have two men in custody. Both admit to being in the church this morning, but they say they had nothing to do with the murder."

"Amazing, isn't it Billy? Nobody we arrest is ever guilty." Donnelly shook his head. "What about the witnesses?"

"Nobody saw it happen, but everybody knows who did it."

The lieutenant tried unsuccessfully to belch. "There's a switch."

The prelate had been killed inside a church and in front of several hundred witnesses. There was also plenty of circumstantial evidence. So, why wasn't this an open and shut case?

For that matter, why weren't there any federal agents knocking on the door, trying to take over jurisdiction? There were always G-men around when a case had national or international implications. Maybe they were too busy to be bothered with one more local homicide – preoccupied with the likes of George "Baby Face" Nelson or Bonnie and Clyde. Every lawman in the country wanted to bring in John Dillinger. So did a lot of amateur sleuths. After all, there was a $15,000 reward on his head.

This week's Justice Department circular reported that there were 400,000 hoods loose in America pulling stick-ups and snatching innocent kids. Even J. Edgar Hoover had manpower limitations. Still, something didn't add up here.

Detectives seized several boxes full of papers at the Armen Garo Club and brought few ARF members into Wadsworth Station for questioning. After about an hour, the cops let them go with a warning "not to leave the city."

As the *Tashnags* were leaving the precinct house, Ara Gureghian approached the desk sergeant.

"Excuse me, please, your honor" he began. "I want to testify."

The desk sergeant considered the young immigrant. During the past ten years that Ara had been living in America, he gave assimilation his full effort. Nevertheless, the Armenian still bore some residual marks of a foreigner: more than a touch of accent in his speech, a hint of imported style about his clothes and a bit of overseas shuffle in his walk. But the most significant giveaway was the manner in which he treated authority figures: slightly too much deference and slightly too much fear.

"Were you there?" the policeman asked tersely.

Ara hesitated before answering. At age 27, he was still occasionally mistaken for a teenager. They said it was the shock of witnessing Turks murder half of his village in 1915. That experience stunted not only his growth, but affected his speech as well. He spoke with a decided stutter.

"Yeah, I was right outside." As Ara's courage mounted, he became enthusiastic. "I was walking toward the church from my apartment a block away on 186th Street," he said. "As soon as I heard all the yelling outside, I ran over as fast as I could."

"But you didn't see the actual murder."

Crestfallen, Ara retreated slightly. The young man felt he had failed twice. First, he hadn't been in the church to stop the assassination (although there was no reason to believe he could have done so). Second, he hadn't been inside to serve as eyewitness. So here he was, confessing to this Irish cop that he couldn't help his vicar, in life or in death.

The sergeant gestured for Ara to follow him. He led the young Armenian to the small room where the dead Archbishop's body was awaiting transport to the mortuary. The Sergeant lifted the sheet that covered Tourian's corpse. Ara was mortified to see the fresh stab wounds on the semi-nude figure, revealed beneath the ornate vestments. As he looked at the body, Gureghian was surprised to see a plain, hand-sewn, cloth patch on the exalted man's long underwear. Ara remembered the first time he met the Archbishop.

> It was a Sunday morning, just after church services. Tourian was due to attend an affair in New Jersey. One of the trustees of the church saw Gureghian standing outside having a smoke.
>
> "Ara, you have a nice car, don't you?"
>
> "Yeah." In fact, Ara had a nearly new Hudson Essex Terraplane, a powerful but not very large sedan which he had just waxed the day before.
>
> "Mr. Kashian, the undertaker, was supposed to be here with his Cadillac. But he's late. The Archbishop has to go to a doing in Paterson. Would you take him?"
>
> "Of course, sure – I'll take him."
>
> Ara was a plain-spoken man who treated everyone the same, whether king or commoner. While not especially impressed, he was perfectly happy to have an important clergyman in his car. And he was always very polite.
>
> The trustee explained the situation to the Archbishop who gladly agreed to ride in Ara's automobile. Two other church officials climbed in, one in the back seat with Tourian, the other in front next to Gureghian. As they were about to drive off, the trustee ran up to the car.

> "Ara, Ara, wait, wait! Kashian just showed up!" He opened the back door and said to the Archbishop, "*Serpazan*, one of our parishioners just arrived with his Cadillac. I'm sure you'd rather ride in his luxury car."
>
> Ara glanced in the rear-view mirror and made eye contact with Tourian. The cleric smiled, and then turned to the trustee.
>
> "This is a very nice car. I have no trouble riding in this fine automobile – as long as the young man is still willing to take us," said the Archbishop, wishing to spare Gureghian's feelings.
>
> "Go ahead, close the door," Ara said to the trustee. "I'll take him." He was moved by the fact that this great man would show such consideration for a person of no special significance. He thought, *That's a real sign of greatness.*

The present political tensions were particularly difficult for Ara since his father, Setrag, had been one of the original members of the *Tashnag* party in Turkish Armenia. A teacher, he was one of the group's leading intellectuals. But Gureghian, the elder, was betrayed by another Armenian who infiltrated the organization and told the Turkish police of the party's revolutionary activities.

The word came down that it was not safe for Setrag to remain in Turkey. He managed to escape to New York. From there, he provided for his family until the start of the *axor* (as Armenians refer to their forced exile into the Syrian desert during the 1915 carnage). He sent for them to come to America, but he would never see them again. While they were en route, Setrag went to the hospital for prostate surgery. He died on the operating table. Ara wondered: What would his old man have thought about all this?

Now seeing the hand-sewn patch on the clothes of this deceased man, Ara remembered the Archbishop's humility. Tourian had lived alone in a comfortable two-suite accommodation that the Church provided on the sixth floor of the swank Seville Hotel at 29th Street and Madison Avenue. But despite his high office and fancy appearances, the Archbishop remained true to his religious vow of poverty. When his own undershirt had developed a rip, the clergyman repaired it by himself.

The policeman dropped the sheet and slammed a fist on the table, shaking Gureghian from his reflection. The young man drew back to where several other Armenians now stood.

"How could you goddamned people kill a man like this?" shouted the Irish cop, he face turned dark red, nearly matching the color of his hair. "He was too fuckin' good for you, he was."

With that, he strode over to the cowering immigrants and spat upon each of them as they hung their heads in shame. Several started to sob. Although these Armenians had not participated in the killing, they felt the guilt of their entire nationality.

It was, to be sure, a condemnation on the whole of the Armenian race – especially painful since Armenians had been highly respected as the world's first Christian nation. Armenians had been considered intellectuals, merchants, pure of heart, martyrs for their religion. Now, they were priest killers.

14

Now

We rode the elevator down to the lobby in contentment and silence. Anna had a hand on my chest. I rested my arm on her remarkably slim waist. We were like a couple of kids, stealing glances at each other, but with a degree of comfort that normally comes from many years spent together. In our case, those were years spent apart. We had the comfort anyway.

Despite our intimacy, we both knew that tonight was the exception, not the rule. I had to finish this research, get back to Florida, and write my book. Anna had a life on the West Coast.

Still, it was difficult to say good-bye again. Painful. As we walked out into the cold night air, the taxi we had ordered was waiting at the curb to take me back to my hotel. I realized that there was nothing else to do but go. We gave promises to stay in touch, knowing that this might be the last time we'd meet. I took her hand and turned to face her.

"Anna," I began.

"No, Tom. Don't."

"What? I just wanted to—"

She put a finger on my lips and shook her head.

"Whatever it is you want to say will just spoil this moment. Anyway, you're a journalist. Let me do the talking for once."

I started to open my mouth again, then closed it abruptly and clamped my own hand over it.

"Good boy," she said. "Now, here's what you're going to do, my love. You're going to take me in your arms, kiss me nicely, and say good-bye."

Slowly, unavoidably, I nodded in agreement.

"Besides, you have important work to do."

I tilted my head down and to the side, tugging on my mustache and hoping to mask the tear that welled up in my left eye. It was no use. She brought out a handkerchief and smiled that smile once more.

Twenty minutes later, I was back in my hotel room, the faint traces of her Chanel No. 5 still lingered in my nostrils. I switched off the lights in the room, opened the curtain and looked out the window over the City, sparkling brilliantly. How many more witnesses were out there? If only I could find the right one. Now, more than ever, I was determined to find out who killed the Archbishop.

15

Then

The cops left Peterson to make his own way back to the Trib from the Armen Garo Club. By the time he arrived at the newspaper office, it was already starting to get dark. The clickety-clack clattering of typewriters filled the air as the deadline for tomorrow's first edition approached.

Tom loved the newsroom. To him, it was truly beautiful, with its scattered piles of paper cast on ink-blotted, scarred, elderly wooden desks; a filthy floor repulsively decorated by years of ground out cigarette butts; file cabinets tilting Tower-of-Pisa-like and threatening to collapse under the weight of their overstuffed contents – all illuminated during the day by tall cathedral windows stained with the city's grime, and by barely radiating light bulbs at night.

The reporter removed his overcoat and hung it on the brass, wall-mounted rack near the door. He tilted his fedora back on his head, tapped a Chesterfield out of the pack and stuck it in his mouth unlit. Then he pulled the folded pages of notes out of his inside jacket pocket and walked briskly to his desk.

"Hey, Peterson, do you still work here?"

It was the accusatory voice of his boss. Stanley Walker had become city editor of the Herald Tribune the same day Tom started there. Walker had worked his way up the ranks. He was the archetypical editor – loud, suspicious and relentlessly demanding. But under that gruff exterior, he was really a hellcat. He was also one hell of a writer, with a particular interest in the underworld. That same year, Walker had penned a book called "The Night Club Era" which his publisher described as "a naturalist's investigation of the astonishing nocturnal fauna of New York – a monograph on the origin of some very strange species…gangsters, racketeers, hostesses, suckers, killers, rats…"

Walker was forever being quoted for saying that news depended on the three Ws: "women, wampum and wrong-doing."

"Where the hell have you been?" He now stood inches away from Tom's bulbous nose waiting for an answer.

"I'm still working on this murder at the church up in Washington Heights," Peterson explained.

"Well it'd be nice to know if we're gonna have something to fill that hole on page one tomorrow," drawled the transplanted Texan.

"Page one?" Tom was stunned. He never expected this story to get such prominent play. "Yes, sir. I have a great story for you."

"Well, let's see some copy."

"And how!"

He plopped into his chair and rolled a blank sheet of paper into the Underwood upright. Among other things, Tom was a very fast typist and the words quickly began to shape his lead. Walker looked over Peterson's shoulder as his writing machine spat out the words:

> **Archbishop Leon Tourian, primate of the Gregorian (Armenian) Church of all of North and South America, was stabbed to death with a nine-inch butcher knife at 10:30 a.m. yesterday in the presence of 400 horrified communicants in Holy Cross Armenian Apostolic church, 578 West 187th Street, as he marched to the altar to preach the Sunday sermon.**

Without looking back, he asked, "What do you think so far?"

"It'll do 'til some real news comes along," Walker replied and walked away. "I need thirty inches in an hour." Then, after a beat, "And take it easy on that thing. Those typewriters cost the paper plenty."

Tom kept pounding hard on the keys, chapeau firmly in place.

"And take off that hat!" the editor shouted before slamming his office door.

As fast as Tom typed, the clock ran faster. He had thousands of great words left on this story, but it didn't matter. The next day, the Trib would give the Tourian murder lead position on the upper right-hand side of page one. The headline blared, "Assassins Kill Archbishop." Unfortunately, a record storm would drop four inches of snow on the city in three hours and New York City would grind to a halt. Even worse, Fiorello LaGuardia was going to take the oath of office as mayor one week from today. Weather and politics were competing for attention as the next big story; Peterson's claim to fame was once again heading for the back pages.

(Copyright, 1933, New York Tribune Inc.)

MONDAY, DECEMBER 25, 1933

LATE CITY EDITION

TWO CENTS In Greater New York | THREE CENTS Within 200 Miles | FOUR CENTS Elsewhere

Roosevelt Christmas Address

By The Associated Press

WASHINGTON, Dec. 24.—The text of the address of President Roosevelt in connection with the lighting of the municipal Christmas tree at the national capital follows:

My friends:

We in the nation's capital are gathered around this symbolic tree, celebrating the coming of Christmas; in spirit we join with millions of men and women and children, throughout our own land and in other countries and continents, in happy and reverent observance of the spirit of Christmas.

For me and for my family it is the happiest of Christmases. To the many thousands of you who have thought of me and have sent me greetings, and I hope all of you are hearing my voice, I want to tell you how profoundly grateful I am. If it were within my power so to do I would personally thank each and every one of you for your remembrance of me, but there are so many thousands of you that that happy task is impossible.

Even more greatly my happiness springs from the deep conviction that this year marks a greater national understanding of the significance in our modern lives of the teachings of Him whose birth we celebrate. To more and more of us the words "Thou shalt love thy neighbor as thyself" have taken on a meaning that is showing itself and proving itself in our purposes and daily lives.

May the practice of that high ideal grow in us all in the year to come. I give you and send you, one and all, old and young, a merry Christmas and a truly happy New Year.

And so, for now and for always, "God bless us every one."

Christmas at Home and Abroad

Summary of Today's News

Holiday Hope Of Joy Voiced By Roosevelt

President Urges Nation to Seek Brotherhood as He Expresses Gratitude to Well-Wishers

White House Party Upsets Precedents

Executive Is Santa Claus to Families of Guards and the Domestic Staff

From the Herald Tribune Bureau

WASHINGTON, Dec. 24.—While the lights of a community Christmas tree glowed before him in the twilight, President Roosevelt addressed to the country this evening his wish for "A Merry Christmas and a truly Happy New Year."

French Grieve For 200 Dead In Rail Wreck

Lebrun Decrees National Mourning as 4 Shattered Cars Smoulder Along Line Near Paris

Many of Injured May Not Recover

Nuns Pray as Relatives Visit Waiting Room to Try to Identify Victims

By James M. Minifie

From the Herald Tribune Bureau

Copyright, 1933, New York Tribune Inc.

PARIS, Dec. 24.—Christmas Eve became a time of nation-wide sorrow for France as President Albert Lebrun decreed a day of national mourning for the worst railroad wreck in the history of the country.

Paul Morel, Undersecretary of the Interior in 1912-'13, in the Cabinets of Raymond Poincare, Aristide Briand and Leon Barthou and Undersecretary of Finance under the late Georges Clemenceau in 1919, was another victim of the wreck. Gaston Poittevin, Radical Socialist Deputy of Rheims,

(Continued on page four)

Murdered in Procession to the Altar

Associated Press photo

Archbishop Leon Tourian in vestments he was wearing yesterday

Assassins Kill Archbishop at Service Here Of Armenians

Head of Church in Americas Is Knifed by 4 as He Marches to Altar in Washington Heights

2 Prisoners Beaten By 400 Worshipers

Slaying Laid to Foes of Soviet Domination of Homeland; Police Raid 2 Clubs, Question 300

Archbishop Leon Tourian, primate of the Gregorian (Armenian) Church of all of North and South America except California, was stabbed to death with a nine-inch butcher knife at 10:30 a. m. yesterday in the presence of 400 horrified communicants in Holy Cross Armenian Apostolic Church, 578 West 187th Street, as he marched to the altar to preach the Sunday sermon.

Two Armenian grocery clerks were arrested for the slaying, which the police described as a political murder by opponents of Soviet domination of Armenia. Two Armenian revolutionary organizations with headquarters at 366 Third Avenue were raided by detectives in the afternoon and books and papers were confiscated.

Worshipers Beat Prisoners

(Continued on page three)

Mouquin Dies At 96; Dean of Restaurateurs

Vintner to 3 Generations Taught N. Y. How to Dine in 64-Year Lesson

Special to the Herald Tribune

WILLIAMSBURG, Va., Dec. 24.—Henri Mouquin, the famous restaurateur who taught several generations of New Yorkers, until the advent of prohibition, the old-world art of embellishing meals with wines, died here today on the estate where he had lived in retirement for nearly fifteen years. He was ninety-six years old.

Despite his illness, he had expressed elation less than a month ago when Utah ratified the Twenty-first Amendment, but his waning health made it impossible for him to celebrate the occasion in proper fashion. It was doubtful, however, that prohibition had deprived him of many of the beverages to which he had become accustomed, for his cellar was known to contain many rare vintages of an earlier era.

... wine merchants, of 10 Washington Street, Brooklyn; Henri Jacques, of Brooklyn; Henri Mouquin 2d, of Staten Island, and Mrs. Louise Harahan, of Brooklyn. There also are five great-grandchildren living.

Regiment's Last Survivor

More than any other man, Henri Mouquin gave to three generations of

(Continued on page seventeen)

Four Die as Car Plunges From Pier in Jersey

2 Women and 2 Men Are Drowned When Vehicle Falls in Manasquan River

Special to the Herald Tribune

POINT PLEASANT, N. J., Dec. 24.—An automobile went off the end of a 175-foot pier at Cedar Street and Manasquan River into five feet of water at 4 a. m. today, drowning four of its five occupants, two men and two women. Those killed were Louis Michaelson, Mrs. Margaret Ward and Joseph Dowling, whose homes were in Belmar, N. J., and Mrs. William Streser, of West Point Pleasant.

William Ward, the survivor, was Mrs. Margaret Ward's husband. He was asleep at the time of the accident and awoke to find himself struggling in the water. He was unable to explain several features of the accident which the police find puzzling.

The pier, to the very end of which the car was driven, is a narrow one.

Suspect Is Arrested In Death of J. W. Brodix

PETERSBURG, W. Va., Dec. 24 (AP).—Less than twenty-four hours after an automobile struck and killed John W. Brodix, fifty-two-year-old brother-in-law of Louis Merryman, National Milk

(Continued on page four)

Mrs. Lindbergh's Air Skill Wins Tribute of Cross of Honor Today

From the Herald Tribune Bureau

WASHINGTON, Dec. 24.—An announcement of the United States Flag Association today said that among the Christmas gifts for Mrs. Anne Lindbergh arriving tomorrow at the home of her mother, Mrs. Dwight Morrow, in Englewood, N. J., will be the Cross of Honor. This is the highest decoration of the association and is the same award which was given to her husband, Colonel Charles A. Lindbergh, seven years ago because of his epochal non-stop flight from New York to Paris.

The cross will be flown to Englewood from Washington for presentation on Christmas Day. The award invests in Mrs. Lindbergh the title of Lady of the Flag ...

... person to have been made a member of the order.

The citation which Anne Lindbergh is receiving with the Cross of Honor reads:

"As navigator and radio operator at times relieving the pilot at the controls, she showed unsurpassable skill, superior aeronautical knowledge, admirable courage and tireless endurance in the most comprehensive and complete survey ever made of trans-Atlantic air routes and one of the most outstanding aviation achievements ever accomplished, in which four continents and thirty-one countries and colonies were visited and 30,000 miles traveled in 230 flying hours, between July 9 and December 19, 1933, on a course extending in variance from over the frozen seas of the Arctic to the torrid jungles of the tropics, surveying a larger area of the earth's surface than was ever before viewed by any voyager. Not only was there secured on this epoch-making flight most valuable data which will help advance the science of aeronautics but the nations visited were thereby brought into friendlier contact which will help establish bonds of understanding and sympathy that will promote the closer unity of mankind.

"In the conspicuous and admirable ..."

Street Drinker Learns Of Repeal From Police

Held for Crashing Bottle on Walk 'to Destroy Evidence'

SACRAMENTO, Calif., Dec. 24 (AP).—J. Hermandez didn't know about repeal today. He does tonight. Hermandez was having a drink out of his Christmas bottle on a downtown street when he saw Police Sergeant L. E. Warren approaching.

Crash! went the bottle to the sidewalk.

"You got nothing on me," he said to Warren. "See, I broke the evidence."

And then he learned.

"I can't arrest you for having a drink. It's legal," said the officer.

"Fine," said Hermandez.

"But," continued Warren, "I've got to arrest you now for breaking glass on the sidewalk."

Boy, 5, with Santa's Toy, Starts Across U. S. Alone

Father Believed Dying Child Is Off to Uncle in New York

SAN FRANCISCO, Dec. 24 (AP).—Parting from his father whom he may never see again, five-year-old Walter C. Hogan, a Christmas toy under his arm, left San Francisco tonight to join his uncle, Lieutenant Walter Clifton Hogan jr., of the Coast Guard at New York.

The father, Captain W. W. Clifton Hogan, a veteran of the Spanish-American and World Wars, is seriously ill in the Veterans Hospital at Palo Alto. Because physicians have told him he may not recover, he has arranged to have his son go to the uncle in New York. Captain Hogan received custody of the child when he and the mother were divorced.

The boy is in the care of the Travelers' Aid Society for the trip.

At 10 o'clock that evening, most New Yorkers – like most Americans – were glued to their radios, listening to Jack Benny. But the Armenians living here had neither the head nor the heart for such comedy that night. They were inconsolable, except for those few who had hated the Archbishop. In some households, the assassination of Ghevont Tourian was cause for celebration.

16

Now

The next morning, with memories of Anna still swirling through my head, I trudged up the twenty-seven steps from the sidewalk to the main entrance of the New York Public Library's main branch at 42nd Street and Fifth Avenue, past those magnificently sculpted lions. (Mayor LaGuardia had named them "Patience" and "Fortitude" but to me the ferocious felines were guarding this palace of knowledge.) I wound my way around the towering colonnade and through the revolving doors, then into the grand foyer which reminded me of the rotunda under the U.S. Capitol building dome. This hallway always makes a powerful initial impression on visitors. I remember reading somewhere that when construction started in 1902, the library was designed to be the largest marble structure ever built in the United States. (Why I remember that I'll never know. Add it to the million other bits of useless information rattling around inside my skull.)

"Where do I find old newspapers?" I asked a uniformed guard at the foot of the stairs.

"Room 100," he said wearily glancing up at me from the front page of the New York Post in his hands. He settled his gaze back on the newspaper. "Down this hall and to the right," he added with a slight nod of his head.

The periodicals room smells clean. It is filled with microfilm. I'm amazed by how accessible these precious resources are. I mean, anybody can walk in and just take what he wants. I guess there are still some things that operate on the honor system. Of course, not everything in the library's vast newspaper collection is in this room. Some of the more obscure holdings must be requested. But the most popular publications were right here in those beige and gray steel file cabinets.

I headed for the drawers from 1933. The papers were filled with ads from that era. I want to go back to a time when a working person could afford the basics of life without going into debt. Ah, nostalgia...

I found the box labeled "N.Y. Herald Tribune: 12-15-1933 to 12-31-1933." Inside, a plastic reel was wound with microfilm from the week of the assassination. I went to an unoccupied machine and loaded the spool. First, it came out upside down and backward. After several more tries (and a bit of help from a very patient librarian) I managed to get going. The black and white images appeared on the screen. I quickly scrolled past the many days of unrelated news until I got to December 24.

At first, I was shocked. Nothing. Not a word about this event. Then it struck me: the murder happened on Christmas Eve but, of course, it didn't show up in the papers until the 25th. I felt a bit foolish, to say the least.

In my article the next day, I wrote that detectives raided the ARF office, "surprising 300 Armenians who were questioned closely." Let me take a moment to explain those words "questioned closely." In 1933, Ernesto Miranda (of "you have the right to remain silent" fame) hadn't even been born yet, let alone been freed by the U.S. Supreme Court for having his Fifth Amendment rights violated. The idea of requiring cops to warn suspects against self-incrimination wasn't even a cliché among law enforcement back then, never mind for the general public. In many police stations, physical force was freely used to "persuade" suspects, based on its fallacious reputation as an effective way to gain confessions.

The year 1933 was a busy one for the cops and the crooks. On February 15th, President-elect Franklin Roosevelt narrowly avoided an assassin's bullets which, instead, killed Chicago mayor Anton Cermak. The two men had been riding past cheering crowds in Miami, Florida when Giuseppe Zangara opened fire on their open touring car.

Meanwhile, gangsters terrorized half the country in the waning days of Prohibition, fighting over illegal booze. I think it was one of my old New York City competitors who came up with the name "Murder, Incorporated" to describe the hundreds of unsolved killings we blamed on gangs. In addition to reaching the highest homicide rate in its history, America saw an epidemic of bank robberies, kidnappings, arson fires and prison breaks.

I turned back to my story. Re-reading this account decades later, I tried to remember what I hadn't included. A few memories started to trickle in through my foggy mind.

I re-wound the last spool of microfilm, thinking my work here was done. I gathered several dozen pages of paper with photocopies of the stories and was about to head back to the file cabinet when I felt someone tap me on the arm.

"Mr. Peterson?"

A bespectacled young man holding a notebook smiled broadly. These days, everyone under the age of 35 looks to me like a high school student. But judging by his library staff badge, he was probably a bit older.

"Yes."

"I understand you're doing some research into an old crime," he said tentatively.

"That's right." I was surprised that anyone here would be paying attention to my reading. "Is there some problem?" The hackles of my suspicious nature began to rise.

"Oh, no. No problem at all, sir. I just thought you'd be interested in these." He held out a list of magazines that had covered the Tourian murder. Many didn't exist anymore.

"Does the library have all of these?" I asked. I was amazed.

"Well, some of them might be on microform. Let me check." And with that, he was off. I wondered how many New Yorkers were aware of the wonderful public resource in their midst. A few minutes later, he returned with a look of disappointment.

"Bad news?" I offered.

"Yeah. We only have a couple of these." He seemed to take the failure personally. "Would you like me to photocopy the articles for you?"

Damn, this was better than hiring a research assistant, I thought. "Uh, sure, that'd be great."

Again, he dashed off. While the young man attacked the Xerox machine, I went back to the file cabinets. I had only perused the New York Times and the Herald Tribune articles. But it hadn't occurred to me that the library might have microfilm of other daily papers. Sure enough, there was spools of stories from the Daily News, the Sun and the Post. This was a real treasure trove.

As I gathered more cardboard boxes full of history, the library employee came back with a fistful of photocopies.

"Nice work," I said.

He beamed. "My pleasure, sir." Clearly, this kid was not a native. He was too nice.

I decided to press my luck. "Do you think there might be any other newspapers from that era?"

Less than ten minutes later, he was back with another list. "I'm not sure how many of these will have the stories you want, but they were all in existence back then." At least he didn't say way back then.

"That's great," I said. "Where do I find these?

For the next several hours, I sifted through almost one hundred editions of newspapers and magazines from around the United States as well as several British periodicals. All in all, I was going to walk away with a thick file full of articles – much more than I had anticipated.

"Hey, one more question."

"Yes?"

"Where do I go to get court transcripts?" I asked.

"The City Archives on Chambers Street," he replied without hesitating.

Somebody should adopt that kid, I thought.

Before leaving the library, I stopped by the reference section to look up the name, Aharonian. It was an eye-opener.

Had I been a better student of my ethnic history, I would have remembered that Avedis Aharonian was President of the first Armenian Republic. He was also editor of the official *Tashnag* newspaper, *Hairenik*, and Vartkes was his son. I wondered whether either of them had any connection with the Tourian murder.

Back at my hotel room, I spread the photocopied articles on the second bed. I decided to create some sort of filing system, piling stacks chronologically and categorized according to subject.

I picked up one sheaf and started to thumb through them. One question kept coming back to me: Had the police arrested the right man?

17

Then

At 5:45 on the evening of Tourian's assassination, two plainclothes policemen brought Mateos Leylegian into a smoky interrogation room.

"Sit down there," said detective Frank Gowrie, pointing to a straight-backed wooden chair. The other cop, Vincent Farese, unlocked one of the handcuffs from the suspect's left wrist and attached it to a heavy iron chain welded to the floor.

Two large flood lamps were focused on the spot. Mateos blinked and unsuccessfully tried to shield his eyes from the blast of light. Gowrie pushed Leylegian firmly into the seat.

"Don't move," he commanded.

Capt. John Lagarenne and Lt. James Donnelly walked in and took more comfortable seats in the back. With them was A.D.A. Cohn. Since Leylegian would only answer in Armenian, the prosecutor questioned him through a civilian interpreter who had come in from the Bronx.

Cohn approached the suspect rather nonchalantly at first. The Assistant District Attorney sauntered back and forth a bit, forced a slight smile and flipped through his notes in the manila case folder. Then he stopped and looked the prisoner directly in the eye, then turned back to the folder.

"What is your name?" he asked mechanically.

"Mateos Leylegian."

"Where do you live?"

"521 West 49th Street, New York, apartment – in back of the store. It is a grocery store."

"What is your business?"

"Grocer."

To a casual observer, Cohn might have sounded somewhat amateurish. But the policemen sitting in that room who knew this prosecutor were well aware of his technique. The A.D.A. continued his interrogation in this rather routine way for several more minutes. He told Leylegian that he was going to be arrested for killing the Archbishop. He gave the suspect an opportunity to refuse to answer.

"Any statement that you do make may be used against you. You understand that?"

"Yes."

Mateos naïvely agreed to speak. He said that he was 39 years old, a naturalized American citizen. He had been in the United States about three years. He was married in the old country, but his wife was dead – a victim of the Turkish massacres. When Cohn turned to the subject of politics, Leylegian's answers became more cautious.

"Are you a member of the Armenian Revolutionary Society?" asked the A.D.A.

The suspect paused for a moment. "Yes, I am a member," he replied.

"How long have you been a member?"

"About – over ten years."

"What is the name of the Secretary?"

What is this guy really doing? Mateos wondered.

"Am I obligated to say it?"

"Yes."

"Why?"

Obviously, this was turning into a very delicate dance. Too little pressure and the prosecutor wouldn't get the admissions he wanted – the evidence to make his case solid. Too much pressure and the suspect might resort to silence or telling lies. Either way, it would be bad. Cohn changed his tone a bit, pressing the suspect more aggressively.

"Are you the Secretary?" he asked.

"No, sir."

"Who *is* the Secretary of this Society?"

"Is it necessary to say?"

"Yes."

"Why do I have to say it?"

Cohn recognized the game. He'd heard hundreds of suspects try to play their way out. It never worked. The A.D.A. got harsh, moving much closer to Leylegian.

"We wish to know who the Secretary of your society is."

Mateos relented. "I am the Secretary."

Of course, Cohn knew the answer all along. It was in the documents Iskenderian and the other cops had confiscated from the Armen Garo Club. But he needed to show the suspect that he could pry the truth out of him. That first victory was the most important one. Now, he had it. From this point, the answers came flowing out. Leylegian nearly sweated the words from his pores.

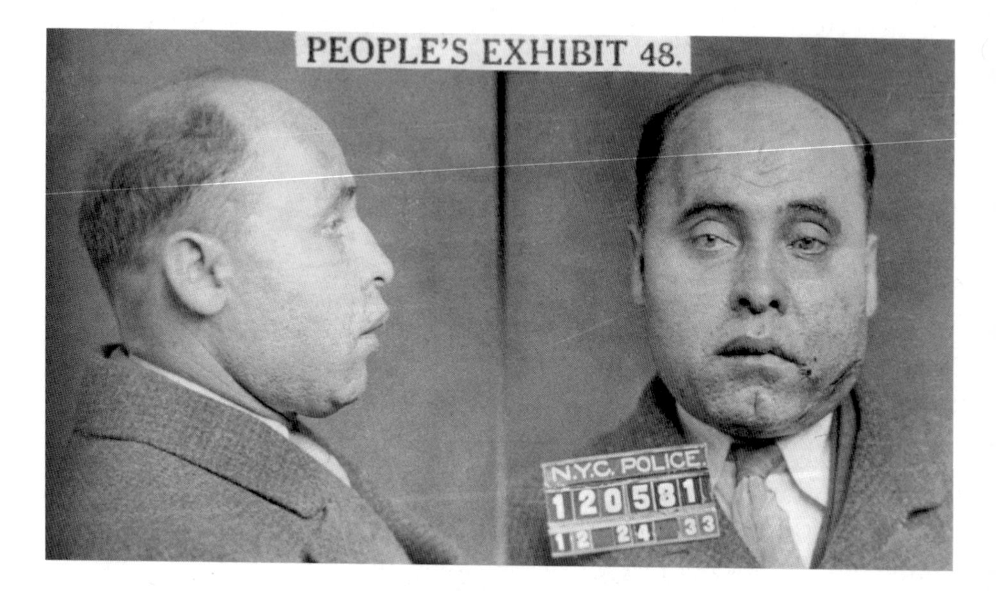

Again, the prosecutor had all this information in writing. He was merely manipulating the suspect toward his real questions. Cohn asked about more minutia: Leylegian's salary, the organization's annual dues, their purpose. Finally, the A.D.A. moved to the key questions which he asked almost off-handedly.

"When did you hold your last meeting?"

"About a week ago."

"Who presided at the meeting as president or chairman?"

Mateos regained some of his composure. "Is it necessary to say?" he asked weakly.

Cohn was firmly in command now. He pressed harder.

"Yes, it is. What is the name of the chairman or president who presided at the last meeting?"

Leylegian gulped hard and said nothing for a long time.

"Why do you hesitate?"

Mateos could resist no longer.

"His name is Vahan Kermoian – was presiding Chairman of the last meeting which was held about a week ago. I don't remember the date."

Cohn was happy. Finally, the suspect was giving up more than he was asked for. The prosecutor considered this a great development. Like a skilled baseball pitcher, he started throwing some change-ups mixed in with the fastballs.

"Where was the meeting held?"

"At our club."

"Where was that located?"
"366 Third Avenue."
"Does the presiding officer live in New York?
"Yes."
Cohn turned to Lt. Donnelly. "May I have a city directory please?" The captain whispered something to one of the detectives who left the room. A moment later, he was back with a book which contained the names, addresses and telephone numbers of every business and residence in the five boroughs. It was a sophisticated version of the regular phone book, with much greater detail and better cross-references. Cohn flipped to the letter "K" and scanned the pages until he found the name.
"Does he live at 560 West 180th Street?"
"Yes."
"His name is spelled on the books K-R-M-O-G-A-N. Is that the name of the man?"
"Yes."
"How many members were present at this meeting?"
Mateos had to think a minute. "There were about – over one hundred members present."
Joseph Cohn abruptly stopped his interrogation, walked to the back of the room and sat next to Capt. Lagarenne. Although they appeared to Leylegian to be in deep discussion, the technique was merely another prosecutor's trick to confuse the suspect. A moment later, Cohn returned to his prey.
The attorney flipped through his notes, and then asked, "Are you a member of the Armenian – of the Holy Cross Armenian Church?"
"No, I am not a member of that church."
"Did you attend the services today, December 24, 1933?"
"Yes, I did."
"How did you happen to attend the services this morning?"
"Because the Archbishop was the first time that he was going to give a mass here. That is why we went over to see him."
Although Joe Cohn never gambled, he would have made an excellent poker player. The man had an eerie ability to keep even the least indication of emotions from his face. But this revelation from Leylegian came as a great surprise to the prosecutor. He never hoped to get the prime suspect in this case to admit that he intended to see his victim.
But the hunt was far from over. He soldiered on, doing his best to remain visibly unexcited.
"Who else attended the mass, the services with you?"

"I went there alone, and I went there and I saw the people there."

So, thought Cohn, *we're back to this game, eh*? The prosecutor quickly debated with himself whether to skip ahead. It was a risk he had to take. *To hell with the groundwork*, he thought. *We'll deal with that in court – if it ever gets that far*. He decided to press further.

"Did you see any members of your Society present?"

"No, I did not."

Now, even the captain was surprised by this bold leap. An experienced interrogator himself, Lagarenne thought Cohn might be pushing too far, too fast. He wondered what the rush was. They had all the time in the world. Still, it was Joe's case.

"Is Nishan Sarkisian a member of your society?" Sarkisian was the alias that Nishan Tuktikian used. During the trial, a judge would require that the prosecutor lay more foundation before asking this question. But here, in the confines of a police interrogation room, the A.D.A. had much more latitude.

"Yes," admitted Mateos without hesitation. He knew that there was no point in trying to protect anyone else now. They were all facing the same threat. Better they should face it together. Leylegian said that Sarkisian had been in church that morning, but they came separately. He also acknowledged learning that Tourian would be at Holy Cross Church about a week ago.

For Cohn, this was another coup. That admission corresponded to the date of the *Tashnag* society meeting. Leylegian must have felt a glimmer of satisfaction from the prosecutor, because he suddenly became more cautious again.

Cohn pushed in for a confession. He wheeled dramatically, pointing an accusatory finger at Mateos and speaking rapid-fire.

"Did you announce at your meeting that the Archbishop was to be at the Armenian Holy Cross Church at 580 West 187th Street?"

Leylegian drew back. "No, we did not announce anything of that sort." His voice was now raised half an octave.

"Your Federation, of course, was opposed to the Archbishop, was it not?"

"The Archbishop is against our flag and we are against him."

"Had you ever attended the services at this church, at the Armenian Holy Cross Church, before?"

"I had been there only once before, last year."

Damn, thought Cohn, *that was an unnecessary distraction*. He knew he was covering old ground, giving Leylegian too much breathing room. Time to refocus. He pushed harder.

"What time did you get to the church this morning?"

"At the time it opened the door.

"Did you come directly from your home?"

"Yes, sir."

"What time did you leave your home?"

"About 7:30 – 8 o'clock."

"Did you make arrangements to meet Nishan Sarkisian this morning?"

"No, I did not."

Cohn had hoped for a slip-up there. He didn't get it. He kept moving.

"Were there many people in the church when you got there this morning?"

"About 50 or 60."

"What row did you occupy?"

"On the left side."

The A.D.A. kept digging for details. He switched interrogation styles, from soft-spoken to manic, alternately trying to appear sympathetic and hostile.

"How many rows away from the door were you?"

"I do not know."

"Did you occupy an aisle seat or end seat?"

"No, in the center."

"Were you waiting for the Archbishop to come up the center aisle?"

"Yes, I knew that he was going to pass through there with the procession."

Even though these answers came through an interpreter, the prosecutor heard panic in Leylegian's voice. The interpreter did an excellent job of mimicking both men, conveying the varying intensity of questions, and fear in the answers. Cohn nearly wanted to comfort the middle man. It was a grueling task. The A.D.A. pressed on.

"When the Archbishop came up the center aisle, what did you do?"

For the first time, Mateos began to break down. Cohn didn't know whether it was the stress of this interrogation or Leylegian's guilt surfacing. Cohn didn't care. The suspect was cracking. His words came out in wave after wave.

"I did not do anything. They attacked him. They attacked the Archbishop. The fight started and then they also attacked me. My enemies attacked me."

"Why did you jump on the Archbishop?"

"I have not jumped on the Archbishop. We were fighting in those aisles, in these rows.

"The Archbishop was your enemy, wasn't he?"

"Yes, we were against him and he was against us."

"Why did you go in the church this morning?"

Cohn truly believed the next words out of Leylegian's mouth would be, *I went to kill him*. Instead, he heard, "I was going to listen to him."

The interrogator was stunned. He had lost his momentum. Cohn marched to a table covered with evidence and grabbed his prime exhibit from: the murder weapon. He hoped this would shock Mateos back toward a confession. Joseph spun on his heel.

"Did you ever see this knife before?"

The A.D.A. waited.

"No, sir."

It didn't work. Dejected now, he persevered nevertheless, raising his voice with each subsequent question.

"Look at it."

"I look at it. I never saw it."

"Doesn't this come from your store?"

"No, sir."

"Didn't you have this knife with you this morning?"

"No, sir."

"Didn't you stab this Archbishop with this knife this morning?"

"No, sir."

The worm had turned. Now it was Cohn who had become desperate. And it showed. No matter what he asked, Leylegian was in full denial. From this point onward, every question about the knife got a negative response. Mateos insisted that he did not have that knife and did not attack Tourian.

Several minutes later, the prosecutor changed course again.

"Are the members of this Holy Cross Armenian Church your enemies?" he asked calmly.

Mateos replied in a similar fashion. "There may be some who are and there may be some who are not."

Suddenly, Cohn decided to switch victims. "Were you attacked in the church?

Leylegian was caught off-guard by the question. "Yes," he said almost gleefully.

So, thought Cohn, *the "good cop" is working now*.

"By whom?"

"By those enemies who knew that I belong to an opposition party. That is why they attacked me.

"Were you attacked after you had stabbed the Archbishop?" He nearly tripped up the suspect with that one. Nearly.

"No, the fight took place." Mateos was searching his memory for the last answer to this question. Unable to remember, he balked. "I do not know when the Archbishop was stabbed."

Cohn again tried to close the snare. "Why did you go to church this morning if the Archbishop was your enemy and members of this Holy Cross Armenian Church were your enemies?"

"There is no difference. Everybody could attend it." Leylegian was slipping again. Both men knew that now.

"Were you invited to attend?" asked the prosecutor with a smile.

"I was not invited, but everybody could have gone to the church." Mateos was defiant now.

"Did you make a contribution to the church this morning?"

"Yes, five, ten cents I dropped."

That's good, thought Cohn. *Focus on the minor, unimportant details.*

"How much did you drop?"

"Five cents or ten cents, I do not know."

And then, the counter-punch. "What did you do with the knife while you were putting the money in the plate?"

Mateos had to think about this one. His eyes widened at first – then, narrowed. "I have not taken a knife."

Cohn's smile immediately disappeared. He would go all the way. It was now or never. The questions and answers came in rapid-fire succession.

"Did you have the knife up your sleeve or did you have it in your pocket?"

"I did not have a knife with me. How could I say it?"

"What did you do with the knife after you stabbed the Archbishop?"

"I have not stabbed him."

"Weren't you the only man that was grabbed by the members of the congregation after the Archbishop fell down with a stab wound in his stomach?"

"No, the fight had started and they had attacked me already."

"Did you have any other knives in your pocket besides this big knife?"

"I did not have a big knife," said Mateos. Then, without reflection, he offered another answer. "But I did have a small knife."

Cohn smelled blood in the water.

"How many knives did you have in your pocket."

"I got two."

The prosecutor licked his chops as he walked back to the evidence table. Cohn picked up a ring handle knife and another small knife about two inches long.

"Are these the two knives?"

"Yes."

"Are you in the habit of carrying a number of knives in your pocket?"

"Yes."

"Why do you carry two knives, two or more knives in your pocket?"

"One day I bought a cigarette lighter and the small one was given to me free."

Joseph Cohn was painfully aware that he was not going to get the key admission he had hoped for. There was nothing like a confession in all of this. The prosecutor knew that Leylegian was guilty. He had plenty of circumstantial evidence to go with. But this case was definitely headed for a jury trial.

At this point in the interrogation, Cohn had to use his powers to finish breaking the suspect's spirit. So, the prosecutor returned to his earlier questions. He saw, in Leylegian's eyes, a certain resignation. That was the look he needed. No matter what Mateos might say now, the authorities intended to convict him. There was no way out.

Still, he stoically repeated his previous answers as if by rote: "I never had intentions to kill the Archbishop. I did not jump in front of the Archbishop. I did not stab the Archbishop."

Cohn tried one more approach, a logical challenge. "Why should these people, members of the church, say that you jumped on the Archbishop?"

"Because they were all hitting me. And have they ever seen any knife in my hand?"

"They saw you jump on the Archbishop, isn't that right?"

"I have not attacked the Archbishop."

The A.D.A. finished by asking about a couple other *Tashnag* society members. Leylegian was too tired to fight, but refused to cooperate.

Cohn's last questions were about the organization's secretary. "Do you keep minutes of your meetings as Secretary?"

"As Secretary, I only get the mail and answer the mail, but the minutes are kept by others."

"Who was the Secretary who kept the minutes of the last meeting?"

"We have an Assistant Secretary who does that."

"Did he take care of the minutes of the last meeting?"

"I do not know whether he kept it or not."

"What is his name?"

The prisoner could barely speak. His mouth was dry and his lips stuck together.

"Vanig Papazian. I do not know where he lives. Look up the book. The address is the club address."

Joseph Cohn stopped and looked at his wristwatch. It was 6:25. For Mateos Leylegian, those past forty minutes felt like forty hours. He was exhausted, barely able to stand on his own. A pair of uniformed police officers re-handcuffed the prisoner and took him away.

18

Now

The New York Municipal Archives were housed in an old building on Chambers Street in lower Manhattan, not far from City Hall. The interior wood panels, heavy brass fixtures and rich marble floors served to absorb all outside sounds from penetrating these walls. That, plus the tons of paper documents stored here, gave a tomb-like hush to the scene.

The facility was remarkably empty. I had imagined there would be hundreds, if not thousands, of New Yorkers seeking personal and business records. Not today. At least not from this area where early 20th century material was kept.

I spent nearly an hour coughing my way through dust-covered folders stacked in the hallways. If there was a filing system, it was a mystery to me. Finally, I did what I should have done from the very start: I went to see the municipal archivist.

"I'm sorry, Mr. Peterson," he said matter-of-factly.

The official file on the Tourian murder was nearly non-existent. One manila folder from the District Attorney's office contained only a few documents. None of them was very interesting. I already had the defendants' names and the dates of their arrests. The only bit of new information was a slight modification to the indictment number.

"That's it?" I wondered aloud. "And no court transcripts?"

The archivist seemed sincere when he told me that the verbatim record for one of the biggest trials in New York's history had either never existed, was destroyed, or had disappeared into the great black hole that is City Hall.

"But how is that possible," I asked incredulously. "This trial was front-page news."

The bespectacled man on the other side of the desk was unmoved. In his defense, files were files. It didn't matter to the bureaucracy how popular or unpopular a case was – any more than a typewriter would care how well-written a letter in it was. To the machine, they were just words on paper.

"You know, way back then…" he began.

Ugh – those words again, I thought and mentally tuned out for a moment.

"…so, a lot of trials didn't get transcribed," he droned on. "And some transcriptions were paid for by the lawyers, so we don't keep them here. You'd have to check with the individual law firms…"

I started to thank him, when suddenly the archivist's eyes lit up.

"There is one other possibility," he said hopefully.

Now he had my full attention. "Yes?"

"You could try the Court of Appeals."

That's right, I thought. *This case had been appealed.*

I started meandering toward the exit. The archivist was about to answer a ringing telephone when another suggestion stopped him.

"And there is one more resource you really should check," he offered. "The Police Department has its own museum. They keep a lot of historical records that precinct houses don't have the space for. Oh, and don't forget about the New York Historical Society."

"Thanks," I called over my shoulder. And thank God for open-minded public servants.

19

Then

Detectives Gowrie and Farese went to get the next suspect.

"OK, boys," said Joseph Cohn. "Let's bring the other one in here."

Meanwhile, the prosecutor and policemen loosened their neckties and stretched their limbs. This interrogation room was rather smoky and Cohn wanted to take a breather. Knowing that he had some time to kill, the assistant district attorney headed for the door.

"Nice job, counselor," said Capt. Lagarenne.

"Thanks, captain. I'm going to get some air. I'll be back in a couple minutes."

"First door on the right," said Lt. Donnelly half-jokingly.

After Cohn had stepped out of the room, Donnelly turned to his superior officer and friend.

"That was a hell of a thing, John" said the lieutenant.

"What do you mean?"

"I never saw an interrogator work over a guy so good without touching him."

The captain snickered. "Yeah, he really put it to him."

"I'm a little surprised the mug didn't crack."

Lagarenne patted Donnelly on the shoulder. "Don't worry, Jimmie. When Cohn is done, these guys'll be begging to confess."

A short while later, the detectives brought in Nishan Tuktikian. Unlike the other man, this suspect was far from docile. He struggled with his escorts the whole time.

"Stop squirming," one policeman said as he tightened his grip on Tuktikian's arm. "You're only making this harder for yourself."

By the time they had reached the interrogation room, the prisoner was winded. The detectives manhandled him into the chair and cuffed him to the chain. He kept struggling against his restraints. Cohn was a bit surprised by this rough scene.

"Tell him to sit still," Cohn said to the interpreter.

The prisoner replied incoherently, but then immediately stopped struggling as the interrogation began. Tuktikian said he preferred to go by "Sarkisian" because it was easier to pronounce. That didn't make much sense to the A.D.A. who found both names equally difficult.

Cohn began with some seemingly innocuous subjects, again going through the interpreter for both questions and answers.

"Where do you live?"

"213 E. 73rd Street, in back of my uncle's store."

"What is your uncle's name?"

"His name is John Tuktikian, same address."

"Where does your uncle live now?"

"He also is living in the back of that store."

"What is your business?"

"I am not working. I am helping him out sometimes."

Cohn did not have the time or the energy to play the same psychological game with this suspect. Anyway, as far as he was concerned, Leylegian was the real killer. This guy was just a co-conspirator.

Tuktikian, alias Sarkisian, answered several more routine questions: He was 38 years old, divorced, had no children, and was never arrested.

"When I was married, my wife had a fight with an Irish woman," he recalled. "And that was the only time I had trouble."

The cops sitting in the back of the interrogation couldn't hold back the laughter. Capt. Lagarenne nudged Donnelly in the ribs.

"Are you a member of the Armenian Revolutionary Federation?

"I was a member but now I go there once in a while." Sarkisian said the last meeting he attended was two months ago.

"Were you in the Holy Cross Armenian Church this morning?" asked Cohn. The suspect said he was there this morning and last Sunday and the Sunday before. He said he had left his seat various times during the service to go outside and smoke a cigarette.

"You were nervous this morning, weren't you, while you were walking up and down smoking the cigarette."

"No, I was just going out, smoking and coming in."

"Didn't you have a fight with the sexton this morning about smoking?"

Sarkisian suddenly became very defensive. "No, I did not have a fight with him. Only he said, 'Stop smoking there in front of the door. It is forbidden.' And then he said, 'If you do not stop, I will tell the policeman.' And then I asked the sexton, 'Why are these policemen here for?' And that is all."

Finally, the prosecutor cut to the chase. "Why did you jump on the Archbishop as he proceeded up the aisle to the altar?"

"I did not hit the Archbishop. I didn't hit anybody. The only thing that when I just got into the church the whole riot started."

Cohn half-heartedly went through the list of questions, not expecting to get anything out of this suspect. Sarkisian admitted that he and Leylegian were friends and had served together in the army. But he denied arranging to meet Mateos in church this morning.

"I have not seen him over three weeks," he said.

"Where did you see him three weeks ago?"

"He was going to buy a coat and I speak better English than he does and we went over and we bought the coat then."

The prosecutor was sure that Sarkisian was lying and decided to let that go. He grabbed the murder weapon. "I show you this table knife, butcher's knife and ask you whether this is your knife. Look at it."

"No," said Sarkisian, defiantly turning his head away.

Cohn closed in, shoving the knife in the prisoner's face. "Did you ever see this knife before?"

"No."

The suspect tried in vain to avert his eyes. Cohn persisted.

"Do you use this in your grocery store?"

"No."

"Is this Mateos' knife?"

"I don't know."

"Did you ever see this in Mateos' possession?"

"No."

"Who uses this knife, you or Mateos?"

"I never. I do not know. In all my life I have never used a knife."

"How many times did you stab the Archbishop?"

"I have never approached him. I never stabbed him."

"Did you see Mateos stab the Archbishop?"

"I saw Mateos was in the church, but I did not see that he attacked the Archbishop."

"Were you sitting in an aisle seat?"

"There was only one woman sitting next to me from the aisle."

"Why did you jump out in front of the Bishop as he passed your seat?"

"I did not jump."

"Were you held by the other members of the church after the Bishop was stabbed?"

"This young man next to me, he came over across the street with a policeman, and he brought me over here" Sarkisian pointed to Detective Farese with his free hand.

"Several members of the church identified you as jumping on the Archbishop. What have you got to say about that?"

"I will raise my hand in the court that I have never attacked the Archbishop."

"Do you want to tell me the truth about this and tell me why you and Mateos jumped on the Archbishop and stabbed him?"

"I have not seen that Mateos attacked the Archbishop. While the procession was passing, I was out and I came in and they were just passed and I took my seat."

"I will give you one more opportunity. Do you want to tell me whether you stabbed the Archbishop or Mateos stabbed the Archbishop? Who stabbed him?"

"I have not attacked – I have never stabbed the Archbishop, and I do not know even how it happened."

In less than fifteen minutes, it was over. Cohn took a long last look at the prisoner, gestured to the stenographer to stop writing, then moved closer and looked Sarkisian straight in the eye.

"Mr. Sarkisian, as God is my witness, I am going to convict you of first degree murder," said the prosecutor in a deliberate and measured tone, "and you are going to die in the electric chair."

Nishan's hard expression softened to a smirk, then a sneer. "*Aghdod huryah shoon*," he muttered. It was too low for the interpreter to hear, so Cohn never understood the slur, "Dirty Jew dog."

20

Now

I came to the New York City Police Museum hoping to get a fresh lead. Instead, I found myself more confused than ever.

This is one of the least known sources of entertainment and information in the five boroughs. Although it has been around since 1929, most tourists have never heard of this marvelous collection. At one time, the museum was part of the police academy. But in recent years, it had moved into its own building, open to the public.

In addition to being a relatively inexpensive form of amusement, this repository of law enforcement history contains many authentic artifacts and records. Unfortunately, the arrest logs related to Ghevont Tourian's murder suspects were not among them. Ordinarily, such records would be kept in the records of the original police station.

I had been to the 34th Precinct earlier in the day, but they weren't much help. Let me correct that: they weren't any help at all. The station house was no longer on Wadsworth Avenue. That building was now an annex to the public school across the street. The cops had relocated to a new facility on Broadway.

The old 3-4 had been a perfect example of a traditional New York City police station. It had often been the scene of much excitement. Take for instance October 30, 1938. That was the night Orson Wells spooked America's radio audience with his "War of the Worlds" broadcast. A terrified man ran into the Wadsworth station, asking police what he should do. The next day, the Philadelphia Inquirer reported that the poor guy heard that "planes had bombed Jersey and were headed for Times Square."

The new station house was much less interesting – a very plain, very functional location which could just as easily serve as a dentist's office. There was an unwelcoming air of detachment about the place which made me feel as if I were invisible. It's not that they were unwilling to help, mind you. But after all these years, many of the old records had been destroyed. To be fair, they probably had something a little more pressing to do than answer unofficial questions about a 40-yer-old case that had already been solved. Nevertheless, I was annoyed.

At least I had hoped for a bit more enthusiasm from the museum. Instead, I felt they were giving me the brush off, too.

"Have you tried the municipal archives?" suggested the curator.

"Yeah, they sent me here," I nodded. "I'm starting to feel like a passenger on a merry-go-round."

"Welcome to New York," he said good-naturedly.

The Historical Society was much more interesting, but no more productive. After spending a few hours sifting through old photographs, old maps, old city directories and other traces of my childhood, I decided that there would be no clues here. This place was making me feel old. I objected to the notion that events in my lifetime belonged in a historical society. I was not ready to accept 1933 as having been "way back then" – not yet.

21

Then

The day after Archbishop Tourian's murder was Christmas. Most of New York was opening presents. Peterson received one gift – this grisly story. Despite the fact that he had been awake half the night, the reporter got up at his habitual time, a quarter to six – a full fifteen minutes before the alarm clock went off.

Outside, it was less dark than usual for this time of day. The sun would not rise for at least another hour, but a two-inch snowfall overnight had blanketed the city. Between the reflected street lamps and pre-dawn twilight, it was bright enough to read the morning paper. Tom dashed outside and dropped two cents into a tin cup at the corner newsstand. He grabbed the Times to see how his competitors were handling the Tourian murder. The headline of their page-one lead story was in large, bold type.

Archbishop Assassinated in Procession to Altar: Laid to Old-World Feud

In contrast to Peterson's own punchy prose, the Times writer began by laying out a straight-forward account of the killing.

> **Set upon by assassins while he was proceeding to the altar to celebrate the divine liturgy, Archbishop Leon Tourian, supreme head of the Armenian Church in this country, was stabbed to death yesterday in view of 200 worshipers at the Holy Cross Armenian Church…**

He continued reading as he walked the half block back to his apartment. By the time he got inside, Tom felt a knot forming in the pit of his stomach. This really was better. It had good background on the victim and even managed to get in some of the complex political intrigue. The article went on to describe the arrest of two unnamed men and mentioned that the police "were holding two others for further investigation."

There was at least one factual discrepancy: Peterson knew that there had been twice as many parishioners in church yesterday as the Times reported. The Herald bested them on that point. But the rest was damned good journalism. Still, Peterson felt good seeing that he had kept pace with his competitors. He set down the paper, reached for his first cup of coffee and was about to pour in the usual two heaping spoonfuls of sugar when his telephone rang.

"Hello."

"Goddamn it, why didn't you have the other names?" yelled the voice at the other end. It was his editor calling. Stanley Walker was shouting so loudly that he hardly needed a telephone at all. Peterson was stunned, nearly mute.

"Wh-what other names?"

Now Walker got quiet. That was a very, very bad sign: it was the same silence a condemned man hears, seconds before the guillotine blade decapitates him. But in this case, the effect would be much more painful.

"The names of the two other guys who killed your priest," he said almost inaudibly through tightly clenched teeth. "The guys you said got away. The guys the New York Times identified on page three." He emphasized "Times" as if it were an epithet. For him, it was.

Peterson listened hard for his boss's next words. "You fucked up, Peterson." Walker was whispering now. The reporter knew there was no point in saying anything. It would only serve to make matters worse.

While absorbing another several minutes of incomprehensible aural sputum, Peterson anxiously scanned the rest of the competing paper's story. Walker was right, of course: they got the names. There it was on page three.

> **Martin Mazian, 41 unemployed, and Oscar Yerganzien, 22, a furniture polisher, both of 321 East Twenty-eighth Street, were taken to the Wadsworth Avenue Station early this morning and fingerprinted. The police said both had been identified by several witnesses as having taken part in the struggle about the Archbishop.**

Shit, Peterson said to himself. They must've stayed there all night. It didn't help much at that moment that the Times had misspelled these names – "Mazian" instead of "Mozian" and "Yerganzien" instead of "Yarganian" – while the names in his own story were (by and large) spelled correctly. The fact is that they had those other names.

When the yelling finished, Peterson croaked back "Yes, sir" and hung up the phone. He was doomed. If not for his personal connection to the story and the fact that he had been the only news reporter to witness the crime, this oversight would have cost him job at the Herald and any hope of employment at every other major daily in the Tri-State area.

"Who was that?" The half-asleep voice came from a redheaded woman in Peterson's bed.

"Sorry to wake you so early, Mary." He leaned over and kissed her on the forehead. She grabbed his face with both hands and returned the favor, full-mouthed.

"Mmmm, that's better," she purred. The mostly naked visitor wrapped a blanket around herself and stood up. Mary McDonald was a cashier at the Horn & Hardart on Broadway and 13th where Peterson ate many of his late dinners. Theirs was a relationship of appetites. Every now and then, they had dinner together – usually at his place. Sometimes she stayed for dessert. Sometimes she was dessert.

"That was my boss," said Peterson.

"He must've been pretty upset. I could hear him from here." She got up and poured herself a cup of coffee. "You in trouble, honey?"

Tom wasn't sure how much he wanted to say about all this. Mary was a nice girl, good company on a cold winter's night. They had been seeing each other for a couple of months now. But Peterson still didn't think of her as wife material – a very narrow-minded and chauvinistic attitude, he knew, but not so unusual for a man of his ethnic origin. The Petrossian in him didn't mind that she was an *odar*, a non-Armenian. Nevertheless, he hesitated to confide completely in Mary. Not yet.

"Nah, it's no big deal. He's always yelling at me."

But in his heart, Tom knew he was in trouble – serious trouble. He had only one chance to redeem himself, and he had to move fast.

By 8 a.m., Lt. Donnelly was already at his desk, working on a status update for the brass.

Police now had another suspect in custody – Juan Gonzales Tchalikian. In the pre-dawn hours, they had canvassed the houses and shops all around Holy Cross Church. A search of one Armenian grocery store turned up a hidden, blood-stained white shirt. Detectives checked the laundry mark and found its owner. They rousted Tchalikian from his bed and arrested him around 1:35 in the morning. This now brought to five the total number of suspects behind bars.

Donnelly wondered what kind of case this was going to make. He flipped through the pages of Tourian's autopsy report. The Deputy Chief Medical Examiner had conducted an examination in the morgue at Bellevue Hospital.

> Two stab wounds were found in the body, separated by two and a half inches. The killer wielded the knife with great rapidity. It was withdrawn partially, but not out of the original wound and driven in again. It passed through the abdominal wall, over the intestines and into the liver. The second wound was fatal, cutting horizontally through the lower left of the abdomen, crosswise two inches on the skin surface. It went backward and diagonally downward and cut the outer portion of the femoral artery.

The lieutenant let the folder fall shut on his desk. *This update is going to write itself*, he thought.

When Tom Peterson arrived at Wadsworth Station, he ran into Iskenderian coming out.

"Where are you off to?"

"I've got to round up more witnesses," said the Armenian cop. "Seems a lot of people in this neighborhood are reluctant to talk to the police."

"Imagine that," said Tom.

"Yeah. We've talked to thirty or forty who were in church yesterday, but so far nobody saw much."

It was no surprise to either man, of course. Immigrants living in Washington Heights knew the penalty for testifying against known killers. This might be the New World, but Old World habits die hard and these folks didn't want to die along with them.

"Hey, by the way, why didn't you tell me about Yarganian and Mozian?" asked Peterson. "My boss is really pissed off that the Times beat us with those names."

"Sorry, Tommy. It happened after I left for the night."

"That's what I figured. Well, OK."

"Don't worry," added Izzy. "There are plenty more scoops for you." The young policeman patted his friend on the chest, then dashed off toward Audubon Avenue. "See you later, alligator," he called over his shoulder. The immigrant loved to use modern American slang.

Tom trotted up the front steps and into the precinct house. Things were amazingly busy for a Christmas morning. The place was jammed with uniformed and plainclothes officers, various city officials, as well as dozens of newsmen and photographers. A major homicide case will do that to a police station.

"Say, Tommy, where was you last night?" It was Peterson's competitor from the Daily News – one of several other reporters now camped out in the neighborhood. "I figured you would've stuck around to get the *whole* story," he chided.

"Well, some of us have deadlines," replied Peterson. But there was no way he could fool his rival. It clearly would've been better to phone in what he had to a re-write man and stay with the cops – all night long, if necessary. Anyway, that was, quite literally, yesterday's news. Today he had to find another angle.

Of course, the Daily News was not exactly the standard by which Peterson judged his work. That tabloid had published a few dramatic photos, but its lurid story included some wild inaccuracies, such as reporting that the Archbishop's weight was "close to 400 pounds."

One idea occurred to Tom: talk to some of the witnesses here in Armenian. Peterson was fluent enough in his parents' mother tongue to get some tidbits that other reporters would likely miss.

"Excuse me," he began to an elderly man sitting near the entrance. "Are you Armenian?" That drew a suspicious look. "*Hye ek*?" he tried again in the man's native language.

"*Ayo*," he replied in the affirmative, nodding with surprise."

Tom learned that this man had come into New York from his home near Boston. While not a witness to the murder, he had seen the attack on Tourian in Massachusetts last summer. Peterson discreetly took notes.

> It happened on August 13th. The Archbishop had gone to a picnic at the Kaprielian farm in Westborough, Mass. The family outing was organized by the Church of Our Savior in nearby Worchester. About 1,500 parishioners were there. Around 6 p.m., just as Tourian rose to bless the congregants, a gang of seven Armenian youths rushed toward the cleric. Some of them repeatedly struck the clergyman. The assault immediately provoked a free-for-all.
>
> Police were called in to stop the brawl and arrested five assailants. The man from Boston was shaking as he retold the

story. His eyes welled with tears as he shook his head and said "*amot, amot*" meaning "shame, shame." He regained his composure, and then told the reporter that the perpetrators had been members of the local branch of the Armenian Revolutionary Federation.

"They brought in a truckload of young toughs to attack Archbishop Tourian," he said in his native language.

As Peterson looked around, he noticed other Armenians leaning in to hear the story. The man pointed at them and said that today there were many other out-of-town witnesses here at the police station – from upstate New York, New Jersey and Pennsylvania. They all had one thing in common: their hatred for the Archbishop's enemies.

The older man put a hand in front of his mouth and leaned confidentially toward Peterson. "Listen, my boy," he said. Do you know how they decided who would kill the Archbishop?"

Tom shook his head.

"It was by fate – *jagadakir*," he said, drawing a finger across his own forehead. The man's eyes narrowed. "They drew lots."

"*Shad shnor hagalyem*," said Tom, thanking the man. It wasn't exactly a scoop, but this might be a good lead. Anyway, it was something his competitors probably missed.

While Peterson was trying to finesse information from the Armenians downstairs, detectives upstairs continued interrogating suspects the old-fashioned way.

22

Then

Margaret sipped her espresso, then set down the demitasse cup.

"So, Tommy, how's the research coming along?" she asked.

I had invited the Moradians to dinner in Manhattan, the only way I could reciprocate for their hospitality – and arranging for me to reconnect with Anna. We were just finishing dessert at Mario's, one of the best little restaurants in Little Italy.

"Not bad," I said and quickly recapped my progress up to this point. "The only really frustrating thing so far is the government bureaucracy."

"I see," said Bob, still sounding very much like a psychiatrist. I was never sure how much of me was on a couch when we spoke.

"Have you checked the Dewey collection?" offered Margaret.

I was puzzled. The only Dewey that came to mind was the Dewey decimal system. She spotted the look of confusion on my face. Dr. Moradian furrowed his brow, equally unsure of his wife's reference.

"I mean the Thomas Dewey papers."

He and I remained nonplussed.

"Thomas E. Dewey," she continued, emphasizing the middle initial. Former governor, presidential candidate, district attorney."

I shook my head, trying to rattle some sense out of this. "What's the connection?"

"Don't you remember?" Margaret looked from her husband to me, and then back again. She seemed genuinely surprised by our ignorance. "He was hired by the Armenian Church as their legal counsel on this case."

Bob and I smiled broadly.

"That's my wife," he chuckled with mock surfeit pride.

"Dear, do you think I spend all my time cooking for you?"

The psychiatrist blushed and rubbed his belly. "Uh, well…"

Margaret took her husband's napkin, dipped it into his water glass and dabbed marinara sauce from his shirt sleeve. "I can't take him anywhere," she said. "Tommy, my sister works in the rare books department at the University of Rochester library. They have all of Dewey's personal papers. You should take a look at them."

I was impressed. "Thanks, Margaret. I'll do that."

Bob reached over and put a hand on my arm. "There's one more person I'd like you to meet," he said.

"Oh?" I wasn't sure my heart could handle another old flame this week.

"A friend of mine from the old neighborhood, George Siravakian." That name was vaguely familiar to me, but definitely not one on my list. "His father had something to do with the case."

My eyebrows shot up. "What—"

"We'll get together tomorrow."

Margaret wrote her sister's phone number on my notebook. "If you go to see Isabelle, tell her to take you to the George Eastman House. It's a fantastic museum."

"OK."

I was feeling ebullient. The pieces of this jigsaw were starting to come together.

23

Then

Thomas Edmund Dewey was born in Owosso, Michigan on March 24, 1902. The three-term Republican governor of New York ran twice for President – once against Franklin Roosevelt and once against Harry Truman. Dewey made his career as a crime-busting prosecutor. But before all that, he convicted scores of mobsters in New York during the 1930s.

The mustachioed lawyer was briefly in private practice at the time of the Archbishop's assassination. The Armenian Apostolic Church Diocese had created an organization called the Tourian Committee to ensure that the cleric's killers would be caught and convicted. That group retained Dewey's services. From behind the scenes, marshalling the Committee's resources, he arranged whatever assistance his former colleagues in the District Attorney's office required – and did unofficially what they could not do.

On the day after Christmas, A.D.A. Cohn interrogated three more prisoners – Yarganian, Mozian and Tchalikian. All three admitted being in the church on Sunday, but all denied playing any part in the death of the Archbishop and all refused to implicate anyone else.

That evening, the pudgy-faced prosecutor walked into the detective bureau, feeling a bit dejected. He found Lt. Donnelly and Officer Iskenderian there, looking equally depressed. Izzy sat in a wooden chair and had his feet up on the edge of a desk. The lieutenant rubbed his eyes wearily and stared at the remnants in his coffee cup.

"I hope you guys have better news than I do," said Cohn. He set his briefcase on the desk and plopped into a chair.

"Do we *look* happy, counselor?" asked Donnelly.

The A.D.A. swiveled toward Izzy. "What about the locals?"

The Armenian cop snorted. "They're worse than the goddamned wops. They're really afraid to say anything to us."

"My people aren't much better," added Donnelly. "Nobody wants to be taken for a stoolie."

"The only Irishmen who come to a police station voluntarily are cops," joked Cohn.

The lieutenant laughed. "Actually, counselor, the bigger problem is that the church was so crowded."

"Yeah," said Bedros. "Nobody got a good view.

"Or they really can't remember what they saw," added Donnelly.

"That's pretty funny," said Cohn. "Too many witnesses."

Iskenderian snapped his fingers. "Wait a minute, Mr. Cohn. Maybe you've got something."

"What? You want fewer witnesses?"

"No. What the lieutenant said. They can't remember what they saw. At least they can't remember *in here*.

"So?"

"So, Loo, where do you go for confession?"

"Not that I've been recently, but – to church."

"Exactly," said Bedros enthusiastically. Let's re-enact the crime – take everybody back to the church."

The other two men looked at the Armenian as if he had lost his mind.

"You've been watching too many detective movies," said Donnelly shaking his head. "I'm not sure—"

"Actually," interrupted Cohn, "that might just work."

Donnelly looked at the prosecutor. "Oh, no. Not you, too?"

"Think about it, Jim. It could jog their memories."

"And it'd be someplace more comfortable for them than a police station," noted Iskenderian.

The lieutenant slowly nodded. "All right. Well, we'd have to clear it with the brass."

Cohn smiled broadly. "I'll call my boss at home," said the assistant district attorney as he grabbed a telephone receiver.

"I'll call the church," said Iskenderian reaching for the other phone. He glanced at his watch. It was nearly 9 p.m. "Maybe I'd better go see them in person."

"How long do you think it'll take to set up?" asked the prosecutor with one hand over the mouthpiece.

"With some luck…tomorrow afternoon," said Bedros.

"Better make it at night," said Donnelly. "We don't want a lot of reporters nosing around."

Except for one, thought Iskenderian. *I owe him a scoop*.

Tom Peterson had just walked into his apartment and was about to take off his hat when the phone rang. He pulled back a shirt sleeve to reveal the time on his wristwatch.

"Jeez," he muttered. "Hello?"

"How'd you like a little inside dope?"

The reporter recognized Iskenderian's voice immediately. "Sure. You gonna tell me who kidnapped the Lindbergh baby?"

"Be at Holy Cross tomorrow night."

"Why? Do they need an extra altar boy?"

"I'm serious," said Bedros. "You want that scoop I promised or not?"

"Sure, sure, Izzy." Peterson took off his fedora. "What time?"

The Armenian police officer gave Tom the details. Then he asked the reporter for a favor in exchange. "You hear anything about Nishan Siravakian?"

Tom thought a moment. "The barber?"

"Right."

"No. What's he got to do with this?"

"That's what I'm trying to find out. I have a rumor that puts him inside the church, right next to Tourian – and maybe even holding the knife."

Peterson hesitated. Until this moment, he had managed to avoid telling anyone that he had observed the murder. Since he was not living in the neighborhood, no one would have recognized him that morning. But this was getting too risky.

"I thought you liked Leylegian for the killer," offered Tom.

"Joe Cohn thinks that Mateos did it. Me? I'm not so sure."

The reporter wanted to help, but was hesitant. "I'll see what I can find out."

"Keep it on the Q-T."

"OK, detective."

"*Keesher paree*," said Iskenderian, wishing his fellow Armenian "good night."

"Don't let the bedbugs bite."

The rumor Iskenderian referred to was actually an eyewitness account. The day after the murder, one of the trustees at Holy Cross Church, Sarkis Deckmejian, told the Armenian cop that he saw Siravakian stab the Archbishop.

"I'm afraid for my life, for my family. I need protection." Deckmejian spoke in whispers.

"Are you sure?" asked Iskenderian. He was surprised, since this was the only witness who had identified a different killer.

"I saw what I saw." A photo engraver by trade, he had a reputation for honesty and excellent vision. "It was him."

Bedros put an arm around Deckmejian's shoulder. "Don't worry. I'll make sure you have a police escort whenever you leave your home."

The other man breathed a sigh of relief. "Thank you, Bedros."

"I'll arrest him myself," said Iskenderian. "As long as you're sure, *Baron* Sarkis."

As Deckmejian walked away, he thought to himself, *same height, same weight, same hat. It had to be him.* Didn't it?

24

Now

I was packing my suitcase when the phone rang.

"Hello?"

"Mr. Peterson, this is Mary Sellers in Albany. Are you still looking for some law records from 1934?"

This civil servant on the other end of the line had dug through a dusty warehouse to find my holy grail. Despite dissuasion from bureaucrats in every municipal agency I had visited, the transcripts did exist. And they sat waiting for me at the New York State Library. When I got there, said Miss Sellers, I would find two bound volumes of verbatim court transcripts, conversations in the judges chambers, photographs, sketches – everything I could possibly hope for.

"I'll be on the next train." Miracles do happen.

Before leaving for the state capital, I called Bob Moradian to let him know that we'd have to delay the meeting with his friend, George. He explained that the son of Sarkis and Elise Siravakian might be able to shed some light on the case.

"I'm sorry to put it off," I said, "but I have to get up to Albany first."

"No problem, Tommy. Just let me know when you're back."

Then I called the University of Rochester. Their library had a fantastic rare books collection. They also had some rather strict rules for copying documents. No more than one hundred pages could be photocopied from any given set. That meant either getting lucky, or going there myself.

"Hello?" It was Margaret Moradian's sister, Isabelle.

"I'm Tom Peterson," I began. Before I could explain my project, she told me about the documents she had already put aside for me to see. Obviously, Bob's wife did more than steer me in the right direction.

"When do you think you can be here?" asked Isabelle.

I hesitated. I didn't relish the thought of Rochester in late December, but I had to know what was in Dewey's papers.

"Can you mail me copies?"

"Only one hundred pages," she reminded me. Rules were rules. "And they cost ten cents each, plus postage."

"Sure. That'll be fine," I said. *Maybe I'll get lucky*, I thought.

The train from New York City to the state capital runs through the beautiful Hudson River Valley. Unfortunately, I didn't see a thing. The rhythmic rail sounds put me right to sleep. Two and a half hours later, I woke up in Albany feeling refreshed. Cheated out of my scenic route but refreshed.

25

Then

Shortly after 7 o'clock on Wednesday night, parishioners started filing into Holy Cross Church. Everyone whispered questions or comments or both.

"What are we doing here?"

"The police are still trying to find out who killed the Archbishop."

"Ohhh...everybody knows who did it."

"Such a waste of time."

"I still can't believe what happened."

Men and women were sobbing. In the subdued light, they had trouble seeing their way around and kept bumping into each other.

"Sorry."

"Excuse me."

"I beg your pardon."

Bishop Hovanesian came out of the vestry, dressed in a simple black cassock. He walked to the front of the altar and raised his hands. The gesture was met by a mixture of shushing sounds and coughs.

"Dear worshipers." He began in English as a courtesy to the police officers present. "*Seerehlee havadatsyalner*," he repeated in Armenian. That finally brought the congregation to silence. From that moment on, the clergyman spoke in his native language.

"As most of you know, the detectives have asked us all to come here to help solve their case. I want you to give them your full cooperation." He turned to Lt. Donnelly and gestured for him to proceed.

"Thank you, pastor." Officer Iskenderian stood next to him and translated. "Ladies and gentlemen, we're going to make this as fast and as easy as we can. First of all, I want all of you to sit in the same places where you sat three days ago."

One by one, the congregants stood up and switched places with each other. Out of habit, most were already sitting approximately where they had been last Sunday, and most Sundays. This process took a few minutes and was remarkably efficient. When the movement had ended, Donnelly continued.

"OK, everybody in your correct seats?" There was a general nodding and grunting. "Fine, then let's go on." The lieutenant turned to Detective O'Shea. "Billy, do you have that floor plan?"

The junior officer brought out a large sheet of paper with a sketch of the church interior. It had been affixed to a piece of cardboard, about three feet square.

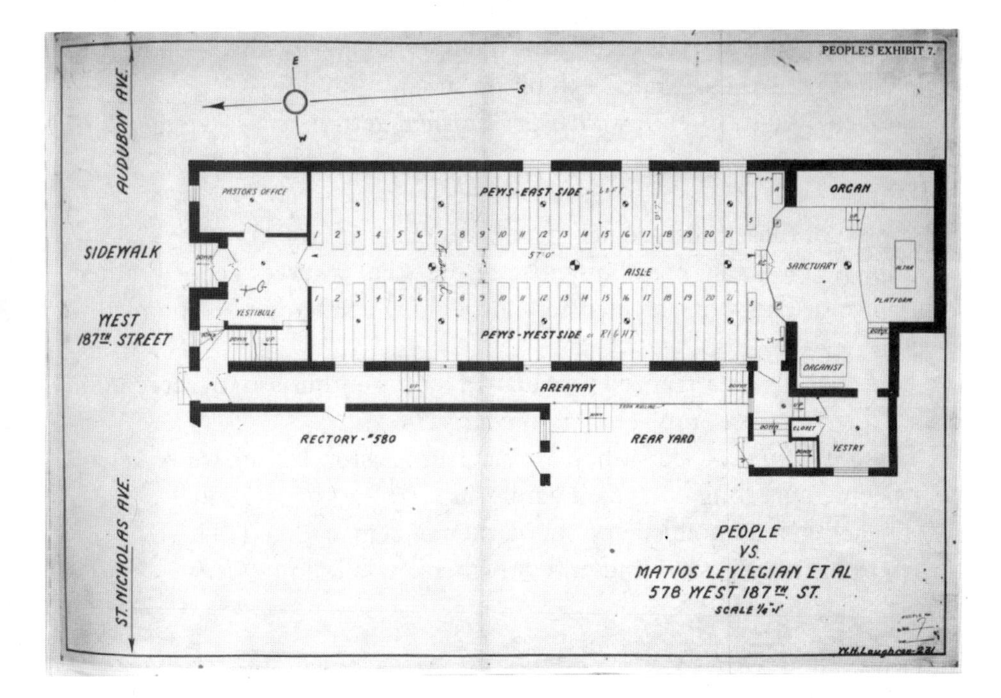

"Good," said Donnelly. "Now, as Detective O'Shea comes around to each of you, I want you to give your names. Then, if anyone is missing from the seats next to you – anyone who was here last Sunday – I want you to give him those names, too."

This was turning into quite a meticulous and ambitious undertaking. While two teams of detectives reconstructed everyone's seating position, half a dozen others asked each person to describe what he or she saw the morning of the murder. In all, nearly twenty men from the 34th Precinct were involved in this investigation.

Joseph Cohn walked from one team to the next, listening to the questions they asked witnesses, and occasionally interjecting an inquiry of his own for clarification. This went on for nearly three hours and nearly everyone got quite agitated. As the night wore on, the scene was far from calm.

"*Vy, vy, vy*!" exclaimed several Armenian women, expressing their grief. They held their heads and shook them from side to side. After the first hour, the tension grew to be too much for many in the church. Every few minutes, a parishioner would sob uncontrollably and have to be helped outside by two others. Many waved handkerchiefs to revive the fainting.

Finally, Iskenderian could see that they had reached their limit. "We've got to let these people go home now," he said to the prosecutor.

"I agree with you. We don't want them to hate us for this." Cohn walked over to Lt. Donnelly. "I think we should stop now."

O'Shea disagreed. "But we haven't finished getting their statements yet."

"Billy—"

"Some of these folks are just starting to open up to us."

"Billy!" Donnelly raised his voice to the point where it echoed rather impressively. The sound immediately brought the sanctuary to complete silence.

Detective O'Shea realized that he had let his enthusiasm obscure good sense. "I'm sorry, sir. You're right, of course."

Donnelly approached Bishop Hovsepian. "Pastor, I think we've kept your people here long enough. Thank you for your cooperation."

The clergyman nodded and shook the policeman's hand. Then, he turned to his parishioners and said in Armenian, "Go in peace."

For the next two days, police continued their work. Harry Sarafian and John Mirijanian were arrested on December 28th.

A.D.A. Cohn interrogated Sarafian shortly before 10 a.m. Unlike his fellow suspects, he denied having present membership in the *Tashnag* society. But he did say he went to the "tea party" a week before Tourian's murder and insisted that he "was always in favor of the Archbishop" – hardly someone who would participate in his murder.

"We have some witnesses who say that you did jump on the Archbishop," said the prosecutor. "What have you got to say about that?"

"That is an absolute false accusation and I can prove it."

As if an actor on stage, Sarafian portrayed a man wrongly accused. As the suspect spoke, Cohn noticed that he kept putting his hand in front of his mouth – a subconscious suggestion that he was thinking, "*I wish I didn't have to say this*." Either that, or he didn't mean what he was saying. The prosecutor also detected that Sarafian spoke confidently when he made self-serving speeches, but not so when in answer to direct questions.

"Someone has something against me," complained the prisoner. "I have a wife and a young child, and there is no reason why I should go through this. I can prove it. God knows I didn't do it."

The A.D.A. sat silently for a moment, watching Sarafian fidget. "Can you tell us who used the knife?"

"I can't tell you that, Mr. Cohn."

"Were you supposed to use the knife?"

"Absolutely not!" Again, the suspect took excessive umbrage. "I couldn't kill a chicken. I am absolutely innocent. This is unfair to me." Then he smiled. "I would be glad to help you if I could."

Sarafian dabbed at the corners of his eyes. *Crocodile tears*, thought Cohn.

By contrast, when Mirijanian was brought in for questioning a few minutes later, he admitted to being a *Tashnag* party member but denied attending the society's recent social event. He recounted spending the night of December 23rd in Washington Heights at the home of Levon and Siranoush Kafafian. The next morning, he went to church with Mr. Kafafian. The suspect said that when the trouble began, the two of them left.

"What happened?" asked Cohn.

"I think there was some fight and I ran out. I told Mr. Kafafian, 'Let's go.'"

"Did you tell Mr. Kafafian, 'Let's go,' because you had attacked the Archbishop?"

Mirijanian seemed genuinely puzzled by the question. "No, because we didn't want to get in a fight."

An impressive performance, thought the A.D.A. – *unless, of course, he* was *innocent*. Two seconds later, the prosecutor shook off that doubt and had the prisoner sent back to his cell.

26

Now

My trip to Albany turned out to be (you should pardon the pun) a capital idea. As promised, the librarian had pulled the two-volume set of transcripts for me. When I opened the first book and started reading, my jaw dropped. There were more than two thousand pages! In addition to a verbatim record of conversations in the courtroom and judges chambers, the official documentation included photographs of all the defendants, the church interior and exterior, as well as a detailed floor plan.

I decided to skip Rochester for now, and asked a graduate student to send me whatever pages she thought would be interesting. I hated to delegate that choice, but this little project was starting to eat away at my savings account.

Back at the Wolcott, I called Ben Archibald to let him know I'd be staying in New York a little longer than I had expected.

"Don't worry about it, Tommy. Shadow's doing fine here."

I was almost disappointed to hear him say that. I had subconsciously hoped my cat would miss me terribly, refuse to eat, maybe even pee on Ben's carpet. No such luck.

"I hope to be back by next week," I said. "What can I bring you?"

"How about some nice weather?" he joked. "It's dropped down into the mid-70s here."

I hate Florida, I thought, watching snow fall outside my hotel room window.

Just as I hung up the phone, it rang. Bob Moradian called to let me know that his friend, George, was going out of town for the weekend.

"Do you think you could meet us this evening?" asked my favorite psychiatrist.

I took a deep breath. All this recent travel was starting to take its toll. I really wanted to stay in tonight.

"To tell you the truth," I began.

"Say no more. "We'll come into the City."

I couldn't very well refuse that. "Thanks, Bob. I appreciate that. How about around seven? I'd like to snooze for a couple hours."

"See you then."

I stretched out on my bed – the one not covered in piles of paper. I wanted to begin digging into the transcripts that I had brought back from Albany. On one hand, I was very curious to re-live those days in court. On the other hand, I suspected the dull legal text would probably put me to sleep. Flipping past the index, the summary statement read like something out of a financial prospectus: b-o-r-i-n-g. Little did I know how much drama was recorded on the subsequent pages.

Anyway, I decided to compromise and finish reading the old newspaper clippings. Ironically, the New York Times had a similarly soporific effect. My eyelids drooped as I scanned the stilted style used to describe what happened decades ago. But before I drifted off, my thoughts turned to Anna. I fell asleep with a mischievous grin.

27

Then

The New Year did not begin happily for Armenians living in the United States.

The Archbishop's body had been lying in repose at a downtown funeral parlor, where hundreds of men, women and children paid their respects. As the New York Times put it:

> Garbed in his elaborate robes, with the brocaded red and gold stole which marked his high rank in the clergy, the body of the Archbishop lay in a huge brass coffin, six feet nine inches long and weighing 600 pounds. Two large crosses, set with diamonds, emeralds and rubies, suspended on a heavy chain of gold, were on his breast.
>
> 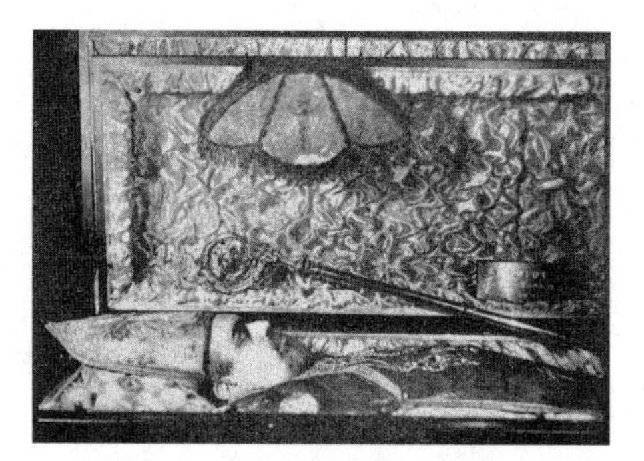
>
> Just above the two crosses was a jeweled medallion of the Sacred Heart and a small plain cross crucifix suspended by a separate chain. Behind the coffin was a large illuminated cross, while vigil lights and 7-foot electric candles burned at the head and the foot of the bier.

On January 1, 1934 (which would have been Ghevont Tourian's 55th birthday), thousands of people gathered at St. John the Divine Church for the Archbishop's funeral. The three-hour service was held at this Episcopalian cathedral to accommodate the large number of mourners. One hundred uniformed and plainclothes police officers were on hand to keep the peace, but there were no disturbances.

But nine days later, hundreds of angry Armenians had gathered in front of the Homicide Court, waiting for police to transport those suspected of killing Tourian. As the prisoners were being led from a paddy wagon into the courthouse, the mob rushed forward.

"Murderers!"

"Monsters!"

The attackers swung umbrellas, canes and fists, but couldn't reach their targets. The cops, badly outnumbered, managed to hold back the crowd. Dozens of reinforcements arrived and a police emergency squad hurried the prisoners into a holding cell inside the building. While officers continued to clash with rioters outside, more Armenians jammed the corridors and filled the courtroom to capacity.

"Silence! Silence in this courtroom!" The judge hammered his gavel so hard he dented the wooden surface. "I will clear the gallery if there isn't quiet." He turned to the bailiff. "Get some more officers in here," he said.

The prosecutor rose. "Your honor, the people would like a continuance. We're still questioning witnesses and—"

The magistrate could hardly hear him. A team of courthouse guards arrived as the judge started banging his gavel again, but to no avail.

"All right, that's it!" The exasperated jurist stood up and pointed his gavel. "Officers, clear this gallery. Now!"

It took only two minutes for the police to empty the courtroom. The judge leaned on the bench. "Contact the clerk when you're ready to proceed, counsel. I'm going on vacation." And with that, he turned around and walked out.

The prosecuting and defense attorneys looked at each other.

"This is going to be fun," said the prosecutor.

"You think so?" answered the other lawyer.

The police continued pushing the now-furious crowd away from the courthouse. After being forced away from the Mott Street exit, the Armenians ran to the other side of the building and gathered near a dilapidated apartment building. As police were taking the suspects back into their patrol van, the mob moved on them again. But this time, the cops were ready. One row of officers spun around, brandishing billy clubs. The protestors immediately stopped advancing, and a few minutes later the van drove away.

On the last Sunday in January, three thousand Armenians from all over New York City squeezed into Mecca Temple on West Fifty-fifth Street. The assembly had been put together by the church-sponsored Tourian Committee. In addition to raising funds to create a memorial, it was assisting law enforcement officials to capture and prosecute those responsible for the Archbishop's assassination.

The Committee wanted to let Armenians know first-hand what progress the police and the District Attorney had made so far. By two o'clock that afternoon, all seats in the neo-Moorish Shriners building were occupied. To thwart any possible trouble, uniformed patrolmen and undercover detectives were posted around the building, along with more than a dozen burley ushers who stood in various strategic spots.

On stage sat more than one hundred representatives from nearly every Armenian organization in town. One group was noticeably absent: the *Tashnag* society. That bias seemed to suit the audience just fine. Whenever a speaker would mention the name of the Armenian Revolutionary Federation, it drew shouts and boos.

One of the first speakers was Thomas E. Dewey. He told the audience how pleased he was by their civility. "You deserve praise for your patience and for your willingness to let the law takes its course, instead of attempting to avenge the murder," said the future governor and presidential candidate.

But the afternoon did not end without incident. Ten minutes after Dewey left the hall, several fights broke out. Police and ushers raced around trying to stop these minor clashes.

On stage, a Mr. Santurian charged that Hitler was funding the *Tashnag* society. A woman sitting in the balcony shouted, "Don't' talk nonsense!" Police arrested Mrs. Apesag Bedrosian, age 40, and later charged her with disorderly conduct.

The defense team was making pre-trial news of its own. Former District Attorney Joab Banton represented the Archbishop's accused killers. He was telling news reporters that Tourian's real murderers were communists sent to America by the Kremlin. That suggestion drew sharp denials from the Tourian Committee. It also provoked a letter to the editor of the New York Times:

> Joab H. Banton, counsel to those accused of the murder of Archbishop Leon Tourian, is quoted as referring to the late Archbishop as a Communist.
>
> As personal physician and friend of the late Archbishop, having had opportunity on more than one occasion to exchange views

on different subjects with him, I know full well that the late Archbishop was never a Communist. He belonged to no political organization and was not interested in politics. He was a true Christian, and his sole effort was to keep his church clear from politics.

M.M. Housepian, New York, Feb. 28, 1934

Over the next several months, tempers remained high. The city's Armenians manifested their anger in many ways, large and small. One rainy day not long after the assassination, Hasmig and Hagop Mahakian were walking to a meeting in Washington Heights. Another couple, Satenig and Misak, were walking behind them. Hasmig raised her umbrella toward the sky and declared in Armenian, "Hail the Tashnag heroes!"

Upon hearing that, Satenig grew irate. She replied in the same language, "Heroism isn't like that. It's like this!" She struck out with her own umbrella and smacked Hasmig on the bottom.

On April 8, about three thousand members and supporters of the *Tashnag* society met inside the Metropolitan Life Building on Madison Avenue. They were there to commemorate the anniversary of the now-defunct independent Armenian Republic. Joab Banton was there to reiterate his accusations that those arrested for the Archbishop's murder were framed.

"I am certain that the young men in custody are there because of perjured testimony," Banton told the receptive audience. "They had absolutely no part in the murder of Archbishop Tourian. In fact, they deplore it more than anyone else."

A detail of police officers were on hand to keep watch over the meeting, because this day had begun rather violently. Shortly before the meeting opened, several hundred anti-*Tashnag* protesters paraded around the building and picketed the group inside.

Initially, it took only a few patrolmen to break up the unauthorized march. But the opposition bunch moved to a nearby subway station and began to hit, kick and even stab *Tashnags* who were arriving. After a quarter-hour of these sporadic assaults, about fifty more officers and detectives were sent in to stop the attacks. One man was seriously injured and about a dozen others had to be treated for minor wounds.

Such clashes were not limited to New York City. That same day, after attending separate church services in Boston, pro- and anti-Tourian factions held political rallies half a block apart. Members from one group challenged the other and young men rushed out onto the street across from the Common to settle the score. Makeshift weapons and fists flew on both sides, spilling Armenian blood in the same spot where American colonialists fought against British Redcoats a century and a half before.

Innocent bystanders were caught in the battle. One non-Armenian called the police. "It's a riot!" he yelled into the telephone. "Please hurry. They'll kill us all." It took two hundred and fifty of Boston's finest to bring the fracas under control.

Meanwhile, a thousand *Tashnag* members were gathered at the West End Women's Club in Chicago. A couple hundred Tourian supporters marched past the clubhouse, protesting the meeting. Some of those inside emerged from the building and began to fight with the protestors. It took fifty policemen to break it up. When the brawl was over, more than a dozen Armenians were injured – some so badly that they needed to be taken to hospitals.

"Well, I don't see why you need me on this case, Joab." Thomas I. Sheridan, himself, had been an assistant district attorney before entering politics as a New York state senator. He was flattered to be asked by his former colleague to take over as lead counsel.

"As I understand it, you have that famous Armenian lawyer, Cardashian, running things." Sheridan sat at a table in a dark corner of a Greenwich Village bar, drinking beer and playing solitaire. The mindless game helped him think, he always explained.

"Oh, him." Banton furrowed his brow. "Well, Thomas, I'm afraid he might not be with us much longer."

"Switching sides?"

"Going to the great beyond." Sheridan stopped flipping cards. "Heart troubles," added Banton.

"Well, Joab, I'm touched that you would think of me." He grinned and shuffled the deck, then handed the pack to his friend. "Cut these for me, will you?"

Banton indulged Sheridan in this minor eccentricity. "You'll have to decide soon. *Voir dire* is calendared for the seventh of June," he said, referring to the process of jury selection.

Sheridan nearly choked on his beer. "Jesus!"

"Yeah, I know. That's not much time."

"Not much time? That's no time." Sheridan started to deal another game of solitaire. "Who's the presiding?"

"The Honorable Joseph E. Corrigan."

Sheridan dropped the deck, scattering cards across the table and onto the floor. "God damn. Corrigan hates me, you know."

Banton chuckled as he helped the other lawyer recover his cards. "Well, at least you'll take the pressure off of me."

Sheridan leaned back in his chair and rubbed his eyes, then looked at his watch. It was nearly 11 p.m. "Joab, my boy, let me ask you one question: Do we stand a Chinaman's chance of getting these gents off?"

"Why don't I send you the files and let you answer that for yourself."

28

Now

In all of South Florida, I never found a restaurant that came close to Gon Mei in New York's Chinatown. The food was fantastic and the prices were very reasonable. I also enjoyed invariably being the only non-Asian person in the place. After all these years, I was pleased to see that nothing had changed. Even the old man behind the register was still there.

"*Nee how ma*," I greeted him with the only Mandarin phrase I knew. One of my hobbies was learning to ask, "How are you?" in as many languages as possible.

"*How, how*," he replied, assuring me that he was feeling fine.

Both Bob Moradian and George Siravakian were vocally impressed by my "fluency" in Chinese. Who was I to disappoint them? We came here because I knew there was little chance of running into any other Armenians. We could speak in relative privacy.

"My parents lived in a top floor apartment at 556 W. 188th Street," George began. He proceeded to tell me the story of how six men asked his father, Nishan, to meet them at Holy Cross Church on that fateful Sunday morning in 1933. By the time the elder Siravakian got there, the murder had already happened.

"Long story short, all hell breaks loose and everybody comes out of that church," said the son. But some of the parishioners thought they had seen Nishan inside with a knife in his hand. "They pointed out that my father was the one who killed the Archbishop."

His mother later told him that of the six visitors, only five were Armenians. The sixth one resembled her husband. "He came in from Chicago – an Italian guy," added George under his breath.

I listened quietly to his story, astonished that none of this had ever come to light at the time of the assassination.

"Do you believe that your father was set up?"

"Now that I'm older, I'm saying to myself, 'Wait a minute, are they setting my father up for the kill here?' Now, you think about it in retrospect, you think there's a good damn chance it could have been that way."

The next day, I wanted to find out what the Armenian press was saying at the time. Fortunately, there was a great source at my disposal.

"Tommy, lunch is ready," Margaret Moradian called from the kitchen. Bob had gone to see a patient, leaving me in the good hands of his wife. "Come on," she said, now standing at the door. "The research will keep."

I looked at my watch, finding it hard to believe it was noon already. "I guess I lost track of the time."

She wrapped her arm around mine and led me to the dining room where a sumptuous meal waited. I deserved a break.

The morning had been quite productive. My new best friends, the Moradians, kept quite a collection of old Armenian newspapers. And even though a lot of them were published in that language which I regretfully could not read, there were also several English editions. I had started with the Boston-based Armenian Mirror. The main page one headline on December 29, 1933 read:

> **Assassination of Archbishop Leon Tourian**
> **Plunges Armenian Communities Into Gloom**

The story reported that police were looking for suspects "in Massachusetts, Rhode Island, Connecticut, New Jersey, and Pennsylvania, and it is believed the Parisian police have been enlisted in cooperation with authorities here – Paris being the central headquarters of the Tashnag."

I was also interested in the "Reflections" column:

> **Homes in an Armenian colony of a Massachusetts town were enshrouded in darkness. People, grief-stricken over the assassination, remained within their dwellings, dismayed and bewildered. Melancholy permeated the whole scene.**
>
> **Nearby in a club, however, the raucous cries of a group of Armenians could be heard rejoicing, drinking and boisterously celebrating some unknown festive occasion – We wonder what?**

Other opinions expressed in this same paper included:

> **The honor of the Armenian people has been impugned.**
>
> **Tourian's death has put a damning blot in the minds of Americans concerning Armenians.**
>
> **The assassination of Archbishop Leon Tourian was the foulest deed ever perpetrated by Armenian cowards.**
>
> **Most atrocious act imaginable.**

The general tone of the paper toward the slain prelate was that he was a saint, a martyr and a hero whose remains should be entombed in Armenia alongside other Church luminaries.

On January 26th, the Mirror published what it described as a private message from *Catholicos* Khoren I to Archbishop Tourian four months before his death. Referring to the prelate's handling of the flag controversy in Chicago, the supreme head of the Armenian Apostolic Church reportedly wrote this:

> **"(T)he Armenian church...is a friend and assistant of the Armenian State, which rules in our Fatherland and works for the improvement and strengthening of the economic life of the Armenian people...That authority, today, is the true government of Soviet Armenia, and the Armenian Church is its friend...**
>
> **"This is the principle by which you have so far been governed in general, and especially in the World's Fair of Chicago at the request of the majority of your flock; and we and the Rt. Reverend members of the Supreme Spiritual Council, consider yours the only correct and beneficial conduct.**

"Continue in your conduct, but be governed by caution and circumspection."

I spotted this display ad in the February 2nd issue:

> **IMPORTANT**
>
> **Send your contribution to the ARCHBISHOP LEON TOURIAN COMMITTEE, that has been formed in New York for the purpose of facilitating the prosecution and punishment of the murderers of the late Archbishop.**
>
> **Checks should be drawn up in the name of ARCHBISHOP LEON TOURIAN COMMITTEE**
>
> **And should be mailed to**
> **Archbishop Leon Tourian Committee**
> **Armenian Prelacy**
> **156 Fifth Ave., New York, N.Y.**

By contrast, the anti-Tourian press accused the Archbishop of plagiarizing his sermons, taking bribes, stealing from orphans and refugees fund, as well as being a notorious womanizer. What's worse, according to his detractors, Tourian sacrificed members of his flock to save his own skin.

"Margaret, this food is delicious. I'm going to gain a hundred pounds if I'm not careful."

Like many women of her generation, she prided herself on having great culinary skills. But in this case, it was more than pride. Margaret's mother had literally written the book on Armenian cooking. Her collection of traditional recipes was a mainstay of every *hye* kitchen from Watertown to Fresno.

"I'm glad you like it," she said modestly, pouring another cup of coffee. "How about some dessert?"

Having spotted a plate of my favorite powdered sugar cookies called *khourabia*, I didn't have to be asked twice. I'm sure they were going to push my cholesterol levels into the danger zone, but I guess that's the price of heaven.

"Mrs. Moradian, your husband is a lucky guy," I flirted.

Unfortunately, lunch was only a temporary distraction from my research. Just as the men arrested for killing Archbishop Tourian could not avoid prosecution, there was no way for me to quit this hunt for the truth.

29

Then

The summer of 1934 was going to be a particularly hot one. But the weather in New York City on June 7, 1934 was still quite nice, not too warm, and typically pleasant. A local announcer on WCBS radio that morning predicted partly cloudy skies, 73 degrees and no rain for this late spring day. However, the climate inside General Sessions Courthouse Part Five was much less temperate. The trial struck a heated note from the very first word.

"The defendants are not ready—"

Defense attorney Thomas Sheridan couldn't even finish his sentence. He was starting to ask the judge for a postponement when the prosecutor objected.

"May it please the court—"

Assistant District Attorney Alexander Kaminsky interrupted to say that he wanted to discuss the matter privately to avoid prejudicing prospective jurors.

"Your honor—"

The Honorable Joseph E. Corrigan knew this wasn't going to be an easy case, but he had no idea that his judicial temper would be tested thirty seconds into the first day, even prior to jury selection.

Both lawyers were on their feet, each vigorously trying to out-shout the other. They struck that quaint orator's pose more familiar to speakers a century before: one hand on the lapel, the other outstretched and chins jutting slightly skyward. After those initial words, neither man could hear anything his opponent was saying. This was more a competition of lung power than anything like a legal debate. The two men competed for Judge Corrigan's attention, each raising his voice slightly more than the other. The court stenographer had trouble keeping up, too, but the prosecutor's last words finally got through to the bench.

"...or some other place out of the hearing of the jury," barked Kaminsky.

The judge held up his hands and glared both attorneys into silence.

"If you are about to say anything that may in any way affect the trial on the merits," Corrigan said deliberately to Sheridan, "I think perhaps the District Attorney's suggestion is a good one. We will go to my chambers."

And with that, he stood and sped out of the courtroom with the opposing lawyers, their co-counsels and the court reporter briskly trailing in the vortex of His Honor's wake, up the back stairs.

Now behind closed doors, the adversaries could relax a bit. Although the stenographer took down every word, everyone was permitted to speak less formally if he wished. To emphasize that point, Corrigan loosened the top two buttons at the collar of his black robe. Nevertheless, counsel for the defense launched into an animated speech explaining why he was not prepared to proceed.

"I have worked during the past two or three days on this case," said Sheridan, mellifluously modulating his voice and gesturing dramatically as if addressing an audience of thousands. "I have worked until 2:30 this morning. I have never done what I am about to do in the past 25 years as a practicing lawyer."

Sheridan looked around at his fellow officers of the court, took a measurable pause, and then dropped the bomb.

"We are going to withdraw from this case rather than have it said that we are not acting with the dignity of a lawyer." Every jaw in the room dropped including that of Sheridan's fellow defense attorney, Joab Banton. The ordinarily implacable native Texan looked at his co-counsel in astonishment and wondered: Was he really going to quit before the trial started? Banton had served as Manhattan's District Attorney until just five years ago, and he knew every trick on both sides. But this move startled him, too. Even the court reporter momentarily took his hands off the steno pad.

Sheridan ended the suspense.

"If your honor directs my assignment, we shall proceed." Everyone breathed a bit easier. Maybe this was just a legal maneuver intended to throw prosecutors off-guard. Sheridan knew which buttons to push. He continued to explain that he had never met with any of the nine defendants, nor had he read most of the available material. But he brilliantly turned an apparent shortcoming into an advantage. Any other lawyer in his place might well be accused of malpractice. But for Thomas Sheridan, this admitted lack of preparation was a powerful weapon. He brandished it like a fencing foil, explaining that he had repeatedly warned the D.A. about his lack of readiness for this case.

Sheridan went into some detail about a lawyer of Armenian extraction named Vahan Cardashian who was also representing the defendants in this case. Cardashian was the most prominent Armenian attorney in the United States. During the Wilson administration, he led the effort to organize statehood for post-war Armenia. But having recently suffered a serious heart ailment, Cardashian was too ill to handle the trial.

"Now, as your honor said the other day, what assurance have we got that this man will recover?" asked Sheridan rhetorically. "They tell me that he has arrived at a point of recovery now," he said, answering his own question. "But in the event the man should die, I think under the circumstances there, as I have stated, a fair and reasonable thing would be to give us a continuance."

The senator went on in this manner for several minutes. Feeling somewhat overwhelmed by Sheridan's forceful argument, the prosecutor decided to bring in some heavier muscle: He called his boss.

The District Attorney for New York County, William Copeland Dodge, rarely appeared in court. It was unusual for any district attorney to prosecute a case personally. That's what an *assistant* D.A. does. But as the second highest elected official in Manhattan, his presence carried a lot of weight. When special cases warranted it, Dodge would show up. This was definitely a special case.

It took only a few minutes for the tall man to walk from his office to the courthouse, just around the block. He was annoyed by his deputy's phone call, unhappy about having a subordinate interrupt his reputedly notorious activities. The newspapers all labeled Dodge as a Tammany Hall man. That corrupt political machine had controlled New York City elections for more than a century. It was widely believed that the D.A.'s campaign was funded by mobster Dutch Schultz. Until recently, he had been what Time Magazine called "an obscure lower court judge."

But Fiorello LaGuardia had just been elected mayor of New York City, ending 16 years of Tammany rule. In the next few years, the D.A. was going to face a showdown with Governor Herbert Lehman who would appoint a special prosecutor to clean up the corruption at City Hall. That man would later go on to become governor himself and run twice (albeit unsuccessfully) for President of the United States. His name was Thomas E. Dewey.

By the time Dodge arrived in the judge's chambers, he had built up enough emotional steam to burst through the doors, ready for a fight. His face was flushed, but his anger was not reflected in the calm voice with which he greeted everyone in the room. Corrigan addressed the D.A. as "Judge Dodge" (since he had also once served on the bench) and explained that Sheridan was again asking for a delay.

"I do not see how that is any concern of the court at all," he said dismissively. "My information is that counsel for the defendants have had as much time to prepare the case for the defense as the district attorney has for the prosecution."

The sandy-haired, bespectacled D.A. insisted that defense counsel was unreasonably attempting to prolong the trial. After a bit of haggling over some details, Dodge finally invoked the power of his office to demand that there be no further delay. That gave Judge Corrigan the extra confidence he needed to overrule the motion and order the hearing to proceed.

"It is going to be a long drawn out case, taking a lot of trouble and time in the hot summer weather," Corrigan said to the lawyers. "But I told you that I will try it and I *will* try it."

Now the judge was building his own oratorical momentum. Still speaking on the record and for posterity, he said, "I am told by the District Attorney – I was told in open court – that his witnesses were intimidated to a certain extent. Also, that there are nine men in the Tombs awaiting trial."

Corrigan went on about agitation among New York's many members of the "Armenian race." He insisted that the case continue without any further delays.

Dodge had won the debate and capped it with the prosecution's most powerful emotional argument. "A murder was committed in this horrifying manner, defying all laws of society," he said, "and we must proceed to prosecute those whom we consider guilty."

Sheridan and Banton tried to have the last word in chambers. They formally withdrew as defense attorneys. But it was nothing more than a final bit of backstage legal theatrics, because the judge brusquely ordered them to represent the defendants. With that, they all tromped back downstairs and into the courtroom.

The rest of that first day – and half of the second – was spent impaneling a jury.

"Are you acquainted with any Armenians?" Kaminsky would ask each prospective juror. "Do you have any racial, religious or political prejudices against the Russian Soviet Government?"

One by one, lawyers would examine those citizens under consideration to hear this case. From a pool of 200 candidates, twelve men were eventually selected as jurors:

William S. Schillinger, foreman
Octavius Spenrath
Harold L. Waters
Frank H. Crehore
Albert C. Bauer
Harry H. Fiedler
Herman Moritz
Howard L. Powell
William F. Hogan
James F. Connor
Herbert S. Bachman
Carl Strauss

Two more – Harris P. Emerson and Charles Meehan – were chosen as alternates. When that was done, the judge sent everybody home for a nice, long weekend with the traditional warning not to discuss the case among themselves or with anyone else.

30

Now

The woman at the other end of the telephone line astonished me.

"Are you sure?"

I couldn't believe this information had been kept a secret all those years. But Margaret's sister, Isabelle, at the University of Rochester was sure. She went through three hundred or so documents in Thomas Dewey's personal papers related to the Tourian murder. Buried deep within this file were several notes on individuals possibly involved in the conspiracy to kill the Archbishop.

"You really should see these memos," she insisted. "The names probably mean more to you than they do to me."

I agreed that a trip to Rochester was inevitable, but explained that it would have to wait at least a few days.

"Well, there is one other thing," she added. "Dewey also dealt with an Armenian law firm in Manhattan."

I hung up the phone just as Bob Moradian walked into his office. "Any luck?" asked my host.

"I feel like I'm a reporter again," I said. "But it's hard to get accurate information so many years after the event."

Moradian nodded, and then handed me a piece of paper. "This might help."

It was a list of people who had lived in the old neighborhood at the time of the assassination. The good doctor thought some might be willing to share their recollections with me. And some were.

> "*Ahreen chreen mertzootzeen,*" said Alice, the first person I reached. "That means, 'by hook or by crook they killed him.' In other words, it was planned."
>
> "Who did it?" I asked her.

"Who else? The Tashnags. I cannot forgive the Turks for the massacres and the Tashnags are the same." Her voice broke and she hung up.

To my surprise, the very next person I called on the list expressed the opposite feelings.

"He deserved it," said Harry. "Anybody who doesn't respect the flag should be shot." Then he added quickly, "As an Armenian, I was not glad. I respected him as a Christian and I respected his rank. But he asked for it."

But most of those on Bob's list would not talk about the Archbishop at all.

Siran put it best. "This incident divided our people, even my own family," she said. We want to forget it. Please just leave us alone."

The list of warm leads in this cold case was getting longer. Before pursuing the Dewey connection, my next stop would have to be the law firm that represented the defendants. Unfortunately, they were no longer in business. But their practice was acquired by another law firm in Manhattan. It was time for me to go back across the Hudson.

31

Then

Bright and early on Monday morning, June 11th, the courtroom was already filled to capacity. Armenians and non-Armenians alike had lined up along the courthouse steps a good hour before the doors opened, to be sure they could get in. The building was under heavy guard. Dozens of patrolmen on foot and on horseback were visible, and undercover detectives circulated among the crowd. Each person desiring admission was subjected to vigorous questioning at the front door.

"What's your name? Why are you here?" Anyone who looked suspicious was given a quick "pat-down" search. Women's pocketbooks were opened.

Inside Part Five, every available spot had a body seated on it and bailiffs allowed audience members to stand at the back. A dozen or so newspaper reporters were corralled into reserved spaces next to the jury box. They – and their editors – regarded this as the trial of the century and didn't dare miss a word. From time to time, litigating parties from other courtrooms poked their heads inside to catch a glimpse of this excitement. Some stayed so long they were late for their own trials. With so many people in so little area, it promised to get stiflingly warm before day's end.

At the crack of ten o'clock, defense and prosecution lawyers were ready to begin delivering their opening statements. At both tables, attorneys unloaded piles of documents from their briefcases, creating miniature paper skyscrapers. It was a bit like the construction contest between the Empire State and Chrysler buildings, each determined to have the tallest and most impressive structure, with one erecting a hidden spire and the other adding a dirigible mooring mast. Both sides in this law competition also had their secret weapons – confidential memoranda which they might never offer into evidence but which they could flash at their opponents to gain some psychological advantage.

There were significant differences in style. The prosecutors were much more conservative, conforming as much as possible to the expected decorum which the occasion demanded. From the moment they entered the courtroom, A.D.A. Kaminsky and his team exhibited a quiet self-confidence. They appeared as much as possible like trusted bankers, hoping to persuade jurors to invest their confidence in the people's case.

By contrast, the defense lawyers took a slightly more melodramatic approach. As Thomas Sheridan stacked notes on his table, he nodded and chuckled self-assuredly. After pausing a moment, he flamboyantly unfolded and then surreptitiously showed a hand-written note to his co-counsel. The two exchanged some inaudible whispers, apparently prompting Sheridan to refold the paper. Finally, with great flourish, he slipped the item in his vest pocket, never again touching it. The whole thing was nothing more than some conjured, fanciful distraction intended solely to worry his opponents. He would never know if his ploy accomplished its aim, although this was an oddly entertaining way to begin a murder trial.

A minute later, the game playing was over. The bailiff stood and cried out, "All rise." Everyone's eyes turned to the bench as the judge entered with ceremonial grandeur. One almost expected to hear royal trumpets blaring.

Joseph Eugene Corrigan was Chief Magistrate of New York City. The balding jurist had been on the bench for more than 23 years. He was also a debonair socialite who was not shy about expressing his opinions – in or out of court. A few months earlier, while speaking at a Kiwanis Club luncheon, the judge suggested that racketeers should be punished with an electric whipping machine. For some reason, that plan was never implemented.

Judge Corrigan took his place in the plush, high-back chair and tapped his gavel twice. Knowing that there would be some language difficulties with so many foreign-born defendants and witnesses, the court arranged for an Armenian language interpreter to stand by, ready to translate. This linguist was the first person to be sworn in.

Before the grand drama could go further, Corrigan had one more preliminary surprise. He turned to the jury.

"Gentlemen, in view of the complexity of this case, which is owing, very largely, I think, to the number of defendants and the fact that Armenian names are unfamiliar to us, I am going to ask to have the roll of the defendants called, and each man answer to his name, so that you will be able to bear that in mind."

As if on a pre-arranged cue, the A.D.A. brought out a large cardboard sign.

"Judge," offered Kaminsky, "we have prepared a chart with the names of the defendants and their numbers, because I will refer to them at times by their numbers."

The chart was posted for the jury to see.

DEFENDANTS' EXHIBIT J.
1. MATIOS LEYLEGIAN
2. NISHAN SARKISIAN, alias NISHAN TUKTIKIAN
3. OSGAN [illegible]ARGANIAN
6. HARRY SARAFIAN
7. JOHN MIRIJANIAN

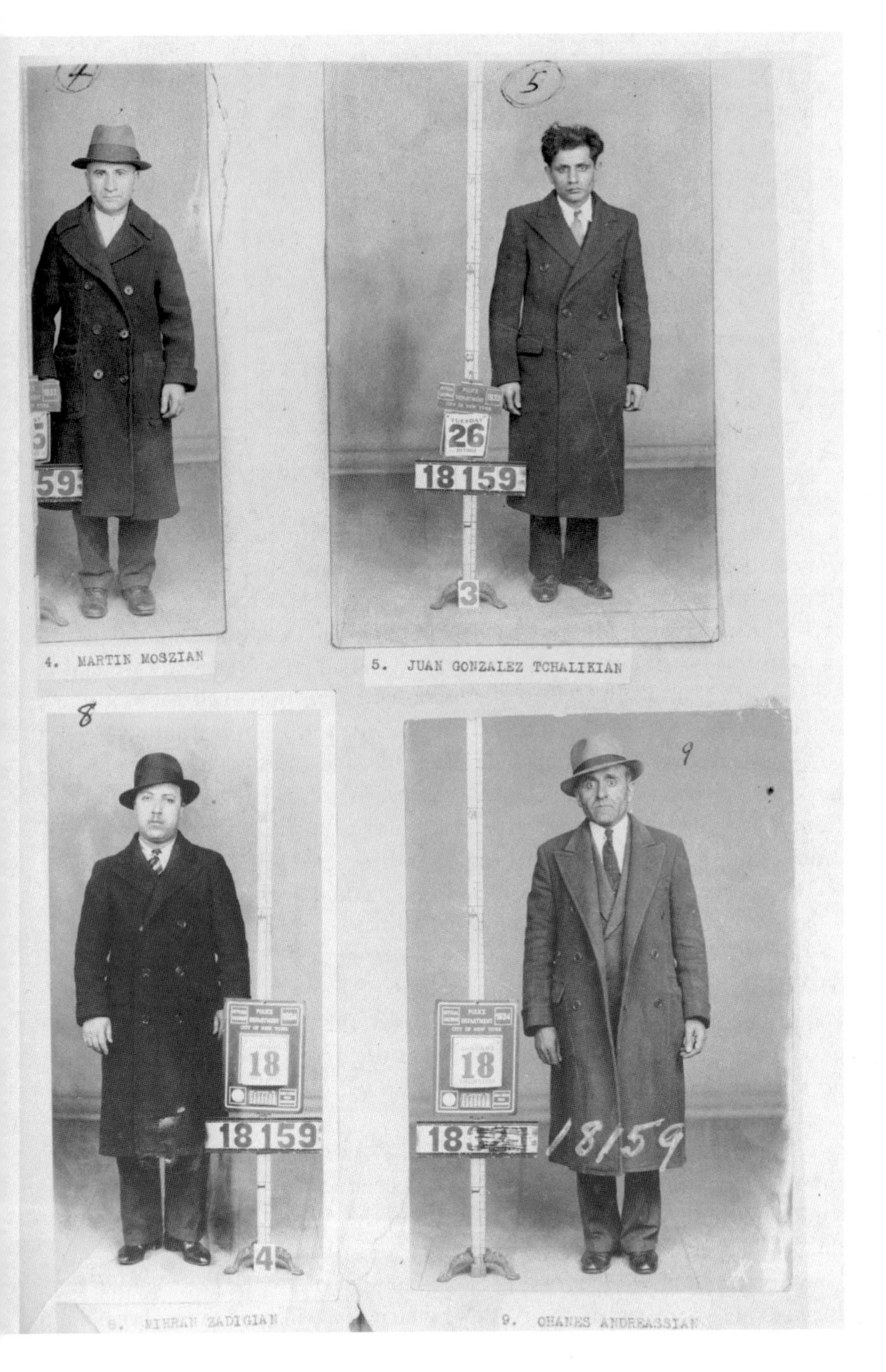

4. MARTIN MOSZIAN

5. JUAN GONZALEZ TCHALIKIAN

8. MIHRAN ZADIGIAN

9. OHANES ANDREASSIAN

Throughout the trial, the nine men with unpronounceable names would be identified by these numbers corresponding to the order of their indictment:

1. Mateos Leylegian
2. Nishan Tuktikian (a.k.a. Nishan Sarkisian)
3. Osgan Yarganian
4. Martin Mozian
5. Juan Gonzales Tchalikian
6. Harry Sarafian
7. John Miriganian
8. Mihran Zadigian
9. Ohanes Andreassian

With that last bit of opening business out of the way, the prosecutor stood and spoke a polite "May it please the court" to the judge. Kaminsky then turned to his right, waited several long seconds, and strode confidently toward the jury, smiling and making eye-contact with each man before saying another word. He wanted to be sure he had everyone's full attention, to focus this essential audience finally on him and him alone.

The room grew uncomfortably quiet. Whispers diminished to nothing. A few final coughs echoed. The balding A.D.A. adjusted his round, wire-rim glasses, rested a thumb in the cleft of his chin and took a breath. He broke the silence with a punchy "Mr. Foreman and gentlemen of the jury." Kaminsky quickly summarized the charges of first degree murder, and then moved into the meat of his opening statement.

"Now, gentlemen of the jury, perhaps it would be well for me to give you the background of the whole situation."

For the next fifty-five minutes, Kaminsky mesmerized the courtroom with what, in any other circumstances might have been considered a complicated and boring history lesson. But in this room and in this case, everything turned on a dozen American citizens coming to understand an arcane conflict born in a faraway land and tragically transported to the United States.

The prosecutor's story began in 1375. That was the end of Armenia's three and a half millennia of sporadic independence and the beginning of Turkish Ottoman rule. For many centuries, the Armenian nation was divided between Turkey in the west and Czarist Russia in the east.

"Finally, somewhere around 1890, a number of groups got together and formed one organization, the name of which you will hear throughout the trial," said Kaminsky. "It is the Armenian Revolutionary Federation, known by the Armenians as *Tashnag*."

The prosecutor took the jury through the World War, the short-lived Armenian Republic and the Bolshevik Revolution. Alexander Kaminsky took a deep breath and let all this sink in. He looked at each juror to make sure no one was being left behind. Once confident that everyone followed his lesson, the A.D.A continued.

"I am not going to discuss the rights or wrongs, the wisdom or fallacies of their leaderships," he said. The prosecutor reminded jurors that this trial was about what happened on December 24, 1933 and not about ancient history. He then moved to Tourian's arrival in the United States on May 8, 1931.

The supreme head of the whole Apostolic Church was *Catholicos* Khoren I. He had sent Tourian to America in hopes of mollifying the rift among Armenians in the New World. But for the next two years, the Archbishop became something of a lightning rod in the Armenian community. Instead of calming that clash, he was the target of *Tashnag* ire. The group accused him of representing a pro-communist church regime and undermining Armenian hopes for freedom.

Kaminsky told jurors about the so-called Chicago flag incident, when the Archbishop refused to speak in front of an Armenian revolutionary banner at the International Exposition the past summer. The A.D.A. explained that the clash had become an important point of reference in the political conflict among Armenians. Those who supported the tri-color and all that it represented subsequently considered Archbishop Tourian an open opponent of their cause.

"From that time on, he was bitterly attacked," said Kaminsky. "He was pursued from church to church."

The prosecutor detailed several assaults that same year in Massachusetts where the Archbishop was stalked and beaten, noting that Tourian's killers were among those who had attacked him in Boston and Westborough. Kaminsky pointed to the accused murderers. The A.D.A. stepped over to the chart with the defendants' names and corresponding numbers.

"Imagine a June day in 1933," he said. "Groups walking along Fifth Avenue. Between 27th and 28th streets, Martin Mozian, the defendant who is mentioned on this chart as Number Four, approaches an old friend of his."

Kaminsky then moved back toward the jury box and began to pace slowly, looking closely from juror to juror.

"They discuss Armenia. They discuss the incident at Chicago."

Joab Banton leaned toward his co-counsel and whispered, "He's lying."

Thomas Sheridan shot him a puzzled look. "The flag incident happened in July. How could they have discussed it in June?" Sheridan smiled and shook his head knowingly.

The prosecutor continued, "And then Mr. Mozian, defendant Number Four says, "It is well for the Archbishop to have a bodyguard with him all the time. Otherwise, we would kill him on the spot." He waited for his words to sink in. One juror nodded ever so slightly – just the sort of affirmation A.D.A. Kaminsky wanted.

"Gentlemen, I intend to connect at least six of these defendants by their own declaration to the fatal event on the 24th of December, 1933." The prosecutor pivoted on his left heel and marched back to the chart. And as he narrated the moments leading up to Tourian's assassination, Kaminsky pointed one by one to the names and numbers.

"This, in short, is the evidence which we hope to present to you against each individual man," concluded the prosecutor. "I know the case is complicated," he said. "It is no easy task. We will present fifty witnesses."

One of the jurors gasped at hearing this. He understood the trial would be long, but fifty witnesses? This was going to take weeks, he thought. Judge Corrigan heard the gasp and raised an eyebrow in the juror's direction. The other jurors also heard the gasp and shared that sentiment, albeit silently. Kaminsky was undeterred by the reaction. He continued toward the end of his opening statement without hesitation, even accelerating his pace slightly.

"Those witnesses will give separate and distinct testimony." The A.D.A. glanced quickly at his pocket watch without pausing. "I hope, gentlemen of the jury, that I have not labored in vain to give you a picture of what the people expect to prove. On summation, I again expect to review the evidence against each individual defendant, to seek a verdict based upon the evidence. Because the people hope to prove fairly, without malice, without prejudice, a case beyond a reasonable doubt against each one of the nine defendants at the bar."

Kaminsky flashed a quick, tight-lipped smile at the jurors, turned around and slowly returned to his seat. He folded his hands on the table and stared straight ahead toward the judge.

Thomas Sheridan now waited for the room to get quiet again. Then, as if awakening from a long nap, the defense attorney rotated his shoulders, rocked his head from side to side, and rose.

"If the court pleases," he began before slowly turning to his right. "Mr. Foreman and gentlemen of the jury." In sharp contrast to his opponent, Sheridan inched his way forward. He wanted the jurors to know that he was as exhausted by the prosecutor's speech as they were. To emphasize that point, he took out his pocket watch and had a long look.

"For almost an hour, the District Attorney most interestingly has presented what he expects to show." There was a hint of sarcasm in his voice, but not enough to draw an admonition from the bench. "There is one thing, gentlemen, and it is very important right now."

He stopped and replicated Kaminsky's eyeballing of each venireman. "Do not be misled by me in this trial. That would be wrong. Do not be misled by my friend. That would be a greater wrong." That drew a faintly audible chuckle from one juror but an embarrassingly loud guffaw from an audience member. The judge quickly tapped on his gavel and cleared his throat. There was no need for further warning and Sheridan continued with a bit more subtlety.

"This is probably a very difficult case for an American jury to pass on. 'The East is East and West is West and never the twain shall meet.' And it is going to tax you during the course of this trial to know, understand and appreciate the nature of the Eastern mind."

Sheridan continued in this manner for the next ten minutes, delving into the psychology and the sociology of the case. At one point, a juror in the back corner stifled a yawn. Whether bored or merely lacking sufficient sleep, the man's attention was slipping away. It was a clear sign to the practiced orator who immediately punched his right fist into his left palm, raised his voice and quickened his pace.

"There is no doubt about it," said Sheridan, "the nine men charged are members of the *Tashnag*. No doubt about it. The nine of them – Armenians – did love their country and love their religion." Coming from any other defense lawyer, those words were the beginning of a confession, possibly even grounds for reversal based on malpractice. But coming from this defense lawyer, these words served to further seduce the jury.

Counsel for the defense then laid out his own version of Armenian history. He told the jury about a rancorous church convention during the summer before Tourian's murder where *Tashnags* voted to oust the Archbishop, prompting the cleric to move from his official residence at the church into a nearby hotel. It left the congregation wondering who was in charge – a question not answered by the Church until after the assassination.

"Now, you men may well say, now Mr. Sheridan, what has all this got to do with this case of December 24th?" Answering his own question, he explained how all this chaos spilled into the chapel on 187th Street. Sheridan offered two alternative theories to the crime. The first possibility, he suggested, was that the real killer got away.

"I don't know who killed the Archbishop," he said. "We are going to show you that one man escaped through the front of the church, was never apprehended."

Following the example of his adversary, Sheridan now paused to let jurors absorb all this before dropping another bomb.

"We have a further theory," he said slowly. "I say this with some apology, because as I said in the opening, it is very difficult to understand the minds of the East."

The defense lawyer then talked about a book written by a former chief of the Soviet Union's state security apparatus, OGPU. It was originally published in French and translated into English, he explained.

"We will show you that this murder might have been the result of a plan on the part of the secret police of Russia itself!"

Upon hearing those words crescendo, many in the gallery could not restrain themselves. They filled the air with a combination of laughs and groans. Once again, Corrigan gaveled the room to silence.

"Is that the book you are referring to?" the judge asked Sheridan, pointing to a small volume in the lawyer's hand.

"No, I will say nothing about the book right now until we get into the evidence, until the proper time," replied the lawyer looking slightly askew at the bench. With that, he turned back toward the jury box and said a few more words about the possibility that Soviet agents acted to discredit the anti-communist *Tashnag* organization.

Ordinarily, judges allow a lawyer's opening statement to the jury a certain latitude. In this case, Corrigan started to interrupt Sheridan with questions, points of law, clarifications. A few times, Kaminsky joined the judge. It verged on harassment. But Sheridan kept going. It began when he tried to mention the absence of the Armenian attorney, Cardashian.

"What is this?" asked Corrigan. "Why bring out all of that?"

"I am going to state it for the record," answered Sheridan.

"Mr. Cardashian? You cannot argue as to what any statements might show if they were here."

"I am not stating as to what they would show if they were here," replied the defense lawyer.

"I suggest you confine yourself to what you expect to prove."

Sheridan moved on. He started to tell an emotional story about one defendant's childhood. The judge interrupted again, asking the attorney to speak louder. Sheridan spoke louder. He misspoke an incorrect pronoun – "she" instead of "he" – and Kaminsky corrected him. Sheridan repeated the correction and moved on.

And at the end of his opening statement – ordinarily a powerful moment intended to leave a lasting impression on the jury – Sheridan barely got the last words out of his mouth when the A.D.A. noisily rose and addressed the bench.

"May we have a five-minute recess?"

"Yes," answered the judge abruptly. "Gentlemen, we will take a five-minute recess." He told the jurors not to talk among themselves.

It was, to say the least, a disappointing start for the defense.

32

Now

I rubbed the fatigue from my eyes and looked at the clock radio on my bedside table. *How did it get to be 9 o'clock already*? I wondered. I got up and poured myself another cup of coffee. From opening statements to the jury's verdict, the actual trial lasted about a month. But at the rate I was reading these transcripts, I could be here until next winter.

As I read the verbatim account of what happened, I tried to recollect how it felt being in the courtroom. I also wondered whether, by today's standards, the suspects got a fair trial. The decision to post a chart listing all nine defendants made sense. But was it not also a bit prejudicial? Did the twelve American jurors look at these Armenians with their strange names and think of them as somehow "less" than they were?

I decided to create a chart of my own to keep track of all the personalities identified in this case. Drawing from news accounts, official court records and my own memory, I counted well over a hundred names. How were the jurors supposed to process all those individuals? I also wondered what the lawyers did not reveal. Can the accused get a fair trial if pertinent facts are withheld from court?

My musings were interrupted by a telephone call.

"Hello?"

"How's my intrepid reporter doing?" It was Anna. I couldn't have been happier if I'd just won the Irish Sweepstakes.

"You saved me from my fourth cup of bad coffee tonight."

She said she was flying back to California early in the morning and wanted a chance to say good-bye again.

"I thought you had already gone back home. If I had known you were still here—"

"You wouldn't get any work done," she interrupted. "Besides, I'm still hoping to get you out on the West Coast when you're done with all this."

I promised to try and wished her a good flight.

"Sweet dreams, Thomas."

I really missed that woman!

33

Then

After the morning's first and only recess, the prosecution called its first witness, Dr. Thomas Gonzales. New York City's Deputy Chief Medical Examiner had been brought to the church shortly after the murder, and so was able to describe in gruesome detail how Archbishop Tourian died. He specified which organs had which wounds, as he had noted during the autopsy. Dr. Gonzales also testified about the markings he made on the cleric's vestments. The A.D.A wanted those clothes marked as People's exhibits.

"Do you wish to put the garments in evidence?" asked Judge Corrigan in slight disbelief.

"Yes, your honor sees the point."

"I don't know what the point is," Sheridan jumped in. "We are not going to have anything brought in for the purpose of inflaming the minds of the jury."

Then, Kaminsky offered the Archbishop's miter as an exhibit. Now Sheridan expressed incredulity.

"Do you want the hat in?"

"If you want it, all right." The prosecutor played along. Sheridan rose in protest.

"I object to the showing of these bloody garments to the jury at this time."

Kaminsky turned back to his witness and asked where he found the miter.

"That came with the clothes," answered the coroner. "It was marked by me."

"I offer it for identification," said the prosecutor.

"What is the purpose of that?" asked Corrigan. Now the judge was confused. Kaminsky seized the moment.

"Mr. Sheridan wanted the hat."

"I don't want anything of the kind." The defense attorney was being played and he knew it and so did everyone else. "I asked the question, what of the hat?"

"Well, I showed you 'what of the hat,' replied Kaminsky with a slight smile.

"Mark it for identification," said Corrigan with no visible trace of a smirk.

Sheridan sat back down and said with exasperation, "Go ahead. No objection."

Throughout this testimony, Kaminsky and Sheridan continued to spar in that vein. Each quibbled over minor details of the other's questions. Each objected over minor points of law. It was entertaining to watch, but everyone could tell that it was exhausting for them to do. Like long-distance runners, both realized they would never survive the duration at this pace. Their verbal sprint had to slow to a steady lope.

"The People call William Loughran."

Loughran was the District Attorney's staff photographer. He took the stand and described the crime scene, showing the jury pictures and sketches of Holy Cross Church. Both prosecution and defense attorneys elicited precise information about the building's layout as well as the size and location of the pews – 21 benches on each side of the center aisle, with every pew holding between five and eight individuals, plus standing room. Their best estimates were that the sanctuary could accommodate as many as three or four hundred people, but there was no way to know exactly how many were there that morning, nor who could see what.

After lunch, the People's next witness was Deacon Sarkis Demurjian. Like most of those who would testify in this trial, the 56-year old antique dealer was born in Turkey. Kaminsky began by asking about one of the defendants.

Initially, Demurjian had very little trouble responding to the prosecutor. But as Kaminsky's questions turned to the assassination itself, the deacon started to get upset. Though not unintelligent, his limited command of English and heavy accent made him sound rather thick. Questions had to be repeated and restated many times, leading to great frustration and finally prompting the judge to bring in the court's official interpreter.

"Do you know a man by the name of Mozian?"

"Yes sir," answered Demurjian. "I know him."

Kaminsky asked the witness to identify Mozian. Demurjian stepped down from the stand, walked to the defendants table and pointed at

Number Four. As he returned to his seat, the deacon recalled an incident a year ago.

> It was in front of a restaurant on the west side of Fifth Avenue, around 28th Street, a very warm afternoon last summer. The two men hadn't seen each other for two or three years. Demurjian asked Mozian how he was doing. As with so many self-employed folks during the Great Depression, Mozian said he didn't have much work these days. With one in four men unemployed, the average worker's wages had dropped by more than fifty percent. The furniture repair business was better than some, but still not enough to make a decent living.
>
> To make matters worse, Mozian's wife had been lingering in the hospital. Sarkis was a bit shocked to hear the other man say he wished that she would die. His three kids were living in an American foster home of sorts, and forgetting their mother tongue. He'd considered moving back to Armenia himself, but working conditions were no better there.
>
> Demurjian changed the subject and noted how terrible it was that the Armenian-language newspapers in America were writing such terrible things about Archbishop Tourian. Mozian became agitated.
>
> "But you heard that they took down the flag in Chicago," he said. "If I have a chance, I kill them. Let them put me in the electric chair."

Demurjian recalled that on the morning of December 24th, he was standing behind and to the left of Archbishop Tourian, marching slowly toward the altar. The prelate was flanked by two acolytes.

"Where, for the first time in that church, did you see Leylegian?" asked Kaminsky.

"I saw only when he came in front of the Archbishop." Demurjian stood up and continued. "And the Archbishop was tall and his shoulders, they came to here on me," he added, gesturing to his own eye level. The deacon went on to describe the motion of Mateos Leylegian's arms, although Demurjian said he saw no knife in the defendant's hands.

"What did you see Sarkisian do to the Archbishop?" asked Kaminsky, referring to defendant Number Two.

Speaking through the interpreter, Demurjian said Sarkisian pretended that he was falling in front of the Archbishop. The deacon said he later saw a bloodstained knife on the floor at the exact spot where Tourian was killed. Kaminsky capped off his examination of this witness with a quick reenactment of the murder.

"Assuming that I am the Archbishop and you are behind me," said the prosecutor, "show me how you were behind me."

Demurjian demonstrated where he had stood that morning, and described the relative positions of Leylegian and Sarkisian as well. When the prosecutor had finished, Thomas Sheridan began to cross-examine the witness.

"Did you ever act out the scene where the Archbishop was standing?" he asked the deacon.

"What do you mean?"

"How many times did you do it?"

"I cannot understand."

As Sheridan continued to question the witness, several jurors called out that Demurjian didn't understand. The witness joined in.

"What do you mean?" asked Demurjian. "I would like to understand that."

Judge Corrigan motioned for the interpreter to assist again. At last, it was clear that the deacon had practiced his testimony with the District Attorney's office several times before coming to court that morning. As Sheridan continued to press the witness on details of his testimony, Demurjian grew more and more agitated, unable to understand or answer questions, even contradicting himself through the interpreter.

Sheridan turned back to the encounter with Mozian on Fifth Avenue.

"When did you tell that story to the police or the District Attorney for the first time after the 24th day—?"

"The 24th day after December, when the Archbishop killed, dead," answered Demurjian.

"On that day in the police station house?"

"No, not on that day. After a week."

"Now, wait, wait, wait."

Corrigan interrupted. "He has not finished."

"I know it, your honor," said Sheridan. He turned back to the witness. "But you did not understand me—"

"Wait a minute," Corrigan told the witness. "Will you please?"

"Only pardon. I will explain something."

"No, no," replied the defense attorney, trying to regain control of his cross-examination. But it was no use.

"I am very well, I know it," continued the witness excitedly. "I told that maybe same day. For what I say, he was in the church the same day also. And he is getting up on the church yelling, throwing his arms up in the air." Demurjian tried to describe in broken English the chaos following Tourian's murder.

Sheridan pointed to the other defendants, one by one, and asked the deacon whether he saw them in the church that morning.

"I don't remember," he answered each time.

The defense attorney stepped back to his chair and sat down. He opened a file folder on the table and casually started turning pages. Demurjian looked to the judge, wondering whether his ordeal had ended. Corrigan cleared his throat to get Sheridan's attention. By this point, everyone in the courtroom was fidgeting a bit. Before Corrigan could say a word, defense counsel looked up.

"Are you out of work now?" he asked the witness.

"I am not out of work," he answered indignantly. "I got one hundred thousand dollars stock in my shop."

"Where are you—" Sheridan started to ask.

Demurjian interrupted again, his face flushed and voice rising. "Do I know the business is different? You are not my partner to ask me!"

Sheridan was taken aback. "You know you are not allowed to act like that."

"You want to make business with me, come on to my shop and talk to me."

Trying to deflate this volatile moment, Sheridan tried a bit of comedy. "I am not anxious to *make business*," he said mocking Demurjian's broken English and accent.

A handful of men and women in the gallery laughed loudly. The witness was undeterred and grew increasingly enraged. "What do you ask me for? You ask what is unnecessary. Unnecessary! What do you ask me?!"

Sheridan now turned back to the bench for help. "I ask your honor—" he said, but again couldn't finish.

"You ask me Archbishop killing!"

"Now if your honor please, I ask that this witness—"

"You ask what happens Archbishop!!" Demurjian's face was bright red. His voice screeched and he nearly levitated from the witness stand.

Corrigan saw that this exchange was out of control. "What do you want me to instruct him?" the judge asked Sheridan.

"Your honor, I think you might instruct him to answer the questions,"

Sheridan replied a bit loudly, to be heard over Demurjian's rant, "even though he does not think they are right or wrong."

And so it went. By late afternoon, the testimony got bogged down in argument over details of what the witness had previously said. Kaminsky jumped back in with suggestions and objections. Sheridan moved on to ask Demurjian what he remembered telling the police about Tourian's murder. The witness stumbled more and more over his words, with or without the interpreter's help. Everyone was hot and tired. Judge Corrigan recommended that Sheridan suspend his cross-examination for the day and the defense attorney finally relented.

"What were you trying to do in there?" Joab Banton asked his co-counsel as the two defense lawyers walked out of the courtroom. "Did you want the judge to hold you in contempt?

Senator Sheridan uncharacteristically loosened his necktie, relenting to the sun's heat and his own. "Joab," he replied winking. "I knew exactly how far to push him." He gestured with the thumb and forefinger of his right hand. "This far and not one inch farther." Sheridan nudged Banton gently in the ribs, then slapped him on the back. "Come on, let's have a drink."

The two men found themselves in the cool, dark sanctuary of a saloon just behind the courthouse. During Prohibition, this tavern remained one of the busiest in New York, completely unaffected by the Volstead Act. Not even Izzy and Moe – those infamous enforcers of the anti-alcohol law – dared touch this watering hole. After all, its clientele consisted largely of cops, lawyers and judges. There was no need for them to visit a speakeasy. Those special customers would freely be served "3.2 beer" with a 100-proof chaser and no fear of reprisal. But now that the ban on liquor had been repealed, even this little fig leaf was removed. Sheridan ordered a very dry Martini. Banton drank Irish whiskey.

"Listen, Joab, I think we're going to lose this case."

Banton tossed back his drink and ordered another. "That's not the sort of optimism I was hoping for on day one."

Sheridan took out his deck of cards and shuffled them. "I mean, I think we'll have to win on appeal." He handed the cards to his co-counsel. "Cut these, would you? I hate to deal without cutting the cards."

As Banton handed the deck back, he frowned at Sheridan. "You think they're stacked against us?"

"I think the other side is holding all the aces. I think the cards are marked. I think they're not going to play according to Hoyle."

The two lawyers sat in silence as Sheridan played and lost three rounds of solitaire. They finished their drinks, stood up and were just putting on their coats to leave when the bartender stopped them.

"Call for you, Mr. Sheridan," he said, offering the receiver.

"Thanks, Flynn." At the other end of the phone line was one of Sheridan's junior partners. He had just received a telegram. The Armenian attorney, Vahan Cardashian was dead. A perfectly awful end to an otherwise perfectly awful day, thought Sheridan.

The next morning, Banton addressed the bench.

"It is with profound regret that I state that Mr. Cardashian, who was the attorney for the defendants, has died."

Judge Corrigan greeted the news with less than effusive sympathy. "Then the adjournment would have done no good." His honor didn't even try to hide his disdain, adding, "He would have been just as dead in October."

Sheridan resumed his questioning of Sarkis Demurjian. But it didn't take long before both Kaminsky and Corrigan pelted the defense lawyer with more interruptions. In exasperation, Sheridan turned to the bench.

"I ask for the privilege of conducting this cross-examination."

"You are getting plenty of privilege," answered Corrigan sarcastically.

Sheridan tried to go on but was waylaid again and again. He wheeled back to the judge.

"I am conducting this examination," insisted the lawyer.

"And I am presiding at this trial," said Corrigan.

"I know it, and I respectfully submit that there should be no aversion, no retorts, no criticism when I come to an examination."

"Where did you learn that?"

"I have learned it from the time I studied law twenty-five years ago."

The two men faced each other for a long moment. "All examinations must be conducted in a proper, legal manner," said Corrigan as if addressing a child.

The judge tried to have the final word. But this was just the beginning. Demurjian sat squirming in the witness box, as sparring between the two lawyers escalated. They argued over whether the questions were fair, whether the testimony was accurately remembered. The stenographer read back the last few moments of the court record. They argued over interruptions of interruptions about interruptions.

Each lawyer used every trick the law would allow – and even a few that defied the rules. At last, Sheridan complained that Kaminsky was answering questions posed to the witness.

"I am not asking *you* to testify," counsel for the defense protested.

"There is no use getting huffy with me," the prosecutor shot back. "I can get as huffy as you."

"I don't care about your huffiness."

Corrigan gaveled them both to silence. The judge was on the verge of losing his temper.

"Will you just wait a minute, and allow me to say something without interrupting me for the first time since this trial began? Now, the proper way for counsel to conduct the trial is not to argue and recriminate among themselves, but if there is an occasion for an objection, to make the objection and then let me make a ruling."

"All right, your honor," said Sheridan standing up again.

"I asked you not to interrupt me." The judge now spoke with a dangerous edge in his voice.

Sheridan lowered his eyes as he sat back down. "I thought you had completed."

"I did not finish." Corrigan took a breath. "Please conduct the trial on the proper lines. All this squabbling between counsel wastes a great deal of time and does no good."

Sheridan waited a moment. "Are you finished, your honor?"

"I have."

The defense attorney stood and surveyed the courtroom. He slowly walked toward the bench and stopped a few feet away – close enough to have intimate eye contact with the judge but not so close as to prompt opposing counsel to join him there. He spoke just loud enough for Corrigan and the stenographer to hear him.

"Now, your Honor, I respectfully object to the statement that your Honor just made because I believe I was strictly within my rights when I interrogated this witness – an important witness for the prosecution – as to whether a certain man was present at a meeting of protest with whom he discussed this case, and also whether that same man was the interpreter at the police station on December 24th. This witness did not answer."

"I beg your pardon," answered Corrigan. "He said, 'I don't remember.'"

"Well, he did not answer until the District Attorney, seeing that I was reaching for the statement of December 24th, interrupts with the statement, 'Yes, yes, the man was the interpreter.'"

Now Kaminsky was on his feet. "May it please the court –"

But the judge shut him down. "I did not ask you for anything."

"I do not want, in the balance of the trial, any more interruptions from the District Attorney," said Sheridan who was using Corrigan's own criticism to gain the upper hand.

The three men continued debating in this manner for several more moments. Demurjian still sitting uncomfortably on the witness stand, felt ignored and now tried to join the conversation.

"Can I talk?" asked the deacon.

Sheridan waved him off. "Please keep quiet." Then turning back to the bench, the defense attorney continued his objections to the prosecutor's interruptions. He spoke almost without taking a breath.

"I ask your Honor during the balance of this trial, if I have any witness under cross-examination, to try to ascertain whether that man is or is not telling the truth, it is grossly unfair for the District Attorney, either by trick, art or device, or by interruption, to interrupt and make a statement, when – unless he is the witness in the case."

"Now you have that on the record," said Corrigan.

Sheridan tried – and failed – three more times to have the judge order Kaminsky not to interrupt. Finally, the defense lawyer sat back down. The courtroom fell silent. Demurjian looked around to see what would happen next. Thinking his ordeal had finally ended, the deacon began to rise. Kaminsky gestured him back into the witness chair and began his re-direct examination.

"When you went into the police station after this murder, did you know the name of the two men, Leylegian and Sarkisian? Did you know them by name?" asked the A.D.A.

Demurjian tried to answer but had difficulty understanding Kaminsky's question. The interpreter intervened but that didn't help. While the question was repeated and translated again, Sheridan's co-counsel stood up and started to move a bit closer to the witness stand.

"Will you sit down?" Corrigan ordered.

"He cannot hear him," said Sheridan.

"I cannot help it," answered the judge. "I did not build the courtroom. He must sit down."

Sheridan pointed to an empty chair closer to the bench. "May he sit over here?"

"Any place he pleases," said Corrigan, a bit annoyed.

"Sit over here but do not stand up," Sheridan told his associate.

The prosecutor sorted out the witness's ability to identify the defendants Leylegian and Sarkisian. But it didn't take long before the two opposing lawyers were at each other again. They were nit-picking over small details and, despite the judge's warnings, constantly interrupting each other. And in the middle of it all sat poor, befuddled Sarkis Demurjian.

On re-cross-examination, Sheridan asked the deacon about a statement he gave police two weeks after the murder.

"Were you confused when you gave that statement on January 16th?"

"Sure," said Demurjian. "For three months, I did not have my brain on me and I lost twenty pounds."

"Did anybody speak to you between the 24th of December and the 16th of January wherein they discussed what had happened in this church?" asked the defense counsel.

"Everywhere, in every home when Armenians met each other." In that one answer, Demurjian captured the mood of his fellow countrymen. For every Armenian living in the United States, the murder of Archbishop Tourian was the number one topic of conversation – no less significant to them than Lincoln's assassination had been for the whole country more than half a century before.

Sheridan drove home the point. "Just as when Armenians gathered they discussed this case?"

"Of course," answered the deacon. "Always and always. He was a very sacred person. No other will come after him."

When Sarkis Demurjian left the witness stand, his shirt was soaked in perspiration. The deacon walked directly out of the courtroom and went home to wash. Unlike most of his fellow Armenians, he expressed no further interest in the Tourian trial. All he knew was that this experience would remain a most unpleasant one – ranking with the death of his parents.

On the other hand, Alexander Kaminsky didn't have the luxury of self-indulgence that day. He called his next witness to testify about the Chicago Exposition flag controversy. But rather than serve his purpose, the evidence provoked another round of sparring with Thomas Sheridan. The defense lawyer focused on an inconsistency between what was said on the stand and what the A.D.A. had said in his opening statement.

"May I have the statement that was given by this witness on January 18th?" Sheridan asked.

"I don't see what right you have to that," said the judge.

The defense attorney stood open-mouthed for a moment, blinked and swallowed hard. Before Sheridan could speak again, Corrigan continued.

"I do not see that either side has the right to call upon the other side to produce its documents," the judge told Sheridan. "You have no more right to call on the District Attorney to produce statements he has taken than he has to call on you to produce statements taken from your witnesses."

Despite that, the prosecutor realized that he was caught in a trap. There was a conflict between witness testimony and the people's summary of its case. To avoid giving the jury a reason to find reasonable doubt, Kaminsky decided to take the blame. He apologized for his mistake and offered Sheridan the statement. That effectively deflected this defense point.

Undeterred, Sheridan soldiered on. At every turn, the two men found opportunities to quibble. Even the interpreter got caught in the middle of this battle, with both sides challenging the accuracy of his English and Armenian translations. An exasperated Corrigan tried once more to stop the seemingly petty disputes.

"Why do you have to fight about this?" asked the judge at one point. "It is too hot for that."

But it was going to get hotter.

"Your Honor?" It was Judge Corrigan's clerk, knocking gently on the door to the jurist's chambers. "There is a member of the jury here to see you, sir."

This is extremely irregular, thought Corrigan. "Very well, show him in."

34

Now

After almost a week in New York, I discovered that my slacks were getting a little tight. All those meals in restaurants and at Margaret Moradian's dining room table had a palpable effect on my waistline. I decided to skip lunch today and instead went directly to the Armenian Archdiocese office.

I had been putting this off, knowing full well that they would give me a very biased point of view. But eventually, I needed to know what they thought. Of course, they had already expressed their point of view on all this in a 1935 publication, "The Martyrdom of Archbishop Tourian." It concluded:

The Prelate was a victim of crazed partisan conspirators. Only "political members who lost conscience and rationality would dare in a church in the presence of children and women commit such a monstrous crime."

In its own way, this was the Armenian version of the Warren Commission Report on the Assassination of President John F. Kennedy.

After an initial momentary shock, the archivist at the Archdiocese was remarkably cooperative. As several others had, he warned me that I was treading on sensitive, painful and potentially destructive ground. I assured him that my intentions were honorable.

"Unfortunately, we don't have much for you to see here," he said. "Most of our information is in that book."

I listened to his summary of what I already knew and thanked him for his hospitality.

"By the way, do you know about the lawyer who advised the Tourian Committee?" he asked helpfully.

"Thomas Dewey?" I said.

"I mean Mr. Simsarian." There was a new name. Dicran Simsarian had a private practice in New York. Apparently, Dewey had a ringer.

"Thanks again for your help."

"Any time," he said. "God go with you."

35

Then

Not everyone in New York was obsessed with the Archbishop's murder trial. On Tuesday afternoon, a lot of baseball fans were disappointed to learn that the Yankees-Browns game was rained out after only four innings. The Yanks had a 3-to-one lead over St. Louis and Babe Ruth had hit his tenth home run of the season.

Thomas Sheridan and Joab Banton were too busy to think about the national pastime. Information had come into their hands about two jurors in the Tourian case. From what the defense lawyers learned, both men had received threatening notes and went to see Judge Corrigan. Both Sheridan and Banton privately asked the jurist to tell them what was in those notes.

"It is a matter of my conscience and my judgment," Corrigan had replied.

The defense attorneys also discovered that Corrigan had met with Alexander Kaminsky. Sheridan reasonably presumed they discussed the matter.

"What can we do about it?" asked Banton. "We already have a lifetime supply of grounds for appeal."

"I know," replied Sheridan. "But this goes beyond the pale. I'm thinking about contacting the Chief Justice in Albany."

"He'll never agree to see you in the middle of a trial."

Sheridan knew his colleague was right. Nevertheless, he felt an overwhelming dread by this example of obvious judicial misconduct.

"Well, then let's just get through this."

The prosecution resumed its case on Wednesday. Over the course of eight days, Kaminsky called a total of thirty-four witnesses. Some testified hearing that the defendants made threats against the Archbishop during the months leading up to his murder. Others identified the suspects and described where they were sitting in Holy Cross Church.

One elderly woman perched especially nervously in the witness chair.

Khanem Deckmejian patted her gray hair and adjusted her thick glasses. She was undoubtedly concerned about her nephew Sarkis, who had sat in jail awaiting charges for his purported participation in this crime. Although he was later released, Khanem feared that the D.A. might arrest and prosecute him if this trial went badly.

She hunched forward and trembled while answering the assistant district attorney's questions. But when he asked her to point out the man she saw kill Tourian, this little old lady rushed to the defense table and forcefully brought her hand down on Mateos Leylegian's shoulder. He winced.

"That's the one!" she declared, drawing bursts of laughter from the gallery and admonition from the bench.

Another local resident who testified was an artist named Dikran Chakmakian. He presented one of the most detailed accounts. Sitting across the aisle from the two murder suspects in church that Sunday morning, Chakmakian said he saw Leylegian holding something white in his hand and striking the Archbishop in his belly. The painter testified that he had stood on his pew and looked down on the scene as he saw Sarkisian hitting Tourian from behind, and several others defending the killers.

But on cross-examination, a few holes developed in the story.

"How long did you remain in the church that morning?" asked defense attorney Sheridan.

"I don't remember." Chakmakian started to fidget in his chair, already feeling rather hostile toward the lawyer who represented Tourian's accused killers.

"Did you go up and say to anybody, I saw the man who did this?"

"No."

As the interrogation continued, Chakmakian revealed that he had told neither his fellow parishioners nor the police what he saw that day out of fear for his life. Several days later, the artist went to the precinct house to get a gun permit. Defense counsel pressed him further, asking why he had kept quiet about what he saw.

"Listen, Mr. Sheridan," Chakmakian said in exasperation. "You put yourself in my position that day and somebody killed a priest, and you would be in condition too like me. I told you a hundred times I am feeling fear now and I don't remember what I said."

Sheridan turned to the judge.

"I want to find out if, when he came out of that church, that his actions and his conduct was the result of fear, or that he is giving something now that he never saw. That is the purpose of my inquiry."

To Sheridan's surprise, Judge Corrigan agreed and instructed the witness to answer the lawyer's question.

"I don't remember, your Honor. I was like crazy. At that time, I wanted to go home, lay down, when I see that man is lying down in blood and with the stomach falling out."

One by one, prosecution witnesses remembered the events of December 24th, both inside and outside Holy Cross Church. It was painful for everyone – those who lived through it, the lawyers who argued over it, and the jury who listened to it. Even Judge Corrigan was desperately hoping for some relief from this daily anguish.

Thursday night, Tom Peterson decided he needed a break from this case, too. The reporter wanted to go to Madison Square Garden and watch the championship fight. Italy's Primo Carnera was defending his world heavyweight title against Max Baer, the "butcher boy" from Oakland, California.

By the time Tom got to the Garden, the good tickets were completely sold out. Ringside seats normally cost $25, but scalpers were getting twice that much. More than 50,000 boxing fans had turned out to watch this much-ballyhooed bout. Even cheap seats were going fast and the line at the box office was around the block. Anyway, the title fight wouldn't begin until 10 p.m. and who knew how long it would last if it went all fifteen rounds.

Peterson had to be in court early the next morning, so he decided to go home and listen on the radio. He regretted it. No announcer could have adequately described what it was like to watch Baer put the champ on the canvas a dozen times, and finally win by a knockout in the eleventh. As one sports writer put it, Max Baer was now the new Jack Dempsey.

Verbal sparring resumed in court the next day. Khosroff Gorgodian was first to take the stand. The Archbishop's bodyguard described what he saw – which wasn't much, since he witnessed the murder from where he had stood more than twenty feet away. On cross-examination, the defense attorney asked Gorgodian to step down from the witness stand and indicate on an enlarged floor plan the spot where he stood during the attack on Tourian. The bodyguard marked it with the letter "G" and then returned to the stand.

The days seemed to drag as attorneys quibbled over details of procedure; the temperature in the courtroom went up and tempers got shorter. Heat rose on the bench, too. Judge Corrigan had the habit of interjecting his personal views on the merits of the case that attorneys presented – particularly defense attorneys.

Thomas Sheridan asked a witness about another suspect who had been arrested and released. Judge Corrigan declared the question to have no importance. Now, defense counsel fought back.

"It was improper for Your Honor to have made that statement to the jury," he said.

"Will you listen while I tell you something?" replied Corrigan irately. "I have tried to rule in accordance with the law, and as to whether my rulings are proper or improper, I do not expect you to tell me again."

Sheridan felt the mercury climb. Corrigan continued.

"I don't ask for your opinion. I don't want it and I don't care about it. You get that just as plain as you want."

Such candor was highly unusual coming from this or any other judge. Sheridan tried to interject.

"I don't want—"

The judge cut him off. "Will you wait until I get through?"

Sheridan recoiled at Corrigan's vituperation. The judge kept going.

"I am conducting this trial in conformity with what I believe to be the law of this state. I am responsible to the higher court for the way in which I conduct it. What any counsel thinks of my rulings is immaterial to me, and I do not care for further criticism as to whether you think my rulings are proper or improper. You have a right to object and to except and that is all the right you have as far as my rulings are concerned."

"I assure you that I will do so," said Sheridan.

"Leave out the remarks," Corrigan shot back.

Sheridan pressed again. "So that this record will clearly indicate everything that you say or do in the course of this trial—"

"That is what the stenographer is here for."

"—both in the courtroom or out of the courtroom."

Corrigan's face instantly flushed and he nearly sprang out of his chair. "What are you talking about, 'out of the courtroom?' What do you mean by 'out of the courtroom?' Where I go to lunch? Do you suppose that is on the record? What I do *out* of the courtroom is perfectly immaterial. What I do *in* the courtroom is material."

Although he was speaking at about the same level, there was such silence in the gallery that Corrigan's voice seemed much louder. Now the judge pressed down on an arm of the chair and actually did rise a bit.

"They are to be tried on what happens before the jury in the court," he said gesturing to the defendants, and then sat back down. After a short pause and with tightly set jaw he added, "You had better show a little courtesy to the court."

Those words hung weightily in the air. There was no explicit threat, but everyone understood that a line had been drawn.

"That is all I want," replied Sheridan quietly. The defense attorney knew that anything further would risk not only a contempt citation for him personally but might irreversibly prejudice jurors against the defendants.

Garabed Zadikian was the last witness of the week. He had participated in the Sunday morning procession, marching behind and to the right of Archbishop Tourian. Zadikian was unable to speak. Surgery to treat cancer of the larynx left him without a voice box. To overcome this physical handicap, he wrote his answers in a notebook.

The District Attorney considered Zadikian to be a key witness, because he observed so much of the crime. He recalled seeing Osgan Yarganian knock the miter off Tourian's head; Harry Sarafian jump at the Archbishop; Martin Mozian leap onto a pew, wave his hands and holler; Nishan Sarkisian grab the cleric's right hand; and Mateos Leylegian stab Tourian.

Zadikian testified that he chased Mozian and Yarganian as they ran outside the church. He said that he intercepted them on the sidewalk, but was himself attacked by Ohanes Andreassian who helped his two accomplices to escape.

Opposing counsel argued about whether the assault charges against Andreassian were admissible, further complicating the case. From the jury's perspective, attorneys were mired in minutia. One juror turned to another with a look of exasperation. Wordlessly, the two men agreed that they were anxious for this day – and this trial – to finish. But by 4 p.m., the prosecutor had not finished questioning Mr. Zadikian.

Judge Corrigan sent everyone home with the same admonition not to discuss the case. Everyone had looked forward to the weekend break. But when it was over, their patience was going to be tested again.

36

Now

To my surprise, the 8-foot tall, solid mahogany door swung open easily.

"I'm looking for a lawyer."

That might have seemed like such an obvious thing to say at a law firm that represented criminal defendants. But here at Kerschner Hastings and O'Brien, most of their clients were other attorneys. This Madison Avenue partnership specialized in cases that were impossible to win. That's why they were brought in on the Tourian matter.

"Are you an attorney," asked the receptionist, flashing a friendly but professional smile.

"No, I'm a retired reporter."

Her smile was replaced by the same look she gave uninvited salesmen. "I'm sorry, but—"

"It's not what you think," I added quickly. "I'm looking for information about a case that this firm handled back in the 1930s."

Now her pretty face displayed puzzlement. Neither this young lady nor this practice existed *way back then.*

"Did you say 1930s?"

Now it was my turn to smile. "Actually, it was a law firm that became a subsidiary of Hastings Kerschner and O'Brien."

That didn't help her much. "So?"

"So, I'm looking for files from a murder case. They're probably in your—" I searched for the right word. I knew it wasn't "morgue" as it would have been at a newspaper. I tried something more neutral. "—your archives."

Then she understood. "Oh, you mean in storage."

I nodded.

"Well, I don't think we can let you look at files, even from way back then."

I cringed.

"You know: attorney-client privilege." She spoke like a first-year law student, knowing just enough jargon to feel self-important.

"Uh huh. Well, tell me—" I glanced at her name plate. "Tell me,

Cyndee, is there a *lawyer* here I can speak with?" (I didn't say *real* lawyer, but that's what I meant.)

I anticipated her next impedimental words as she opened the appointment book. To my relief, at that very moment Richard Kerschner walked into the lobby.

"Hey, Cyndee."

"Good morning, Mr. Kerschner." I recognized the senior partner's name.

"Any messages for me?" he asked.

As she flipped though her call records, I seized the moment.

"Mr. Kerschner, my name is Tom Peterson. I'm a retired reporter and I'm writing a book about a historical case your firm worked on. I'd like to ask you a question," I blurted out. It worked.

"Really? Well, sure, Mr. Peterson. I think I can spare a few minutes for an author. Come on in." A lawyer with a healthy ego – who would have guessed?

Kerschner invited me past the opened-mouthed receptionist. "Hold my calls," he told her as we moved into his office. "Please, Mr. Peterson, have a seat. Can I offer you some coffee?"

To my astonishment, this powerful and busy man was more than happy to put aside real business to spend time with a stranger who was interested in writing about an obscure part of his practice. However tangentially, he considered my book to be a priority.

I explained my dilemma as he listened intently. Richard Kerschner's success was due in no small part to his unsurpassed memory. He clearly and completely remembered everything that he considered important. That included past clients, even those represented by associates.

"Mr. Peterson, I have some good news and some bad news," he began. "First, Al Callaghan was the attorney who handled this matter for our subsidiary firm. Unfortunately, he is no longer living. But luckily for you, his son Al Callaghan Jr., is also a lawyer – with the Justice Department. My guess is that Callaghan talked about the Tourian case since it was such a big trial at the time." (Thank God he didn't say "way back then.") "He might even have some personal notes."

I was somewhat encouraged but not quite optimistic. Kerschner gave me Callaghan's contact information and wished me luck. He also gave me a signed photograph of himself, shook my hand and hinted at appreciating my support if he ever ran for District Attorney.

Scratch the skin of a good attorney and you're likely to find a politician.

37

Then

Monday, June 18th turned out to be the longest day of this trial. Zadikian, the witness with no larynx, was back on the stand. Opposing counsel were back at each other's throats, so to speak. But with help from Judge Corrigan's "impartial" rulings, the People's case was looking stronger and more solid than ever.

A record number of witnesses testified that day – eleven men and women in all. After the midday lunch break, the prosecutor was ready for a young man who most desperately wanted to see justice done.

"Call Ara Gureghian," said Joseph Cohn.

"Ara Gureghian," repeated the clerk.

The shoemaker approached the witness stand with a combination of pride and panic. This was his chance to do the right thing, he thought. If only he could find the strength to talk in front of all those people. It was the only fear he knew. After being sworn in, Ara sat down.

"Mr. Gureghian, do you speak English?" Kaminsky began.

"A little bit."

"You mean you speak but I cannot hear you." The prosecutor tried to put Ara at ease.

"I can speak a little bit."

"That is fine. Now, speak as loud as that."

"All right, sir."

The A.D.A. had Gureghian establish that he was outside the church on December 24th. He asked the shoemaker to step down to the defense table and point out the men he saw immediately after the murder. Ara indicated that he had seen defendant Number Two, Nishan Sarkisian, running away from the church that morning. He then returned to the witness stand.

"Now, will you tell the court and the jury where you were standing when you saw the second man, Sarkisian, running away from the church?"

"I was right in front of the door of the church."

"Will you tell the court and the jury what you saw this man do?"

"He ran out of the church. He was fighting his way out. He rushed out of the door and went across the street."

For several minutes, Ara's testimony went smoothly. He felt confident, helpful. Next, Kaminsky asked Gureghian if he had seen Garabed Zadikian holding two of the suspects. Ara returned to the defense table and identified Yarganian and Mozian.

Back on the stand, the witness said another man came along. "He pulled them away from him and kicked him on the shin and he called him—" Ara hesitated a moment. "—a son-of-a-bitch." "And he never let the men go."

That expression drew titters from the gallery, not accustomed to hearing vulgarities in the courtroom up to this point.

Judge Corrigan was taken aback, too. "Called him what?"

"Son-of-a-bitch," Ara repeated matter-of-factly.

As the audience continued giggling, defense counsel also wanted to participate. "Called him what?" asked Sheridan

"Son-of-a-bitch," said Ara a third time.

"In English or Armenian?" asked Sheridan.

"In English."

Kaminsky tried to restore some decorum. "Can you step down from your chair to the table and, with the court's permission, show the man or recognize if you can the man who tried to pull them away?"

Gureghian left the witness chair and pointed to defendant Number Nine, Ohanes Andreassian. Back on the stand again, Ara testified that Andreassian ran to a light green sedan parked across the street from the church and said, "What are you standing here for? Come on, they killed them."

On cross-examination, Sheridan interrogated Ara at great length, asking and re-asking what he saw, what he told police as well as what he had said earlier to the prosecutors. Despite any misgivings, Gureghian remained calm throughout. By the time he had finished, the shoemaker felt proud to have done his civic duty – and honor the memory of his Archbishop.

Tuesday morning, Siranoush Kafafian had taken the stand to answer the prosecutor's questions about defendant Number Seven, John Mirijanian, whom she had known for about seven years. Mrs. Kafafian said that on December 23rd, she encountered Mirijanian in the butcher shop on St. Nicholas Avenue. After Siranoush finished shopping, Mirijanian accompanied her home and spent the whole night playing cards with the Kafafians and another couple from New Jersey.

"Towards morning, did he say anything to you about sleeping?" asked Kaminsky.

"Well, then my husband went to sleep," she said, "so, I asked Mr. Mirijanian if he would like to sleep someplace in my house. He said, 'When the church bells ring, wake me up.' I said, 'You never be in church before,' like a joke."

"Now, after this conversation did Mr. Mirijanian...go to bed?"

"He went in the parlor and he laid down right in the parlor couch.

"How long did he remain sleeping?"

"About ten or fifteen minutes."

"Did anybody wake him up?"

"No."

"Did he say anything to you at that time?"

"No. I asked him, why are you not sleeping? He said he cannot sleep. He is going out. I said it is too early. He told me the Archbishop is going to mass in the church, and we didn't know it."

She testified that her husband went to the church with their guest. Under cross-examination, attorney Sheridan elicited an admission from Mrs. Kafafian that she had visited Mirijanian at his home, several weeks before the murder. But she denied that anyone threatened her husband for taking Mirijanian to the church. She added that Mirijanian's brother told her if his sibling had been involved in attacking Tourian, "the word came from headquarters" to "teach the Archbishop a lesson."

By Wednesday morning, everyone's nerves were frazzled. It was the final day for the prosecutor's case in chief and Mr. Kaminsky was anxious to end on a strong note. He gave his last witness a challenging task: not to mention the name of a person the lawyers would refer to as "Mr. X." This mystery man had been indicted once before, but was not currently charged, let alone under arrest.

The defense objection came from Sheridan's associate counsel, Joab Banton.

"With all due regard to the rights of the People," he began, "I think that would be highly prejudicial to the defendants."

Judge Corrigan didn't buy this assertion.

"Well, how?"

"In many ways," the defense attorney feigned.

"Tell me why," Corrigan insisted.

Banton tried to persuade the judge that Mr. X might be the very person who actually killed the Archbishop.

"I suppose by this time everybody knows who we are looking for," admitted Kaminsky. Defense lawyers agreed to keep the name secret and the prosecutor showed opposing counsel the name. On that conciliatory note, he began his final examination.

Sixty-two-year-old Manoog "Mike" Hagopian worked as a cook in the Arax Restaurant, about a block from Holy Cross Church. He testified that defendant Number Nine, Ohanes Andreassian, came in with Mr. X on the morning of the murder. The two men had coffee.

"Will you tell the court and this jury as nearly as you can remember…what did Mr. Andreassian say to Mr. X?" asked Kaminsky.

"Andreassian took the coffee and began to speak. He said, 'Today we have arranged everything. The Archbishop cannot escape. We will kill him today.'"

"What else did he say at that time?"

"He said that Aharonian's wife took the knife in."

"After Andreassian told that to Mr. X, what, if anything, happened?"

"They immediately left…and went to the direction of the church."

Hagopian said he later saw defendant Number Five, Juan Gonzales Tchalikian, with blood on his shirt, in the grocery store next door to the restaurant. The cook testified that Tchalikian told him, "We killed the Archbishop." Then, a second man put his hand over the defendant's mouth and told him to shut up. As they emerged onto the sidewalk, Hagopian said he saw defendant Number Nine come along.

"What did Andreassian say?" asked the A.D.A.

"Run away, run away. He died. Don't stay here."

Under cross-examination, this last prosecution witness became just as combative with the defense attorney as the People's first witness had been a week earlier. Attorney Sheridan kept trying to get Hagopian to testify in English. After several minutes of banter, the stubborn cook exploded.

"I cannot speak. I cannot explain to you right, and you want wrong. I don't want it. Do you want right? I talk in Armenian!"

"Give me right or wrong. Give it to me in English," insisted Sheridan.

"No, no!"

That exchange provoked shouts from several Armenian women sitting in the gallery. The judge tapped his gavel, but with no effect.

"We have got to have some order here. If these women cannot behave themselves, put them out."

Uniformed court officers hushed the disruptive observers and restored a more tolerable level of noise. Meanwhile, Sheridan finally relented and asked his questions through the interpreter. But even that was not free of vitriol.

"Did you get any money for what you are telling today?"

"Am I a lawyer that I should get money?"

"Or am I a liar that I should get money?"

Kaminsky was watching his last witness come apart. "I object to that, your Honor."

"Not necessarily for being a lawyer," continued Sheridan, "but for telling your story. Did anybody promise you anything?"

The cook retorted, "It is my conscience that I am talking, not for the money."

"Did you have a conscience between the 24th of December and the 18th day of January?"

"What is meant?"

And so it deteriorated until both frustration and fatigue led the defense attorney to say, "I am finished."

A bit later that afternoon, Alexander Kaminsky stood facing the bench. He kept glancing back over his shoulder and waited for the courtroom to be quiet. Judge Corrigan gaveled the gallery to silence.

"May it please the court," the prosecutor said matter-of-factly, "the People of the State of New York rest their case against these nine defendants."

After the People rested, Judge Corrigan had granted both sides a much-needed breather. The prosecution team agreed to spend their entire four-day recess preparing for cross-examination of defense witnesses. On the other side, defense lawyers got together for only two dinner meetings, but took most of the time off to rest. Sheridan got in some relaxing games of solitaire. But since Joab Banton spent the weekend in the Catskill Mountains, Tom had to cut his own deck before dealing.

Tom Peterson decided to invite Mary to a movie that night – despite the fact that they always had to negotiate over which flicks to choose. He wanted to drool over Dolores del Rio in "Flying Down to Rio," while she preferred the new Clark Gable film, "Men in White." They compromised and went to see Shirley Temple in "Little Miss Marker" at the Loew's cinema.

Afterwards, they celebrated with a late supper and an all-night snuggle.

"Make me a good little girl," she said, quoting a line from the movie.

"I'm afraid it's too late for that," he teased, blowing smoke rings toward the ceiling.

She rolled toward him and propped herself up on one elbow. "Do you think they did it?"

"Who?"

"Those Armenians."

That broke the spell. He was back in the moment.

"Probably." Tom took another long drag, then exhaled. "I don't know." He inhaled again. "I don't care."

And then, to push the present out of this night, he put his arms around Mary once more.

"Yes?" she asked with mock surprise, dramatically batting her eyelashes.

"I want to make you a *bad* little girl."

38

Now

I never imagined that I would be detained by the FBI.

And yet, here I was, inside an interview room in New York City's main office for the Federal Bureau of Investigation. It was on the sixth floor of a high-rise building in lower Manhattan. The walls must have been super-insulated, because I could hear absolutely no traffic noise. Of course, it didn't hurt that this room also had no windows. The artificial lighting was rather subdued and cast a slightly blue tint. Everything was painted flat blue-grey. The whole scene made me feel a bit lethargic, despite the fact that I was understandably quite worried.

The young man who led me into this small, chilly chamber had promised that someone would be here "right away" – about 45 minutes ago. Were it not for my innate sense of curiosity and the distinct feeling that there might be unpleasant consequences, I would have walked out by now. But then I imagined that the door was probably locked and I wasn't going anywhere unless someone released me.

And what landed me in this peculiar spot? That same inquisitiveness I relied on as a news reporter, the one which always got me good stories – and occasionally into a little trouble. All I wanted to know today was whether the Justice Department had investigated Tourian's murder. OK, maybe my methods weren't too smart. I suppose, in retrospect, I shouldn't have peeked inside that window.

It's not what you think. The window belonged to Al Callaghan Jr., an assistant U.S. attorney for the Southern District of New York. At least that's what the sign on his office door said. And why, you might wonder, was I going to see him? As I discovered, Callaghan's father had worked for the law firm that handled the defendants' appeal – their unsuccessful appeal, I might add. As such, he was one of the last attorneys connected with this crime. Although the elder Callaghan was now deceased, I hoped his son could shed some light on what happened. It was a long shot, I'll admit. But maybe, just maybe they had talked about the Tourian murder before the old man died. Or maybe there were some case notes in Al's inheritance.

I guess it would have been better to call ahead for an appointment. Or stop at the secretary's desk rather than slip past her while she was away. Or write a letter. But I was afraid Callaghan would never agree to meet with me. So instead, I decided to use the old "ambush interview" technique. I tried turning the knob. When it wouldn't budge, I peered in through the little window next to his door. (If they didn't want me looking into his office, why did they put a window there?) That's when I felt the firm hand on my shoulder.

"Can I help you, sir?" The uniformed guard with the *basso molto profundo* voice was one of the largest human beings I'd ever met. Even without the gun and badge, I would have displayed some deference.

"I'm looking for Al," I tried.

"Mr. Callaghan is not here, sir." He spoke with absolutely no inflection and almost inaudibly. "You'll have to come with me."

Yes, I did.

I stole a glimpse of this anthropomorphized mountain. On his peak, a bald dome lay hidden beneath the paramilitary-style hat. A café latte complexion and indistinct facial features revealed no certitude of race or ethnicity. His ancestors could have come from almost any continent. All I knew for sure was that he had Herculean strength.

The officer grasped my right upper arm resolutely. He didn't have to squeeze. It was clear that this man could crunch the bones of anyone stupid enough to resist. He directed me out of the office area and through a door marked "Authorized Personnel Only." We walked a few hundred feet to a service elevator, went down to the basement, and into the caged back seat of a waiting car. The unidentified driver of this black, unmarked sedan zipped us out of the underground garage.

We didn't go far, driving right across Federal Plaza and into another sub-street garage. My escort led me through a long corridor and up another elevator that stopped at the front lobby of the FBI's division headquarters – easy walking distance from the other building.

"This gentleman was the code three at Attorney Callaghan's office," he said to the smiling receptionist. She stopped smiling. Her lips remained frozen in an upward curve, but her gaze had turned deadly serious. She picked up the telephone receiver and pressed a button.

"Your code three is here." She hung up the phone and said to my guard, "Thank you. We'll be taking it from here in a moment."

The officer nodded. He released the grip on my arm, but I didn't bother to turn around. There was no need. I could still feel his enormous presence behind me. I glanced at the wall behind the desk, noticing framed portraits of several government officials. Among them were the President of the United States and the Attorney General, as well as several faces I didn't recognize.

After a few minutes, a tall, young man walked in. His medium blue blazer and light gray slacks weren't exactly a uniform, but he had an official photo identification with the word "SECURITY" in large block letters hanging on a chain around his neck. Clearly he was also in some authority here. The young man made eye contact with the receptionist. She nodded and he turned to me.

"Please come with me, sir." He sounded pleasant enough. It wasn't so much of an order as it was an irresistible invitation. A few minutes and half a dozen floors later, we arrived at Interview Room Number Eight.

And that's how I found myself in this peculiar spot.

I now sat on a hard, straight-backed chair behind a gray metal table. There was a pair of handcuffs welded to the tabletop. Thankfully, they were not attached to me. But the sight of these "bracelets" made me shudder. The only other items visible were a yellow legal pad and a ball-point pen.

Finally, two men in dark suits entered and firmly closed the door behind them. The taller one walked casually toward me, reached into his coat, pulled out a black leather card holder and flashed FBI credentials.

"I am Special Agent Stephen Montgomery. This is Special Agent Jules Cooper."

Montgomery held a brown file folder with a Justice Department logo stamped on the front. He kept moving in my direction as he opened the dossier. Cooper stood just inside the door with his arms folded and stared blankly at me.

I eyed these two G-men and contemplated whether or not this would be a friendly conversation. My strong suspicion was that it would not.

"Am I under arrest?"

"What makes you say that?" asked Montgomery. Cooper didn't budge.

"Well, it's just that – oh, I don't know." I wanted clarity. "Why am I here?"

"Why do you think you're here, Mr. Peterson?" Montgomery revealed nothing. I bet he was one hell of a poker player.

"Oh, come on," I said. He was testing my patience.

"Weren't you looking for information about..." He paused, opened the folder and looked inside. "...the Leon Tourian case?" Montgomery continued his style of responding to my every question with a question.

Cooper stayed stationary.

How on earth did they know? I wondered. Now I was really annoyed.

"What is your interest in Leon Tourian, Mr. Peterson?"

Now I folded my arms and looked at Cooper, then back at Montgomery. Obviously, I would have to give them something they wanted if I was going to get anything back.

"OK," I nodded, "Fine. I think one of the Archbishop's killers got away." I took a chance. "I'm working on a book." And one more pause for dramatic effect. "This might have been a KGB assassination."

Montgomery raised an eyebrow. Apparently, that little speculative detail was not in his notes.

Even Cooper stirred. He surprised us both by speaking. "You're writing a book about the KGB?" His partner glanced back at him.

"I'd be happy to tell you what I know," I teased. Cooper moved forward, took the notepad and pen from the table in front of me. "But first, I need answers to a couple of questions."

Both agents grimaced simultaneously. Montgomery spoke first. "You want to ask us questions about the Russian secret service?"

"Just a few," I said good-naturedly. I decided to try one more angle and gestured toward the file. "What do you have in there on the Armenian Revolutionary Federation or the *Tashnag* society?"

The agent snapped the folder shut. "Sorry, that's classified," he said severely. Cooper crossed his arms again.

His strong reaction told me two things: one, that there was something in the FBI file on A.R.F.; and two, that this federal agent considered whatever it was important enough to keep from me. Before I could ask anything else, the door burst opened. In marched the Special Agent in Charge.

Robert W. Smith was one of several SACs in the New York office. Ordinarily, an agent at his level would not participate in routine interviews. But in very high profile cases or matters involving particularly sensitive material, an exception might be made. In this instance, I suspected it was more for dramatic effect than anything else.

Smith wore a well-tailored gray three-piece suit and walked with military bearing. That was not merely coincidental. He had risen to the rank of lieutenant commander in the U.S. Navy. After two tours of duty in Southeast Asia, a good university education and a law degree, he joined *the Bureau* (as agents like to call their agency) to fight communists in America.

"Mr. Peterson," he began quietly, "you have the right to remain silent. And I'd encourage you to exercise that right while I explain why you are here."

I took the hint and said nothing. Smith paced deliberately in front of me with his hands behind his back, as if on the bridge of a ship.

"The FBI has reason to believe that you are delving into matters of national security," he said. "As much as we like to cooperate with the press, many of these matters are classified and cannot be discussed with anyone lacking the proper clearance. I am, however, authorized to disclose non-classified information to you. But before going any further, we will need to find out what you already know."

"Am I under arrest, Mr. Smith?" I asked again, now out of more than just curiosity.

He stopped pacing. "Why do you ask?"

"Well, you didn't mention that I have the right to an attorney, or that anything I say will be used against me in a court of law." I did my best to mockingly repeat the famous Miranda warning.

Smith grinned and chuckled softly. "Let's just say that we'd appreciate your cooperation. After all, I don't want to make a federal case out of this."

I wondered how often he had used that line before. Hundreds of times, I supposed. Anyway, it had its intended effect. I relaxed a bit, smiled and let out a slight sigh.

"All right," I said. "As long as we're just having a friendly little chat."

Smith unbuttoned his coat, pulled out a chair and sat directly across from me at the table. "Now, why don't you just tell us what you can about this case," he said. "Then, you and I will talk – off the record, of course."

"Of course," I agreed.

For the next fifteen minutes, I recapped the high points of my recent research. Cooper took notes, although I presumed a hidden microphone and recorder somewhere also taped my words. Montgomery flipped through the file folder periodically, apparently comparing my story to the official version.

When I finished my narrative, Smith rubbed a hand over his mouth a few times.

"Excellent, Mr. Peterson," he said, "excellent." He reached out toward Montgomery who understood to hand his boss the file folder. "You two wait outside," he ordered them. "Oh, and switch that thing off," Smith added, clearly referring to the recording system.

When we were alone, the SAC laid the file folder on the table and leaned back a bit in his chair.

"Thank you, Mr. Peterson. I appreciate your cooperation." He reached into his shirt pocket for a pack of cigarettes, tapped out a few and offered them to me. I instinctively reached for the smokes, then stopped.

"No thanks. I'm trying to quit."

He hesitated a moment, then pushed the exposed cigarettes back into the pack and returned it to his pocket. He then shrugged, placed both hands flat on the table and stood up. Smith turned toward the door.

"Wait a minute," I said, caught off-guard by this. "What about your part of the bargain?"

He didn't turn around. "I'll be back in about five minutes," he said as he walked out the door.

I sat there, dumbfounded. *What the hell just happened*, I wondered. I thought that perhaps I was being snookered. Then I noticed that Smith had left the file folder on the table in front of me. Without hesitation, I opened it.

Inside were dozens of pages clipped through punched holes at the top. Unlike the typically redacted photocopies that reporters get to see under the Freedom of Information Act, these documents were uncensored. Quite a departure for a government agency famous for its secrecy.

The first few pages were a chronology on the life of Ghevont Tourian. It began with his arrival in the United States, covered the major events until his murder, and ended with the conviction of his accused assassins.

Then came the first big surprise: a memorandum for FBI Director J. Edgar Hoover. It was written by Assistant Attorney General Joseph Keenan four days after Tourian's death. An official at the State Department had information about Vahan Cardashian, the original attorney for those accused of killing the Archbishop. According to the memo, Cardashian had once threatened the life of the Turkish Emperor. Interesting, but hardly big news.

I flipped over to the next pages. There was correspondence between Hoover and Royal S. Copeland, a U.S. Senator from New York. He was also Dr. Copeland, a noted eye surgeon and advocate for homeopathy – derisively known among his colleagues on Capitol Hill as the senator from the American Medical Association. And because of his loyalty to the Rockefeller family (which had financed his political campaign), he was also called the senator from Standard Oil.

Copeland forwarded to the Director a handwritten letter he had received from an Armenian informant, naming several suspects in the Archbishop's slaying who were not yet in custody. Hoover wrote back that there were no plans for an FBI investigation into the Tourian case. Hmmm…this was getting rather meaty.

On subsequent pages, I found an exchange of mail to and from President Franklin Roosevelt's uncle, Frederic A. Delano. As a member of the so-called kitchen cabinet, Delano had easy access to high officials throughout the executive branch. He had also received a note from the Armenian informant – whom he presumed was a "nut" deserving of an FBI investigation.

One more page turn. And there it was: THE NAME. My jaw dropped. Before I could finish reading the last few documents, the door opened. By reflex, I closed the file and dropped it onto the table.

"I'll take that, Mr. Peterson." Smith scooped up the folder. "I hope you had a satisfactory, um, visit."

What a strange thing to say, I thought.

At the risk of being rude, I decided to press my luck again. "May I ask you one more question, Mr. Smith?"

The agent cocked his head slightly, listening.

"After all these years, is this still a matter of national security – still, somehow, of interest to the federal government?"

He rubbed his mouth again. "Off the record?"

"You bet."

He hooked a thumb in his vest pocket.

"Mr. Peterson, we are always interested in anyone who uses violence to achieve political goals in our country. This group has shown a propensity to do that." Smith paused and tapped the file folder with his index finger. "But it's complicated by the fact that they are anti-communist."

I drew back. The other shoe was about to fall. All it needed was a little encouragement from me. Just a *really?* Or a *go on*. But as I started to open my mouth, Smith stopped abruptly.

"That is really all I can say." He reached into his inside coat pocket for a folded sheet of paper and flattened it open on the table. It was a Non-disclosure Agreement. "I'll need you to sign this," he said matter-of-factly.

There was no point in arguing or even in reading the document's fine print. Clearly, it was my ticket out of here. I scrawled my signature. Smith re-folded the form and extended a hand.

"Thanks for coming in, Mr. Peterson," he said as we shook. "The agents will show you out." Rather than releasing my hand, Smith tightened his grip a bit and looked me coldly in the eye. "One other thing."

"Yes?"

"You weren't serious about that KGB reference, were you." It was more of a statement than a question.

"Of course not," I replied – clearly understanding that was what the G-man wanted to hear.

He smiled ever so slightly and let go of my hand. "Forget about it."

Montgomery and Cooper stood at the door, waiting to usher me out of the building. A few minutes later, I exited the lobby and walked into the bright, winter sunlight – happy to be free but wondering where to go next. And still curious to know how the FBI had become aware of my interest in Ghevont Tourian. The answer to that mystery was not likely to be revealed to me anytime soon.

Anna was right: there was a lot more to this story than I knew. The FBI confirmed that. And now I had a name to check out.

39

Then

They all spoke at once.

"Mr. Sheridan, anything to tell us?"

"How's it going so far?"

"Who are you going to put on the stand first?"

Thomas Sheridan ran the rhetorical gauntlet as he passed reporters waiting inside the General Sessions Court on Monday morning, June 25th.

"No comment, boys." He waved them away with an uncharacteristically sober expression.

The defense had more witnesses than the People did. In addition to the nine defendants, there were more than thirty men and women to provide alibis, character references and alternative theories. Sheridan had an enormous challenge to overcome. So far, the evidence had been piling up against his clients.

He decided to begin by putting each of his nine clients on the stand. It was a risky strategy to say the least. But at this point, both Sheridan and co-counsel, Joab Banton, felt that a bold move was essential. One by one, the accused men insisted on their innocence.

First to appear was Mateos Leylegian. Defendant Number One, as he had come to be known to the jury, took the oath. He talked about his early years, about coming to America, about returning to Armenia during the War, about how the Turks killed his wife but his only son survived.

"Are you well known among the Armenians?" asked Sheridan.

"Yes, in my own circles," said Leylegian through the official interpreter.

"Are you a member of the *Tashnags*?"

"Yes."

The defense counsel asked his client to describe what he did on the day of the assassination. Mateos testified that he had gone to Holy Cross Church alone, although he did not remember what time. He sat in the middle of a pew on the right-hand side, about four rows from the altar. By his own account, that would have put him ahead of the procession – contrary to testimony from numerous prosecution witnesses.

"What did you do when the procession came down the aisle?"

"When I was standing there, I saw the procession was stopping in the direction of the entrance of the door and was not moving."

"What did you see, if anything, in connection with the Archbishop?" asked Sheridan.

"I saw one in front of him and other men behind him," replied Leylegian. "I saw so much."

Mateos went on to deny that he had moved into the aisle, denied that he attacked Tourian, and denied that he had a knife. He insisted that the attack began before the procession reached his row of pews. Leylegian said that he was beaten by other parishioners in the pew where he stood. The next thing he knew, a policeman grabbed him from that very spot – not in the aisle as had been alleged by others.

The defendant said he was taken to the station house, paraded in front of about thirty other Armenians from the church, and then beaten by the police. He also accused the Armenian lawyer, Dicran Sinsarian, of orchestrating witness statements at the 34th precinct.

"He said, 'Say, say. Say that these are them.'"

Thomas Sheridan walked back to the defense table and was about to sit down, prompting the prosecutor to spring to his feet. Kaminsky opened his mouth, about to cross-examine, when Sheridan asked one last question.

"Did you in any way attack the Archbishop?"

The A.D.A. threw his hands in the air, sighed loudly and sat back down. Leylegian was momentarily distracted by the prosecutor's ungraceful movement.

"I have never come out of my pews," replied the defendant, "and I did never have any intention of the sort."

Opposing counsel looked at each other. Sheridan decided to play Kaminsky one more time.

"You may examine," he said. Kaminsky slowly rose to his feet. "Just a minute," continued Sheridan. After looking through his notes, he said, "Yes, you may examine."

Kaminsky simply stood in place, waiting for a few titters in the gallery to die down. He shot several hard looks over his shoulder at Sheridan, like a pitcher trying to keep a man from stealing second base. Finally, the prosecutor buttoned his coat and approached the witness.

"Now, Mr. Leylegian, you are the secretary of the *Tashnag* organization in New York City, aren't you?"

"Yes."

"As the secretary of that organization, you are the only person who can call the committee of seven together, isn't that right?"

"Yes."

For the next several minutes, Kaminsky tried to ask the defendant about alleged terrorist policies and activities of the *Tashnag* organization. But Sheridan objected to nearly every question. Finally, the prosecutor abandoned that line of inquiry and turned his attention to statements Leylegian made to A.D.A. Joseph Cohn.

"Why did you deny to Mr. Cohn at first that you were the secretary of the society?"

"I have never denied it," said Mateos. "I have told him I am the secretary but probably the interpreter by the name of Dirad has done so." Leylegian's answer constituted a central part of the defense strategy – that his previous statements were inaccurately interpreted or incorrectly transcribed. In response to one question after another, virtually every defendant would stick to this tactic.

Feeling frustrated again, Kaminsky gave up and switched topics once more. The prosecutor asked Leylegian to describe what he saw happen to the Archbishop in Holy Cross Church on December 24th.

"How can I see? I was not looking towards there. I was looking at the altar."

"Didn't you testify that it is the custom when the Archbishop comes in the church that everybody should rise?" Kaminsky was beginning to lose his temper and raise his voice.

"As I said before," replied Leylegian calmly, "before they reached us, a quarrel had begun. They had not reached us. I was just looking to the alley."

Interrogator and witness discussed the details of what happened during the several minutes leading up to and following the assassination. Mateos remained remarkably calm, while the prosecutor demonstrated his ire.

The assistant district attorney culminated by asking – nearly shouting, "So all that time that you sat in the fourth row, when you saw the turmoil in the church, at no time did you see with your own eyes the figure of the Archbishop?"

Leylegian flashed a look of total innocence. "No."

That answer pushed Alexander Kaminsky beyond the boiling point. But the experienced prosecutor knew he had to regain control, and to do it quickly. He turned away from the witness stand, looked directly at the jurors and smiled a Cheshire cat smile – as if to say, *Now I've got you.* And now, Alexander Kaminsky tried to do what he did best – expose a lying suspect.

For the next ten minutes, the A.D.A. went at Leylegian, point by point, verbally twisting the defendant around his little finger. Mateos struggled to withstand the inquisition, nearly pleading with his eyes to be finished. Even opposing counsel was caught off-guard by this aggressive turnabout. Sheridan opened his mouth several times to object, but each time it was too late. Kaminsky had moved on to a new topic. The prosecutor even managed to cast aspersions on the court interpreter.

Finally, the defense attorney jumped back into the fight.

"Just one minute," said Sheridan. "I object to the remarks that are made about the interpreter. We did not pick him. We are not responsible for him."

"Mr. Sheridan threw a harpoon into the lake and tries to muddy the waters," retorted Kaminsky. "It is just a trail of the red herring."

"Please, I may object if it is necessary."

Judge Corrigan had heard enough. "Really, when you get through squabbling – I had hoped that if we took this long adjournment, your dispositions might be improved."

"Oh, not I," answered Sheridan indignantly. "I am very much surprised—"

Corrigan cut him off. "I think we ought to get along better."

Meanwhile, Alexander Kaminsky was fuming. "I do not like to have my cross-examination interrupted," he complained.

And with that, the prosecutor realized that all his clever interrogation techniques had been deflated. The defense strategy had been left firmly in place, suggesting to the jury that the defendants were victims of poor interpreters.

Kaminsky tried one last, futile attempt to derail Leylegian. "Have you ever seen the Archbishop before that morning?"

"No."

"And you now say that being in that church, at no time did you see the Archbishop in the procession or anywheres in that church, yes or no?"

"I have not seen him."

When the morning's session was over, Mateos returned to the defense table and Judge Corrigan declared a lunch break. Court resumed at two o'clock that afternoon and A.D.A. Kaminsky recalled Leylegian to the stand for a few more questions. He did not want to leave the jury with that last, nearly triumphant image of the main defendant.

The prosecutor asked whether the defendant had ever written for an Armenian newspaper or magazine under a pseudonym. He asked about his friendship with the other eight defendants. He asked about what Leylegian had worn the morning of Tourian's murder. And he asked how long he waited in church for the Archbishop to arrive. Each question implied guilt, but each answer affirmed innocence. For Alexander Kaminsky, it was not his finest hour.

While the prosecutors were putting papers back into their briefcases, a bailiff approached.

"Mr. Cohn?" said the court officer as he handed him a note. The A.D.A. unfolded the paper, glanced at it, and then handed it to his co-counsel. The prosecutor read the message.

Kaminsky and Cohn, come to my office immediately. /Dodge

Upon entering the District Attorney's private office, Kaminsky and Cohn noticed that most of the lights were off. There was no mistaking the patrician figure of William Dodge seated behind his opulent desk. In the plush high-back chair next to him sat another man, his face cast in shadows.

"Sit down." The boss gestured toward a pair of leather wingbacks opposite the desk. "So, are you going to convict these sons of bitches?" asked Dodge forcefully.

Alexander Kaminsky knew better than to answer with a prediction. "It is going very well, sir."

Joseph Cohn nodded in agreement. "The evidence is all on our side and the jury is clearly sympathetic to the People's case."

"That's not the way I see it." The man in shadows spoke in exact, mellifluous syllables while neatly stroking his moustache. "Your own case was pretty good, but the defense keeps coming back at you like gangbusters." Thomas Dewey leaned forward into the light, giving both assistant prosecutors a start as they leapt to their feet.

"Tom!" Kaminsky was effusive. "Have you been in court?"

"Back row, left side. Friend of the bride." Dewey stood up and shook hands with his former colleagues. Smiles all around, it was the first time they had spoken in weeks. Most of the former prosecutor's help had been communicated indirectly.

The D.A. pulled out his pocket watch. "Gentlemen, the lunch recess ends at two o'clock," said Judge Dodge. "I want to talk about a plea."

Kaminsky and Cohn were shocked. Dewey cut them off before either could protest the suggestion.

"That might be a little premature, Bill. Sheridan still has thirty or forty witnesses to call."

"Take it from me," said Dodge dismissively, you're sitting on a razor's edge. "If your cross-examination does not go well, I want you to offer a plea bargain." The D.A. rubbed his chin. "Make it first degree manslaughter for the two murderers, second degree for the rest."

"That's quite a bargain," said Cohn.

"A bird in the hand, Joseph." Dodge stood up. "Now, let's get back in there and finish off these rats. I don't want any of them to finagle out of this."

As the four men walked out of the D.A.'s office, none of them seemed to notice a stranger discreetly loitering in the reception area. They had not indicated any awareness of his presence near the slightly open door while they were talking earlier. On the other hand, perhaps this stranger should have found it surprising to overhear such an important private conversation so easily.

When court resumed after the lunch break, Thomas Sheridan was ready to call his next witness. But he was a bit concerned about his co-counsel. Joab Banton was never late during a trial. Just as the defense attorney was about to ask defendant Number Two to take the stand, Banton walked into the courtroom.

"Where were you?" whispered Sheridan.

"I've got news – big news," replied Banton fervently.

Sheridan looked toward Judge Corrigan and realized that there was no way to ask for a recess at this moment. The lawyer grimaced, tapped Nishan Sarkisian on the shoulder and gestured him to go to the witness stand.

"Nishan Sarkisian," he announced.

"Nishan Sarkisian," repeated the clerk who held a Bible for the witness. "Do you swear that the testimony you are about to give shall be the truth, the whole truth, and nothing but the truth, so help you God?"

"I do."

Banton urgently tried to relate the pressing news, but Sheridan refused to listen. Instead, he gestured for his colleague to write it down, and then pressed ahead with his direct examination.

Sheridan asked Sarkisian (a.k.a. Tuktikian) essentially the same sorts of questions as he had asked the first defense witness. But jurors were less sympathetic toward defendant Number Two. He seemed less open, less trustworthy than his accused co-conspirator.

It began with trying to explain the alias. Americans had trouble accepting Nishan's explanation that his adopted last name was easier to pronounce than his original family name. To members of the jury, both Sarkisian and Tuktikian were equally foreign-sounding.

And then there was the matter of going in and out of the church several times during services on December 24th. The defendant said he had gone out to smoke a cigarette when Tourian was attacked. Several jurors shook their heads, visibly rejecting that alibi. Finally, Sarkisian/Tuktikian insisted that he was outside when the fighting started. He came back into the church with a police officer, but then went out again. Nishan said he was standing across the street when the policeman returned and arrested him.

"When you were arrested, did they take you back to the church?" asked Sheridan.

"Yes, to the small room."

Kaminsky leaned toward his co-counsel and whispered, "He's making this sound so complicated."

"Look at the jurors," Joseph Cohn whispered back. "They're not buying any of it."

"I'll make sure on cross." Alexander Kaminsky sat back, feeling self-satisfied.

Meanwhile, Joab Banton needed to find a way to let his associate know what he had just learned. The defense lawyer thought about Sheridan's odd obsession of playing solitaire, and then wrote the following cryptic note.

A.K. will cut the deck for you.

Thomas Sheridan looked at the words and immediately understood that this was, indeed, momentous news. No matter what happened, Sheridan had to keep Nishan Sarkisian for another day. He needed time to prepare a strategy.

But it was too late. After a quick cross-examination, the prosecution was finished with this witness. Sheridan came up with only a few questions on redirect. He had run out of time. Judge Corrigan adjourned until tomorrow. Defense counsel's only hope was to avoid the prosecutor until the next day.

Sheridan threw his papers into the briefcase and hurried out of the courtroom with Banton closely in tow.

"Let's get the hell out of here," Sheridan said breathlessly. The pair talked as they dashed into a taxi. "How did you find out?" he asked.

"An old friend of mine in the D.A.'s office—"

"Never mind that." Sheridan needed to think. He reached for the deck of cards again, then stopped himself. *Too obvious*, he thought. Still, he was impressed by his associate's clever message.

Banton had noticed that Sheridan always asked him to cut the deck before he would deal cards when playing solitaire. It was a little joke between them, as if Sheridan wanted to make sure the game was honest. This note meant Joab Banton somehow discovered that the prosecutor was willing to take a plea in exchange for lesser charges. By cutting the deck, "A.K." – prosecutor Alexander Kaminsky – would then offer a "deal" to settle this case. Unfortunately, he had to quickly come up with a prospective response.

"There's no way we can agree to let them take a plea," said Banton.

Sheridan nodded. "You're right. But still, we need to talk with them about it."

"Maybe not. My friend said they would offer a plea agreement if cross-examination of Sarkisian went badly for them."

"Hmmm." Sheridan tried to decide who had won today's battle of witnesses. "He might be pretty happy with himself."

"Yes, especially the way we ran out of there."

"Then again—"

Banton stopped his colleague. "No, Thomas. We can't even entertain the notion of a plea at this point. We're working for acquittals."

Sheridan nodded again. "Agreed."

After court had adjourned for the day, Kaminsky and Cohn returned to the D.A.'s office. Dodge and Dewey were waiting for them, four glasses of Scotch already poured.

"Well done, boys." Dodge walked to the office entry, glanced around the now-empty reception area, and then firmly shut his door.

"You think they got our message?" All four men laughed at how well their theatrical disinformation trick had worked. There never was going to be a plea offer, of course.

"And how," said Cohn. "You should have seen how fast they ran out of court, Bill."

"But we need to do even better with the next witnesses," said Dodge.

Dewey put his hand on Kaminsky's shoulder. "The way I see it, Alex, you can clinch this case by recalling the same witness."

The A.D.A. scratched his head. "Sarkisian?"

"On re-cross, you need to tear him apart. Start slowly, wait for an opening, then rush in for the kill." Dewey punched his palm for emphasis. "He's no match for you. Dollars to donuts the jury doesn't like him anyway. He looks guilty."

Cohn put in his agreement. "You almost had Leylegian until defense counsel tripped you up at the end."

"And you did fine with Sarkisian the first time. Just don't let Sheridan interrupt you," added Dewey. "Don't let him get to you."

Kaminsky nodded slowly. "Maybe you're right, Tom." He looked at his boss. "Maybe Tom's right."

"Well, it's your funeral, Kaminsky," replied Dodge. He added with mock gravity, "I still think a plea bargain is a good idea." Everyone laughed and drank their drinks.

That night, Tom Peterson got home in time to hear Lowell Thomas's renowned radio signature.

> "...So long until tomorrow," said the famous reporter and commentator.

After a brief pause, the Blue Network announcer said, "Now, please stay tuned for *The Amos 'n' Andy Show* which follows immediately on most of these NBC stations."

Just then, Tom's phone rang.

"Did you hear that?" It was his favorite law enforcement buddy, Iskenderian. "Lowell Thomas just called the *Tashnags* a terrorist organization!" The Armenian detective was very excited.

Although Peterson had managed to miss the program, he said, "I suppose the jury heard, too." Of course they did. In 1934 virtually everyone in America listened to Lowell Thomas. The National Broadcasting Company had scored a big coup a few years before by stealing the globe-trotting newsman from CBS.

"I'll bet the defense lawyers heard it, too," added Izzy. "And it'll really burn them.

In fact, defense attorney Thomas Sheridan did mention the broadcaster's remarks in court the next day. But the prosecutor wouldn't take the bait. He ignored any suggestion of prejudice. Instead, to opposing counsel's surprise Kaminsky recalled Nishan Sarkisian to the stand.

Following Thomas Dewey's suggestion, the A.D.A. launched into this defendant with merciless, rapid-fire questions. Inside of a few minutes, the witness was backpedaling on nearly everything he had said the day before, even doubting his ability to count the number of pews in church.

Finally, Alexander Kaminsky pulled a rabbit out of his hat. "Do you know a man, a legionnaire, whose name is Mateos Araquilian?"

The witness didn't stop to think, answering before Sheridan could object.

"Of course, that is Leylegian. The Armenian of it is Araquilian."

"That is all."

Judge Corrigan looked at defense counsel. "Is that all?"

"That is all." He didn't want to let the jurors see that he had been caught off guard. Sheridan decided to let this little revelation go by. Instead, he called the next two defendants in sequence. Both Osgan Yarganian and Martin Mozian went through the formalities of stating where they had been on the morning of Tourian's murder. Both categorically denied having any involvement with the assassination. Both held up rather well to the prosecutor's hard-hitting cross-examination.

Kaminsky was fully warmed up as he sat waiting for defendant Number Five.

Juan Gonzales Tchalikian took the stand and told his lawyer that he was born in Panama of a Spanish mother and an Armenian father. The 28-year-old immigrant fretfully twisted the tip of his forefinger and squirmed in his chair. Tchalikian tried to answer questions in English, saying that his parents had been massacred by Turks and that he, himself, was taken as a slave.

"How old were you at that time?" asked defense counsel.

"Seven or eight." Tchalikian fought back tears and slumped down into the witness chair. "I came to this country first time 1929."

The defendant said he worked as a busboy at the Belmont café. Then he told the jury what he saw on the morning of the murder.

"Did you see Gorgodian, the Bishop's guard?" asked Sheridan.

"Yes.

"What did he say?"

Now, the words flooded out. "He told me, 'I think there is going to be trouble over here. Please don't get trouble you.' I said, 'Gorgodian, what are you talk about? In church you are going to have fight?' He said he heard something maybe is going to be fight. He said you not get into fight. No trouble."

"When the fight started, did you do anything?"

Tchalikian cried out, "No, sir!"

Sheridan let the words hang in the air, then asked the witness to describe the aftermath of Tourian's assassination. He said Gorgodian grabbed him as he tried to get away from the brawl, and said the bodyguard struck him in the head with his pistol. He left the church with blood streaming from the wound and got cleaned up at the grocery store next to Arax Restaurant. A friend put him in a taxi and took him home.

The next day, said the defendant, he was arrested and taken to the local precinct where several police officers beat him.

"And the next day, December 26th, did you give a statement to Mr. Cohn?"

"After I go, police take me headquarters. Sleep station house. Next morning, I go to District Attorney's." Tchalikian slumped further into the chair.

A.D.A. Kaminsky sat listening to all this, biding his time. When Thomas Sheridan had finished his direct examination, the prosecutor launched into the witness with newfound aggression.

"There is no question about you belonging to the *Tashnag* Society, is there?"

Tchalikian suddenly sat up straight. "I am a *Tashnag*."

"How long have you been a *Tashnag*?"

"I am a *Tashnag* all the time!" The witness thought a moment. "About 1923."

"Did you read the constitution of the *Tashnag* Society?"

"Yes, sir."

That's exactly what the prosecutor wanted to hear – a dedicated party member. Kaminsky grabbed a document from his table and approached the witness. "Isn't it a fact that the Central Committee under that constitution has the right to declare terror against those whom they consider to be traitors to Armenia?"

Men and women sitting in the gallery gasped loudly. The witness nearly bolted up out of his chair.

Thomas Sheridan was on his feet. "I object to that!" he shouted.

"I never saw that," added Tchalikian.

The two lawyers went at each other, arguing over the admissibility of the document and the propriety of the question. Several minutes later, Judge Corrigan intervened.

"Are you all through, Mr. Sheridan?"

Defense counsel knew that like so many others, this decision was not going to be in his favor. He closed his eyes and said, "Yes."

The judge did allow the document and the question. But while the lawyers were arguing, the defendant had already thought ahead. He said he was loyal to the cause of Armenian liberation.

Kaminsky plowed ahead. The prosecutor ran through more than two hundred questions, covering every aspect of the case with this one witness. After more than half an hour on the stand, Tchalikian's head was spinning. After the A.D.A. finished his cross-examination, Thomas Sheridan stood up to try to repair the damage on re-direct.

In a very calming voice, the defense attorney approached his client. "Did you see a fight in the church?"

The defendant sighed. "Yes."

"Will you kindly tell us now your best recollection of what you saw in that church with reference to this fight?"

Tchalikian was wiped out. He turned to the official interpreter and continued in Armenian. "Slowly, slowly," he began, "the Archbishop was coming with the procession."

The interpreter translated into English the words repeated so many times in the past two weeks. "And they were all mixed to each other."

That phrase caught Judge Corrigan's attention. "Well, in what group?" he asked.

"The procession."

His Honor was confused. "Do you mean the fight started among the members of the procession?"

"I saw so. Something happened in the procession," replied Tchalikian. "I am not a prophet," he added.

"Well, nobody asked you to be a prophet," said the judge testily. "You are just an observer."

"Yes."

To everyone's astonishment, the judge kept questioning the witness on this point. "Well, did the Archbishop start the fight?"

Sheridan sprang to his feet again. "I object to that! I object to a statement on the part of the Court."

"That was not a statement. That is a question," declared Corrigan.

Sheridan took a step toward the bench, then remembered his place. "Well, if that is a question, I ask that the Court refrain from asking a question of that kind."

Defense counsel implicitly accused the judge of having asked a prejudicial question. Corrigan dismissed that suggestion and returned to the witness.

"Now, I am asking him, did the Archbishop start the fight?" he repeated.

"No."

"Did the choir start the fight?"

Tchalikian understood he was treading on dangerous ground and began answering with greater precision. "From the procession began instantaneously something."

Corrigan moved ahead, point by point. "You say the choir was all around the Archbishop, front, back and on both sides?"

"Yes, sir."

"Did you say that one of the choir started the fight?"

Again, Sheridan jumped in. "I object to this! Just one minute. I object to the question. No evidence in this case and no testimony that anybody of the choir—this witness has—"

"I know what the testimony and the evidence is," said Corrigan angrily.

"I know it!!" Sheridan was blind with rage. "I watched the expression on your face for the last three minutes and the smile, and the shake of the head." Defense counsel had clearly lost all self-control. He pointed accusingly at the judge. "The asking of the Bishop, the asking of the choir. And I ask for a withdrawal of a juror on the ground that your conduct is prejudicial."

Corrigan didn't hesitate. "Well that motion is denied, and I will tell you now and leave it to the jury, that any expression has been correct and proper through this trial. And that is simply a way of making a record which may be used later."

Sheridan was relentless. "No. No, it is not! It is only my duty as a lawyer that I make this. I do it with reluctance. And a description of the expression on your face would sound so harsh even in a record that I reluctantly refrain from stating it."

The judge smiled broadly, and then responded. "You do it with great reluctance, I know. I consider it absolutely untrue. It is a method of getting something on the record."

"I am watching your face, your Honor. You are not watching it."

"I am watching yours, and you have made many grimaces as anybody in the courtroom since the trial started."

"I note an exception on the record."

Defendant Number Six was the youngest man accused of complicity in this homicide case. Twenty-five-year-old Harry Sarafian was a dapper fellow. Born in Bulgaria, the Armenian immigrant earned his living as a restaurateur, but was also an amateur actor. His appearance on the witness stand underscored his theatrical bent, speaking with great poise and self-assurance. Unlike his fellow defendants, Sarafian used to be a regular worshipper at Holy Cross Church.

"Now, did you jump on the Archbishop?" asked Sheridan.

"I did not."

"Did you strike at the Archbishop?"

"No, I did not."

As Sarafian continued to testify, the judge suddenly interrupted.

"We will stop now," said Corrigan abruptly. He turned to the witness. "You may step down." The defendant returned to his seat. Sheridan started to object, but the judge cut him off.

"Since this trial began, it has been called to my attention that one or two members of the jury have received anonymous communications." The judge somberly asked each juror whether he would be affected by the existence of such messages. Each in turn said he would not.

Thomas Sheridan made a passionate speech describing how he had asked the judge about a visit from two jurors and a private conference with the assistant district attorney. Corrigan shrugged off the defense counsel's plea, then asked the jurors whether they could continue to try the case fairly. Each man said he could.

Judge Corrigan showed the notes to opposing counsel and then instructed the clerk to enter the messages into the record without reading them publicly.

> **Mr. H. Fredler, 67 Park Avenue, New York. Postmarked New York, N.Y. 5, June 24th, 4:00 A.M., 1934. Mr., You like live, aquite (*sic*) our boys or we will kill every one jurier (*sic*). /L.T.**

> **Mr. W. Schillinger, 500 W. 171st Street, New York. Dear Sir: You better help our nine boys if you value your life we have been watching all of you. We will kill. /T.**

Defense co-counsel Joab Banton then moved for an immediate mistrial, which Corrigan summarily – and predictably – denied.

After Harry Sarafian finished testifying, Thomas Sheridan called defendant Number Six. John Mirijanian also tried to speak in English, but with some difficulty. When it came time for Alexander Kaminsky to cross-examine him, the prosecutor took advantage of the witness's language limitations. In more than an hour of testimony, the A.D.A. managed to confuse Mirijanian with a complex series of questions about who was in the procession, how many were priests, what they were wearing, and so on. The interrogation sounded like an Abbott and Costello routine. Defense counsel was unable to rescue his own witness, who finally stepped down from the stand in shambles.

Judge Corrigan called a short recess to allow the lawyers to calm down. When they resumed, it was clear that the break didn't really help. Everyone's nerves were still frazzled.

"How much longer will be consumed in putting on your defense?" he asked testily.

Sheridan was surprised by the content and the tenor of Corrigan's question. "I don't know, your Honor. It is difficult to specify time. I thought the examination would proceed faster than it has in the last two days." Without fully considering the impact, he added, "We will have about twenty more witnesses."

Now it was Corrigan's turn to be surprised. "How many?" That inquiry was accompanied by a low but audible groan from the jury box.

"There will be," Sheridan paused, then continued, "about twenty more witnesses. It is very difficult for me to approximate how much time."

The judge glanced at the jurors. "Without indicating any cynicism at all, do you mean twenty witnesses?"

Now co-counsel Joab Banton rose to shoulder some of the increasingly apparent burden. "Yes."

The prosecutor wanted to savor this subtle moment. When the judge estimated that the trial would continue through the next week, Kaminsky said, "If they have thirty witnesses, I guess it will be necessary." Again, several jurors whispered their discontent.

Sheridan knew he had to do some damage control here. Defense counsel decided to shift some of the blame to his opponent. "I don't know whether Mr. Kaminsky will take as long examining them as he did with the others."

But Judge Corrigan refused to allow another verbal sparring match to begin.

Instead, he turned to the question of whether the jury should visit the crime scene – something both sides had requested, but which the judge was reluctant to grant. "It would take about three hours," he said. "It would take a whole session and quite an expense to the City."

"Well, we could go by subway," suggested Sheridan sarcastically.

But the judge ordered jurors to be delivered there all together in police vehicles.

"When? Tomorrow?" asked defense counsel.
"Why not do this, Judge?" added Kaminsky.
"How about 11 o'clock tomorrow morning?" offered Corrigan.

That evening, Franklin Roosevelt gave his first fireside chat in several months. His popular, folksy speeches were meant to explain his administration's policies for extricating the nation from economic depression. The President spoke in easy-to-understand terms about some complex matters. He sought to reassure citizens.

> Let me put to you another simple question: Have you as an individual paid too high a price for these gains? Plausible self-seekers and theoretical die-hards will tell you of the loss of individual liberty. Answer this question also out of the facts of your own life. Have you lost any of your rights or liberty or constitutional freedom of action and choice? Turn to the Bill of Rights of the Constitution, which I have solemnly sworn to maintain and under which your freedom rests secure. Read each provision of that Bill of Rights and ask yourself whether you personally have suffered the impairment of a single jot of these great assurances. I have no question in my mind as to what your answer will be. The record is written in the experiences of your own personal lives.

FDR listed the many accomplishments of Congress in the past six months and noted, among other things, that lawmakers "strengthened the hand of the Federal Government in its attempts to suppress gangster crime." That phrase caught the attention of Tom Peterson. The reporter laughed at the line.

"What's so funny about that?" asked Mary. She was sitting next to him on the living room sofa.

"Do you really believe the feds care about suppressing gangster crime?"

"Well, isn't that what the FBI is doing?"

Tom took his girlfriend's hand. "Kiddo," he remarked, "J. Edgar Hoover no more wants to wipe out the mob than doctors want to eliminate disease."

She stared at him blankly.

"What do you think the G-men would do without organized crime?" he continued.

Mary shook her head. "You reporters have some pretty crazy ideas, you know that?"

Meanwhile, Roosevelt concluded his remarks.

> While I was in France during the War our boys used to call the United States "God's country." Let us make it and keep it "God's country."

40

Now

Back at my hotel, a small crowd had gathered just inside the entrance. The Wolcott doesn't have a restaurant, so I knew these folks weren't there for the early bird special. I noticed that everyone in this group of young people wore formal clothes – which is rather odd to see in the middle of the afternoon, even in New York City. Then I spotted the center of their attention. She wore an elegant, white, satin and lace bridal gown. I guessed that this was where a wedding party was staying tonight.

After my ordeal with the FBI, I needed a shower and a shave. I wanted to take a nap, too, but that would have to wait. For the moment, I had a murderer to find. It was time to call in a favor.

"Ahmed al-Isaacs," announced the voice at the other end of the line. As far as I knew, this son of my high school friend was the only Arab-Israeli (sorry, Israeli-Arab) spy in America. Ari, as he preferred to be called, spoke a dozen languages fluently, played a lovely flamenco guitar, and according to his ex-wife, was not a bad tango dancer. I liked to imagine that he could probably kill with one hand, too.

Since Ari had such an eclectic personality, I was never surprised by what he knew and could do. That's why I turned to him to accomplish that which could not be done by mere mortals. In all the years I lived in New York, and ever since retiring from the Trib, I never asked for help from Isaacs – until now.

"I need the impossible."

"Consider it done."

We met at his favorite steak house in Hell's Kitchen. As he dove into a 24-ounce prime rib, I nibbled at a Caesar salad and laid out my dilemma. With a photographic memory, he never took notes. Instead, he kept nodding in-between bites.

"And you want this yesterday, I suppose?" he asked when I had finished.

"No, later today would be soon enough."

"Fine." He took the check for dinner and handed it to me. "Here's my bill." That was his standard arrangement for friends: In exchange for professional services, all he wanted was the dinner of his choice – no questions asked. Seemed fair to me.

"I'll call you."

We walked out of the restaurant separately, a token gesture of security. I wasn't sure for whose benefit.

41

Then

The trial dragged into the next month. Owing to the excessive heat, Judge Corrigan decided to limit sessions to half a day. In addition to putting the nine accused men on the stand, defense attorneys had already presented more than a dozen character witnesses. On Monday, July 2nd, Thomas Sheridan called Araxie Apikian.

"Were you in Holy Cross Church on December 24th, 1933?" asked the defense attorney.

"Yes." The witness explained that her son was in the choir that morning. When the melee began, she immediately grabbed the boy and took him toward the altar, away from the fighting. "I went to the vestment room."

"And did he take off his vestments?" asked Sheridan.

"Yes, and I take him out," she replied in heavily accented English.

Thomas Sheridan walked slowly to the defense table and picked up the blueprint of the church. Turning back to the witness, he held up the drawing and asked, "And you took him out?"

"Yes. Out the side door. I walk down the alley."

Members of the jury had visited the crime scene a few days before, so the church building's layout was still fresh in their minds. Nevertheless, having this visual aid made her testimony perfectly vivid.

"When you got into the alley, what did you see?"

Despite her accent, Mrs. Apikian spoke loudly and clearly. "I saw choir vestment on the ground. Some choir girl pick it up, and one shadow passed out from the door to the street."

From the public gallery and the jury box, those who heard this bombshell let out various oohs, ahs and gasps. Joseph Cohn could not restrain his anger and struck a fist on the prosecutor's table. That had the unintended effect of startling his co-counsel.

But Alexander Kaminsky would not let the defense witness go unchallenged. "Madam, were you an enemy of the Archbishop?"

"Never."

"You know it is your duty as a good citizen to assist the District Attorney to punish people who commit crimes, isn't it?"

"Yes."

"You were willing to tell Mr. Cohn all about what you saw, isn't that right?"

"Whatever he asked," she replied.

"All right, he asked you what you had seen. Did you tell him that you saw a shadow running through the alley?"

The witness squared her shoulders and looked directly at the prosecutor. "Before I gave a reply, Vartan Dirad said that she is not interesting." Mrs. Apikian said she was questioned by A.D.A. Cohn in his office for only about one minute before being sent home. Apparently, she said, the prosecutor did not want to hear about the shadow man in the alley.

Next, her husband took the stand. Gir Apikian had not gone to church the morning of Tourian's murder. He confirmed that his wife came home in an agitated state – "in an excited mood, in terrible shape." A short while later, he went to the 34th precinct.

"What did you do when you got into the station house?" asked Sheridan.

"I saw people there," answered Apikian. "My willingness was to cooperate with the authorities and find out or clear the crime committed in the church." He described A.D.A. Cohn's attempt to question witnesses, while Dirad and other local Armenians influenced the testimony.

"I saw a terrible mood of hate," said Apikian. "People around there were talking about getting other *Tashnags* into the station house, arrest them and bring them over there." He tried to complain, but said he felt ignored.

Kaminsky began his cross-examination by challenging the witness's credibility. The prosecutor accused Apikian of engaging in business fraud, of serving as a Turkish spy, and of trying to insinuate himself into the murder investigation in order to exert his own influence on the outcome.

"I protest!" shouted Apikian. "Absolute lies!"

The prosecutor shouted back. "What do you call a man that goes in and tries, if you pardon the vernacular, suck around the District Attorney to get information from the inside?"

"I was there to do my duty as an American citizen, and as an Armenian!"

Both men had beet red faces, grimacing dangerously at each other. Kaminsky asked why, if the witness felt there was prosecutorial misconduct, he didn't report it to Judge Dodge.

"I did not know!" yelled Apikian at the top of his lungs.

"Wait a minute," retorted Kaminsky. "I can shout as loud as you!"

And then suddenly, there was silence as the two simply stared at each other. After nearly forty-five minutes of verbal warfare, the combatants had run out of steam. Kaminsky had one last line of questioning.

"Didn't you tell Mr. Cohn you loved the Archbishop?" asked the prosecutor calmly.

"I respected him, certainly," replied Apikian quietly.

"And you were looking for his murderer?"

"Certainly, more than anybody is." The witness clenched his teeth. "Surely. What do you think of it?"

"Shall I tell you?" asked Kaminsky under his breath, but loud enough for opposing counsel to hear.

"No, don't," answered Sheridan.

The parade of defense witnesses continued. Among them were several more character witnesses as well as a few who offered alibis. The last to testify was Aram Proudian, an Oriental rug cleaner. He, too, was a *Tashnag* and one of several men called as character witnesses. The defense attorney asked whether Mateos Leylegian had a reputation for peace and quiet.

"I think he is a very fine and honest man," replied Proudian. He gave similar answers for the other defendants, all fellow *Tashnags*.

On cross-examination, Alexander Kaminsky had only two questions.

"Do you do typewriting?"

The witness stared at the prosecutor for a moment, then turned to Sheridan who merely shrugged.

"Yes, I can."

"When you studied typewriting, did you hear or practice that famous motto—"

"Beg pardon?"

"—Now is the time for all good men to come to the aid of their party?"

Joseph Cohn slapped a hand over his mouth to suppress a laugh. Even Judge Corrigan had to bite his tongue.

"Isn't that what you are doing?" continued Kaminsky, poker-faced. "You are coming to the aid of your party?" Finally, the prosecutor allowed a smile to peek through. "That is all."

Thomas Sheridan was fuming. The assistant district attorney had had the last laugh.

"All right," he said at last, regaining his composure. "That is all. The defense rests."

Cool as a mountain spring, the prosecutor rose to his feet. "Shall we proceed?"

"Yes," answered Judge Corrigan, wiping a tear of laughter from his eye.

The prosecutor called six rebuttal witnesses. One of them, George Kasangian, had been in the procession ahead of the Archbishop. He strode resolutely back to the witness chair.

"You have testified that you ran out of the church and chased somebody," said the A.D.A.

"Yes, sir."

"How were you dressed?"

"White robe."

"The white robe you wore in the procession?"

"Yes, sir." Kasangian said he removed the robe and threw it to the ground, on the steps in front of the church – but not in the alleyway.

Next came Vartan Dirad, the Prelacy secretary who served as interpreter for A.D.A. Cohn and the 34th precinct detectives. He simply defended his competence as a translator. Lt. Donnelly also appeared to swear that the investigation was conducted in a professional and orderly manner.

And finally, Joseph Cohn took the stand. After Kaminsky established his colleague's *bona fides*, he asked Cohn whether anyone had complained about him not doing his duty.

"I object to all this," cried Sheridan. "I think it is a violation of one of the basic rules of the canon of ethics for an attorney in the trial of a case to take the stand, and I object to these statements."

Kaminsky argued that it was perfectly proper and that there was precedent for such testimony.

"Don't be silly," said defense counsel.

"There is a question that is—"

"Don't be playing up."

Finally, the judge was fed up. "Will you stop that!" Sheridan smirked at his opponent. "I mean you," said Corrigan, pointing at the defense attorney. "There has been quite enough of that." He ruled that Kaminsky could continue.

Sheridan accomplished predictably little on cross-examination – hardly making an effort. It was the prosecutor who scored well with the jury on re-direct.

"By any chance, you are not one of the lawyers who got $60,000 from the Tourian Committee that has been testified to on the witness stand?" asked Kaminsky, smiling broadly.

"I don't think so," replied Cohn with equal good humor.

"That is all." Kaminsky turned to the judge. "And that, may it please the court, is the People's case against these nine defendants."

42

Now

After dinner, I dove back into the documents I had amassed in the past week. The newspaper clippings alone made a stack several inches tall. I had copied stories from all the New York City dailies as well as several out of town publications. Unfortunately, there was no evidence of Mr. X in any of those articles. The transcripts were even more impressive – 2,214 pages of verbatim court records. But I knew I wouldn't find the name of the tenth suspect there, either.

Just as I was about to call it a night, Ari called.

"I may have something for you."

I was stunned.

"Can you meet me in the same place tomorrow at noon?"

"Uh huh, sure."

"Ta." He hung up.

I sat there holding the receiver in my hands for what must have been a long time. It was only when I heard the warbling alert tone that I was shaken back to reality. I can't tell you what I was thinking during those several minutes, but I still had a silly grin on my face as I undressed and got into bed.

Damn, I thought to myself. *I'm going to crack this case.*

The restaurant was crowded. Ari and I had to wait fifteen minutes for a table. I kept glancing at him, hoping he would tell me what he knew before lunch. No dice.

On his suggestion, I tried the porterhouse steak. It was quite good, very filling, and more red meat than I had consumed in years. I was sure my colon would never recover. To my astonishment, Ari put away twice as much food as I did, and was thinking about ordering dessert. Amazing.

Finally, over coffee, he looked at me expressionlessly. "So, which do you want to hear first," he asked, "the good news or the bad news?"

I needed a boost. "What's the good news?"

“I have the identity of Mr. X.” He grinned with self-satisfaction. Then, reaching into his shirt pocket, he pulled out a folded piece of paper and slid it across the table. “Or perhaps I should say ‘identities’ as in more than one.

My hands shook visibly as I reached for it. Before I could bring myself to look at what was written on this note, I had to ask. “Identities?”

“Well, as you’ll see, he had an alias.”

I wanted to know everything about how he got this information, if he used any secret agent connections or spy equipment, or whether it was simply a matter of basic research. Had I overlooked the obvious? Rather than asking any of those questions, I unfolded the paper.

And there it was: the name of Mr. X.

43

Then

Thomas Sheridan was one of those rare men who could hold the attention of an audience no matter what he said. Whether it was the timber of his voice or some immeasurable human magnetism, the former New York State Senator had the gift of many great orators.

That said, he also risked relying too heavily on that gift rather than fully preparing for some speeches. Years later, he would regret the degree to which his summation in this case was ad libbed.

"If the court please." Sheridan rose to face the jury box. He held the typed transcript of the trial in his hand.

"Mr. Foreman and gentlemen of the jury. This case has proceeded to trial since June 7th. Now, I think it would be a waste of time, it would be almost an insult to your intelligence for me to take the three volumes of testimony and say, turn to page 363 to some unpronounceable name, that probably after half an hour you would forget the name."

And for the next hour and twenty minutes, the defense counsel cajoled jurors with his analysis of this case. First, he recapped the highlights of the crime itself.

"You are dealing with zealots, extremists, fanatics," he declared, being careful to stay as far from the defendants as possible. "And you are dealing with a type of mind that is just a little bit different from your Western mind."

Then he stood very close to the jury box, modulating his voice to sound confidential. "I don't know who killed the Archbishop. I can say one thing though, that we have shown you in this case that the theory of the prosecution has taken quite a few setbacks."

Sheridan tried to push every emotional button. He mentioned the suffering of the Armenians at the hands of the Turks. After dropping to a nearly inaudible volume, the defense lawyer punctured the air. "You are here to do the highest act known to man: Justice! Justice!"

About halfway through, Alexander Kaminsky startled both opposing counsel and the jurors by interrupting with a factual correction. But Sheridan took it in stride. A few minutes later, the prosecutor did it again by objecting to a misstatement of the law. This time, Sheridan turned on him.

"You have no right to interrupt me now," he bellowed, "and don't do it again!"

Judge Corrigan concurred. But that didn't stop the assistant district attorney from jumping in a third time. Finally, Corrigan reprimanded Kaminsky. Nevertheless, the damage had been done. Sheridan, without a clear plan, limped to the end of his closing argument. Ten minutes later, he stumbled to a stop.

"I thank you for your attention."

It was not yet noon, but the temperature in the courtroom was already unbearable. The defense attorney noticed that he was drenched in perspiration as he sat down.

The judge turned to Kaminsky. "I assume that you would like to follow our plan, to make your speech tomorrow."

"Yes, I would like to. I am not prepared to start today."

Sheridan objected, but it was to no avail. Court was adjourned.

Alexander Kaminsky sat in the catbird seat. He had the prosecutor's traditional advantage of giving the last word, and he had the fresh start of the morning. And he had one more advantage. It was Thursday. Years of personal experience and centuries of collective wisdom told him a jury was more likely to rule in favor of the People when it got the case at the end of the week, rather than the beginning. So, Alexander Kaminsky was quite happy when he rose to deliver his summation.

The prosecutor closed his eyes and silently recited his favorite Latin quotation: *Nunc aut numquam* — now or never.

"May it please the court," he began. In sharp contrast to his opponent, Kaminsky did not make a comparatively quick or seemingly extemporaneous speech. And he made sure that the jury knew that.

"I must begin my address to you by a plea for patience, by a plea for tolerance, and by a plea for indulgence," he said.

And patience, indeed, was what the jury required. The prosecutor went through every witness and every piece of evidence presented over the course of the past five weeks. He started by castigating his adversary.

"Mr. Sheridan's function is just to throw dust, speak of generalities, resort to oratory," said Kaminsky.

On the other hand, the prosecutor heaped praise on defense co-counsel

Joab Banton. He reminded the jury that Banton was not only the former District Attorney of Manhattan, but the man who hired fellow prosecutor Joseph Cohn.

Following such preliminaries, Kaminsky engaged Sheridan in his own rhetoric. "And I tell you that he called the turn when he said, 'Who could kill him?' And I quote his words, 'zealots, extremists, fanatics,' and I point to those nine men and I say to them: zealots, extremists, fanatics."

The defense attorney bristled to have his own remarks used against him. Sheridan decided to fight back with the only weapon left him – interruptions. He repeatedly broke in to ask the prosecutor for page numbers of the testimony quoted in his summation.

But Kaminsky charged ahead. "Now, gentlemen of the jury, let me characterize the defense for you to show how ridiculous it is." The prosecutor spent the next fifteen minutes throwing rhetorical rocks at Sheridan's theories.

At the end of forty-five minutes, A.D.A. Kaminsky asked for a recess, to give jurors a respite from what was going to be one of the longest closing arguments in New York State legal history. Following a five-minute break, the prosecutor worked through all of his witnesses as well as those of the defense. Shortly before one o'clock, everyone was getting antsy. Even Judge Corrigan felt the need to wrap things up. He suggested that they conclude tomorrow.

"I would like to get through today," replied Kaminsky. He promised only forty-five minutes more.

But the clock approached 2 p.m. as the prosecutor reached the last of his summation.

"Now, gentlemen, I am sorry that I have delayed you too long, but the case is an important one, and I want to be fair with you," he said. Kaminsky stood facing the jurors one last time, to drive home his final point.

"I have labored with this case. You have been very, very patient, very kind. I leave you with this last word, that one phrase that summarizes the subject over which volumes may be written: Be true to your oaths, do your duty fearlessly, so that justice may prevail."

The prosecutor bowed slightly to the jury, to the judge, and then walked slowly back to his table and sat down. Four hours.

The next morning, Judge Corrigan issued his jury instructions. They included a rather unusual statement.

"I hate to speak of this, an unpleasant subject for me to touch on – but at various times during the trial…it was said that I had a whimsical appearance on my face." The jurist was determined to maintain a neutral look as he took a deep breath and continued. "Gentlemen, I do not know whether I had or not. If I had, I assure you that it indicated nothing but a fleeting impression, and you should not attach any significance of any kind to it. You should disregard it." Corrigan gave a quick nod to Thomas Sheridan who offered a reciprocal gesture.

At about half past noon, the jurors retired to deliberate. Over the next thirteen hours, they stopped only a few times: once to have the definition of homicide repeated; twice to have some testimony re-read. Shortly after one o'clock in the morning, a bailiff brought the following message to the court clerk:

Jury has reached a verdict.

It was a remarkably quick decision. Everyone hustled back into the courtroom. Despite the hour, there was still a large crowd of spectators. At 1:25 a.m., the clerk began his formal inquiry.

"Please rise, Mr. Foreman. Gentlemen of the jury, have you agreed upon a verdict?"

William S. Schillinger was on his feet. "We have."

"The jurors will please rise," continued the clerk with this formal ceremony. "Jurors, look upon the defendants. Defendants, look upon the jurors. How say you, gentlemen of the jury?"

44

Now

Shadow seemed very happy to see me when I got back to Miami. Ben had taken good care of my feline roommate and I was grateful.

"Dinner is on me, pal."

"At least," he said half-jokingly. "But first, there's something I've got to ask you. Did you find the killer?"

"Maybe you'd better sit down."

I told Ben what I had learned, including the identity of Mr. X. I showed him the piece of paper that Ari Isaacs gave me:

Arsen Arsenian, also known as Hampartzoum Zirakian

"Who the hell—"

"The unnamed defendant," I replied preemptively. "His name was in the original secret grand jury indictment, but removed from the final one. All ten men were charged with first degree murder. It was later amended to list only nine accused killers."

"That—that's great news!" he said enthusiastically.

"Yes, good news."

But judging by my expression of disappointment, Ben must have thought there was more to this story. He was right. "So you wrapped up all the loose ends, right? Now you can write your book?"

"Well, now I know who Mr. X was," I replied. "But—"

I looked away, unwilling to let Ben see all the self-doubt that must have been evident in my face. My trip to New York did not provide very much certainty at all. The only thing I knew for sure was that the assassination of Archbishop Ghevont Tourian didn't solve anything. On the contrary, it was the final straw that broke any hope of reconciliation among the divided Armenian community.

"But was Mr. X the real killer?"

"Probably not," I said. Then I let the other shoe drop. "It's possible none of these defendants killed Tourian." I finally looked back at my neighbor. "I think the jury made the wrong decision."

45

Then

Mateos Leylegian and Nishan Sarkisian were both found guilty of first degree murder, and the other seven defendants were convicted of first degree manslaughter.

Ten days later – July 24, 1934 – court reconvened. On that bright, summer day, the Honorable Joseph E. Corrigan prepared to pronounce sentences. Defense counsel first went through the formality of moving to set aside the verdict.

Mateos Leylegian interrupted his lawyer. “I am innocent,” he said.

“Please, now—” Sheridan tried to calm his client.

Judge Corrigan denied the defense motion and laid out the punishment for the nine convicted men. Leylegian and Sarkisian would die in the electric chair sometime during the week of September 3rd and the other seven defendants would serve a term of ten to twenty years each.

Immediately after sentencing, the Armenian convicts were rushed out of the courthouse and into the state police bus parked behind the building.

46

Now

On a cold, early spring morning in Watertown, Massachusetts, Ara Gureghian stood in front of his red brick, Cape Cod house at the corner of School and Porter streets. Every winter since 1951, he shoveled snow off that driveway, wrestled with the oil burner in the basement, and swore that this winter would be his last one here. Over the years, he had removed many times his weight in the white stuff until his eldest son, Warren, gave the old man a snow blower. He bought it the middle of summer, with the first paycheck from his first job after graduating from high school.

"What the hell am I supposed to do with that?" Ara remembered asking.

"It's a labor-saving device," the son explained. "Think of all the work it'll save me someday," he joked.

"I thought it was a hood ornament for your Rambler, Pop," added Warren's smart-aleck younger sibling, Richard.

Ara was never sure whether to laugh or discipline the boys. Fortunately, it didn't matter. They would both become successful engineers one day. Warren was going to design automotive electrical switches, and Richard's destiny would be in technical sales. Then there would be wives and grandchildren and a nice, quiet retirement for himself and his spouse, Victoria. Soon.

The 66-year-old former shoemaker pulled up the collar on his leather jacket and adjusted the brim of a black fedora. Early this morning, he got a phone call from a lifelong friend. It was long-awaited news that he greeted with both gloom and relief. Without telling anyone, Ara slipped out of the house.

Gureghian walked about a mile to the historic Mt. Auburn cemetery in adjacent Cambridge. Billing itself as "America's First Garden Cemetery," Mt. Auburn was where many Boston-area celebrities were buried. It was not the final resting place for most of Watertown's Armenians. That would be Ridgelawn Cemetery on the other side of town. But those who were better-off liked to have their remains laid to rest near Oliver Wendell Holmes, Henry Cabot Lodge, Henry Wadsworth Longfellow, Mary Baker Eddy – in short, the sort of folks whose station in life merited the routine inclusion of a middle name.

Half an hour later, Ara arrived. He stopped at the entrance to re-light the stub of his cigar, and then moved in past the graffiti on a low concrete wall. "Goddamn neighborhood kids," he cursed in his adopted language and spat.

Waiting a few hundred yards away was Ara's best friend, Mousheg Derderian. He stood at the grave of his own mother. The two men had grown up together on New York's Upper West Side, and both relocated to this suburb of Beantown after the Second World War. Despite their occasional differences, Ara and Mousheg felt a close, unbreakable kinship through their roots. They also shared a mutually deep commitment to justice.

Mousheg began in Armenian, "*Eench gah, chee gah*?" The phrase was usually translated as "What's new?" but literally meant "What is there, isn't there?"

Gureghian talked about his wife and kids. The old woman was still wearing out vacuum cleaners keeping the house constantly spotless. The boys were growing up fast. The younger one was still a troublemaker who nevertheless made his old man proud. Derderian reciprocated with his family stories. It was all prelude, but all vital to bind their tribe.

"He'll be out next week, you know," Mousheg said, finally getting down to business.

Ara nodded. He reached into his pocket and pulled out an awl. The iron tool with its worn wooden handle and curved blade was one of the only souvenirs he had kept from his old shoemaker's shop. He used it to gently clean a spot of dirt from under his left thumbnail.

"I heard he wants to join his brother in California," continued Mousheg, watching Gureghian with bemusement.

"Fresno," said Ara. "My two sisters live there now."

Mousheg nodded.

"I'll leave on Saturday," Ara said.

"You know the time and the place?" It was less of a question than a rhetorical confirmation.

Ara grimaced and grunted twice. They gave each other no details, needed none. The pair put their hands on the upright gravestone in front of them, then made a sign of the cross and sighed.

Gureghian put his arm around the other man's shoulder. "She lived a good life." He fought back a tear.

"*Paree janapahr*," said Derderian, wishing his friend a good trip in their native language.

Ara slept during most of the long, overnight cross-country flight. But it was a fitful sleep. Once, a flight attendant had to wake him because he was shouting something in a language the other passengers did not understand. It was just as well. The Turkish obscenities would have embarrassed a Las Vegas comic.

The jet landed with a thud and everyone was expressively glad to be on the ground again. The travelers quickly deplaned and shuffled through the airport. Ara told no one he was coming, so there were no friends or relatives at the small terminal to greet him. He retrieved his suitcase from baggage claim and moved briskly out the front door.

Gureghian immediately felt the difference in temperature: Fresno was at least 25 degrees warmer than Boston. *Why do I listen to my wife*? He wondered. *We should have moved here long ago.*

Ara approached the lone taxicab at the curb and leaned into the open window.

"Say, mister, do you know where the Armenian cemetery is?"

The toothless cabbie looked at Gureghian a long moment, rubbed his unshaven chin and hummed several times.

"Just a minute, buddy." The driver got out of his vehicle and walked to a uniformed dispatcher sitting on a nearby bench. The two spoke for several minutes, and then the cabbie returned.

"Sure, I can take you there." He opened the door. "It'll cost you ten bucks."

Ara breathed an audible sigh of relief. "OK." He got in.

Fifteen minutes later, the taxi was on a narrow dirt road entering Fresno's Ararat and Masis Armenian cemeteries on the west edge of town, near the Southern Pacific railroad tracks. Both of these burial grounds were dedicated to that ethnic group, shared without discrimination by the various religious and political factions. Finally, in death, they stopped separating themselves.

The taxi parked in front of a small, white painted brick building with a simple sign that read "Office" over the front door. Ara handed the driver a twenty dollar bill – twice the fare.

"Mister, will you please wait for me?"

"You bet, buddy." He smiled a broad, gummy smile.

Gureghian hesitated. While the driver was busy putting the money into his wallet, Ara nervously unzipped the overnight bag and reached inside. He discretely pulled out a small object, slipped it into the left pocket of his jacket, closed up the valise and put it back on the rear seat of the cab.

"I'll be back pretty soon."

"Take your time," chuckled the driver, waving his fare away. "Don't worry. I'll watch your grip."

Ara nodded, then ambled into the cemetery office. A few minutes later, he emerged with the information he needed and strolled off toward a large monument in the center of the grassy memorial park. This ten-foot tall granite obelisk – topped by a brass eagle with wings spread wide and talons clawing a snake – was the grave of Soghomon Tehlirian.

By his own account, Tehlirian shot and killed former Turkish Interior Minister Talaat Pasha – the *Grand Vizir* who ordered the extermination of Armenians in the Ottoman Empire. The assassination happened in a suburb of Berlin, Germany on the morning of March 15, 1921.

> Tehlirian had trailed Talaat to a street near the city Zoo. At 11 o'clock in the morning, he ran up behind the Turk, pulled a revolver from his coat pocket, and then shot him in the head at close range. The execution was purportedly planned and ordered by the *Tashnag* party. A German court subsequently found Tehlirian not guilty.

As Ara approached the elaborate marker, he kept his left hand in the jacket pocket. Only one other person was there. Hearing footsteps, he turned around abruptly. This gaunt fellow was neatly dressed, in his early 70s, balding, with a grey stubble and sallow complexion, but very dark eyebrows. He was an old Armenian who had lived a tough life.

The man stared at Gureghian for quite awhile before recognizing him, smiled weakly and then tentatively extended a hand. The two shook, but neither spoke a word. They stood

nearly touching, breathing each other's air.

At last, Ara broke the silence. "You look well."

The other let out a quiet grunt, then coughed. "Thanks, Ara. How are you?"

Gureghian nodded, shook his head, then nodded a bit more. The second man responded in kind. Their "conversation" went on in this manner for several minutes, saying a lot without speaking at all.

Finally, Gureghian couldn't hold back any longer.

"Tell me the truth. Did you do it?" he asked with some difficulty. "Did you kill Tourian?"

The other stared blankly at Ara for what felt like minutes. Then his words spilled out in a steady stream, with a quiet and deep voice like whiskey on sandpaper.

"What do you think? You were there that day. You know me." He paused and took a deep breath, then extended his right arm to Gureghian, palm upward.

"Ara, I swear by my parents, there is no blood on this hand, but still I am guilty. We were all guilty – for what we did, for what we didn't do. And I'm not sure God's heart is big enough to forgive us. Anyway, what happened, happened." And then he let out a long-stifled belch.

Ara was stunned into silence, cocked his head slightly, blinking back his feelings. Then he nodded. "I see," he replied slowly.

Gureghian squeezed the object hidden in his pocket, held it for a moment, then released his grip. It was the awl. He jerked his empty hand out of the pocket.

"You know, I wanted to kill you back then," said Ara, gesturing angrily. "And now." His voice trailed off. "Now," he started again, made a fist but couldn't finish. He put his hand back into the jacket pocket.

"I know," the other added emotionlessly. "What's the point?"

"But I don't understand. Why?"

He looked at Ara with those same sad eyes, spoke to him in a tragic voice and answered this question for the very last time: "My boy, we were young and we just did what we were told."

47

Then

Sing Sing Prison was built in 1828 along the Hudson River, about 30 miles north of Manhattan – whence comes the expression, "sent up the river." Over the years, this particular penitentiary developed a nasty reputation. But in 1920, Lewis Lawes took over as warden. He transformed the penal facility into a model institution by introducing educational programs, sports teams and even a marching band.

A prison bus arrived at Sing Sing on July 24, 1934 carrying the nine men convicted of killing Archbishop Tourian.

"Empty your pockets," said the officer as he filled out a receiving blotter for each man.

Mateos Leylegian handed over $10.35, and Nishan Sarkisian put $12.25 on the table. The others also surrendered about ten dollars each. Martin Mozian carried nearly fifty dollars and a ring. John Mirijanian turned in the most money – $76.00 cash.

After signing for their property, they were separated according to sentence: Leylegian and Sarkisian went to the death house, while the other seven headed for the general population.

Warden Lawes personally opposed the death penalty, but the law required him to execute the two men convicted of murder. Their trip to the electric chair was scheduled for September 3, 1934. The New York State Court of Appeals rejected efforts to reverse the verdicts of Leylegian and Sarkisian, but Governor Herbert Lehman was more generous. On April 9, 1934, he commuted their sentences from death to life.

The law also provided procedures for sentences to be shortened. So, due to good behavior, Osgan Yarganian, Martin Mozian, John Mirijanian and Mihran Zadigian were released on parole in 1940. Juan Gonzales Tchalikian, Harry Sarafian and Ohanes Adreassian got out the following year.

From 1943 to 1955, Thomas Dewey was Governor of New York. As long as he served in the state house, Leylegian and Sarkisian remained locked up in the "big house." But Dewey's successor was W. Averell Harriman who, among other things, shared the *Tashnag* Party's anti-communist views. Despite vigorous lobbying by Dewey and others, Governor Harriman granted an application for parole. He ordered the Archbishop's convicted murderers to be released by the end of 1958. Within 25 years, all nine men convicted in the Tourian homicide were freed.

On the day he got out, Leylegian had expected his attorney to meet him at Sing Sing. Unfortunately, the lawyer had taken ill, so Mateos had to make his own way back to Manhattan. When he arrived at the attorney's apartment in New York City, the lawyer's wife and newborn infant were home. Leylegian was immediately drawn to the child.

"May I hold him?" asked Mateos.

The mother cautioned him that this baby was always fussy and would probably cry. He took the child in his arms. Rather than cry, it looked at this stranger and smiled. For the first time in many years, Mateos Leylegian felt joy.

48

Now

Unlike old soldiers, aging journalists do die eventually. But I'm not ready to go just yet. As I approach the end of the time of my life, I find myself repeating the famous final words of William Saroyan: "Everybody has got to die, but I have always believed an exception would be made in my case. Now what?"

There was no exception made for Mateos Leylegian. He died in Queens on February 19, 1964.

No exception made for my friend, Bedros Iskenderian, either. He retired after spending twenty years with the New York Police Department. In 1949, he took the wife and kids and moved to Southern California. I'm sorry I never got to see him again. Our last conversation on the telephone was a good one. He reminisced about coming to America as a young man, remembered our time together after the Archbishop's murder, and told me how much he enjoyed retirement.

I decided that Florida was no longer for me. My neighbor Ben passed away, and it was not as much fun to ogle beach bunnies by myself. Every day that I wake up is a gift. After removing my left lung, the oncologist found a suspicious spot on the other side. He gave me six months to live. That was ten years ago. Doctors.

Anna and I had stayed in touch, but her visits were infrequent. I didn't fly anymore. Transcontinental train trips were impractical. Telephone calls and letters were not very satisfying. And e-mail messages? Forget about it. Anyway, I was too old for a long-distance relationship.

Anna persuaded me that we should live in the same time zone, and eventually under the same roof. So, our residence is now the Armenian Home for the Aged in Fresno, California. Yes, I know: My pathological fear of earthquakes should have precluded this eventuality. What can I say? I guess I just got over it. Besides, with a woman like Anna at my side, I can face anything.

After we returned from breakfast this morning, the phone rang. Anna answered.

"You have a visitor," she told me after hanging up.

I was expecting no one, but tried to be sociable. Over the years, I had come to welcome company.

"It's a priest," she said. My mood shifted somewhat to the dark side. Men of the cloth were not always my best friends these days. Ever since writing about the Archbishop's assassination, I felt that I was considered a bit of *persona non grata* – at least in some Armenian churches.

A moment later, there was a knock on the door. The clergyman entered wearing relatively casual clothes and carrying a briefcase.

"Good morning, Mr. Peterson."

This fellow seems young enough to be my grandson, I thought. "Good morning, uh—"

"I'm Father Kabrielian, but please call me—"

"How about *Der Hayr*," I said, suggesting his Armenian title rather than a more casual form of address." He smiled knowingly.

I returned the smile. "What can I do for you?"

He opened his attaché and took out a copy of my book.

"You want an autograph?" I teased.

"Well, actually, yes." The priest paused with embarrassment. "And the answer to a question."

"If I can," I replied. "But I, myself, always have more questions than answers."

"That makes sense for a journalist." The priest handed me the book. "On the other hand, you are probably the only person who can solve this particular mystery."

I grinned and started to think of an appropriate inscription. "All right, *Der Hayr*. I love a good mystery. Shoot." I gestured for my visitor to sit down.

"I read your book from cover to cover. It seems to have every detail about what happened. And still…"

I smiled. "Still?"

"Still, I'm not sure I know." He fumbled a bit. Finally, the priest blurted it out. "Who do you believe killed Archbishop Tourian?"

That was the question: whodunit? It was, strangely enough, the one question I had not answered in my book. Strictly speaking, of course, the court had found nine men guilty. But I always wondered whether the jury had convicted the real killer. Who was really to blame for the brutality that took one man's life and tore asunder an entire community?

"To tell you the truth, I don't know and I don't care."

The priest drew back slightly.

"Please, sit down." The clergyman drew up a chair next to me.

"At first, I suspected that this Mr. X might have been the real killer," I said. "Unfortunately, I never found out why he wasn't charged along with the others. Anyway, it doesn't matter, because he probably didn't kill the Archbishop, either."

Now Father Kabrielian became agitated. Before he could object, I continued to lay out my theories.

"Actually, I did find a strange connection to the Russian secret police. The defense attorney, Sheridan, mentioned it in his opening statement. Frankly speaking, I'm pretty sure the jury never saw the real assassin."

The priest stared slack-jawed. I went on.

"You might remember from the book that the FBI was also aware of some non-Armenian criminal involvement."

"Turkish?" asked Father Kabrielian.

"Italian." I paused to let that sink in. "My guess is that, for some reason, there was a cover-up."

"But the people who did this needed to be brought to justice," he said. "After all, they killed our Archbishop."

I frowned. How strange to hear a man of the cloth talking about the need for earthly punishment. "Unfortunately, father, you fall into the same trap as everyone else. There is no 'us' and 'them.' Anyway, where do you draw the line? Today, it's capital punishment for murder, tomorrow it's armies bombing villages to prevent terrorism."

He quickly caught himself. "Of course, there will also be God's justice in the next life. But don't you think somebody should be held responsible in this life?"

"OK, I'll give you that. On the other hand, we don't necessarily need to know who that person is. Whether any or all of them really murdered the Archbishop will forever be an open question. Besides, it's not the point. Whoever held the knife, that assassination did happen. Even if we do know who actually killed Archbishop Tourian, it changes nothing."

I opened my book, quickly penned an inscription and signed it. Then I took the priest's hand. Anna took my other arm and they helped me get to my feet.

"*Der Hayr*," I said, "you're too young to have heard of him, but there was once a great writer named H.L. Mencken. He said, 'For every complex and difficult problem, there is an answer that is simple, easy and wrong.' I'm sorry to sound so cynical."

The priest looked at me as if I had just told him that there was no Easter Bunny. Then he smiled. "I prefer the Gospel according to John: *And the truth shall set you free*."

We shook hands and I gave the book back to him. Some time later – I don't know when, because I wasn't there to see – Father Kabrielian opened it and read the inscription on the inside front cover: "We are all responsible."

Epilogue

Then

His nickname was Pugnale. In his native language, it meant "dagger." According to the police description, this Italian thug from Chicago stood five feet, two inches tall, weighed 135 pounds, had a dark complexion, brown eyes, dark bushy eyebrows, brown hair and a very receded hairline. According to Elise Siravakian, this man bore a striking resemblance to her husband, Sarkis.

Early on Christmas Eve morning in 1933, Pugnale walked up Audubon Avenue along with five tough-looking Armenian men to the Siravakian apartment. They told Sarkis to meet them at Holy Cross Church around the corner, and then they went there to wait for him.

Half an hour later, Sarkis had still not shown up. As parishioners began to enter the church, Pugnale and the others decided not to wait any longer. They moved inside and took positions in various pews. Pugnale sat five rows from the altar. Next to him was a woman sitting right at the aisle. Shortly before the service started, she took something out of her coat sleeve and slipped it to Pugnale.

> *I knew what was coming next*, the assassin recalled later. *The organist played a loud chord, everybody stood up, turned away from the altar and faced the front door. I watched as a man walked backwards swinging an incense burner. Next came about twenty members of the choir – men and women, girls and boys – all holding candles, all marching solemnly forward.*
>
> *I switch places with the woman, putting me on the aisle. The procession kept moving. They started to pass me. Finally, I saw him – the big man, dressed in all his bejeweled splendor, with gold and green vestments, a tall white miter, carrying a staff in one hand and a cross in the other. He turned from side to side, blessing the congregation. When he reached the fifth row – my row – a pack of men sprung into the aisle, surrounding this clergyman. I wrapped a white handkerchief around the grip of the finely honed, double-edged butcher's knife.*

I drew it out of my coat pocket, hiding it behind my other forearm. I slid into the aisle. I stabbed him twice in the belly, tossed the knife to the other side of the aisle, and retreated behind the human circle surrounding my victim.

Several others began to shout and drew the congregation's attention away from where I stood. As I backed away from the crowd, two tall men screened my movement. They walked with me past the altar and into the vestry. My accomplices blocked the doors as I took off my overcoat, put on a policeman's uniform jacket and hat, and exited directly into a side alleyway. I stepped quickly to the street, turned away from the church, got into a waiting taxi.

Two hours later, the man called Pugnale boarded a train back to Chicago – and got away with murder.

THE END

AUTHOR'S NOTE

I trace the roots of my family tree to Asia Minor. Half of our heritage is Armenian, and the other is Greek. From my mother's side, there is the anecdote about a messenger who brought bad tidings to the King of Armenia in the first millennium B.C. That man was rewarded for his excellent job performance with summary execution. Hence, the old Armenian proverb that says, "He who tells the truth must have one foot in the stirrup."

Then there is my ancestor, Phillipidis (our original surname). He was the legendary Marathon runner who died of exhaustion 2,500 years ago after announcing to Athens, *nenikíkamen* – "We have won!" Both tales are dubious at best, but both contain a kernel of truth. And both underline the need for caution when reporting the news.

I first heard the story of what happened to Archbishop Ghevont Tourian when I was a child. My mother and her family attended the church in New York City where that notorious crime occurred. Not since the 12th century assassination of Thomas à Becket had such a high religious official been murdered at the altar.

Fact or Fiction?

As a journalist, I'm committed to the truth. My dilemma: how best to tell this tale? Writing a fact-based novel turned out to be the most effective way to achieve my goal.

After years of research, I uncovered a lot of previously unreported information about the Tourian case including eyewitness testimony and recollections from the descendants of those portrayed in this book. Much of the trial dialogue is drawn directly from the actual court transcripts. Print and broadcast accounts cited here are authentic.

Honest people can differ as to the interpretation of facts. To the best of my knowledge, nothing I've written conflicts with what actually happened. Nevertheless, this dramatization is not intended to be pure history, nor should the reader treat it as such.

The historical characters named in this book are portrayed as accurately as possible. A few wholly fictitious characters were insinuated among real personalities. The New York Herald Tribune did not provide bylines for the reporter (or reporters) who covered this story. Tom Peterson serves as a composite character; however, most of those with whom he interacts (except, notably, Anna Rosen) were real. The existence of "Pugnale" is inferred from various sources, but cannot be proved based on the available evidence.

Many have expressed concerns about the crowded cast of characters in this tome. The reader will find some guidance in the following section to help alleviate any confusion.

DRAMATIS PERSONÆ

(An asterisk indicates the character is fictitious.)

Aharonian, Vartkes	Son of ex-Armenian President Avedis Aharonian
Amanatian, Arousyag	Child resident of Washington Heights
Andreassian, Ohanes	Defendant Number Nine
Apikian, Araxie	Defense witness
Apikian, Gir	Defense witness
Archibald, Ben*	Peterson's neighbor
Arsenian, Arsen	Unindicted co-conspirator also known as Hampartzoum Zirakian
Ashjian, Haig	Child resident of Washington Heights
Bachman, Herbert S.	Juror
Banton, Joab	Defense Attorney
Bauer, Albert C.	Juror
Boyajian, Anahid	Child resident of Washington Heights
Boyajian, Leo	Child resident of Washington Heights
Callaghan, Al*	U.S. Attorney
Cardashian, Vahan	Defense Attorney
Chakmakian, Dikran	Member of Holy Cross Church
Cohn, Joseph	Assistant District Attorney
Connor, James F.	Juror
Cooper, Jules*	FBI special agent
Corrigan, Joseph E.	Judge of General Sessions Court, Part 5
Crehore, Frank H.	Juror
Dekmejian, Khanem	Member of Holy Cross Church
Demurjian, Sarkis	Deacon of Holy Cross Church
Derderian, Armen*	Ara Gureghian's friend
Desteian, Antranik	Trustee of Holy Cross Church
Dewey, Thomas E.	Private counsel to the Tourian Committee
Dirad, Vartan	Translator and secretary to the Armenian Prelacy

Dodge, William Copeland	New York District Attorney
Donnelly, James	NYPD Lieutenant, 34th precinct
Emerson, Harris P.	Alternate juror
Farese, Vincent	NYPD Detective, 34th precinct
Fiedler, Harry H.	Juror
Garabedian, Hovsep	Bishop and Holy Cross Church pastor
Gonzales, Dr. Thomas	Deputy Chief Medical Examiner
Gorgodian, Kosrof	Archbishop Tourian's bodyguard
Gowrie, Frank	NYPD Detective, 34th precinct
Gureghian, Ara	Shoemaker
Gureghian, Richard	Ara's son
Gureghian, Victoria	Ara's wife
Gureghian, Warren	Ara's son
Hagopian, Manoog	Arax restaurant cook
Hogan, William F.	Juror
Isaacs, Ari Ahmed al-*	Spy
Iskenderian, Bedros	NYPD Officer and temporary detective at 34th precinct
Israelian, Krikor	Member of Holy Trinity Church, Boston
Israelian, Puregh	Member of Holy Trinity Church, Boston
Kabrielian, Father*	Priest
Kafafian, Levon	Member of Holy Cross Church
Kafafian, Siranoush	Member of Holy Cross Church
Kaminsky, Alexander	Assistant District Attorney
Kasangian, George	Deacon of Holy Cross Church
Keosayian, Kalouste	Choir boy at Holy Cross Church
Kerschner, Richard*	Lawyer
Lagarenne, John	NYPD Captain, 34th precinct
Lawes, Lewis	Warden of Sing Sing Prison
Lehman, Herbert	Governor of New York
Leylegian, Matios	Defendant Number One
Loughran, William	District Attorney staff photographer

McDonald, Mary*	Peterson's friend
Meehan, Charles	Alternate juror
Minassian, Nishan	Censer bearer of Holy Cross Church
Mirijanian, John	Defendant Number Seven
Montgomery, Alexander*	FBI special agent
Moradian, Dr. Bob*	Member of Holy Cross Church
Moradian, Margaret*	Member of Holy Cross Church
Moritz, Herman	Juror
Mozian, Martin	Defendant Number Four
Peterson, Thomas G.	*Reporter
Poochigian, Armen*	Tourian's childhood friend
Powell, Howard L.	Juror
Proudian, Aram	Defense witness
Roosevelt, Franklin D.	President of the United States
Rosen, Anna*	Peterson's friend
Sarafian, Harry	Defendant Number Six
Sarkisian, Nishan	Defendant Number Two (a.k.a. Nishan Tuktikian)
Schillinger, William S.	Jury foreman
Schmarion, Herman	NYPD Stenographer
Sheridan, Thomas I.	Defense Attorney
Simsarian, Dicran	Attorney for Tourian Committee
Siravakian, Elise	Resident of Washington Heights (Nishan's wife)
Siravakian, Nishan	Resident of Washington Heights (Elise's husband)
Smith, Robert W.*	FBI Special Agent in Charge
Spenrath, Octavius	Juror
Stepan, Father*	Priest
Strauss, Carl	Juror
Streyckmans, Major Felix	Chicago Int'l. Expo Committee Chairman
Sutton, Willie	Bank robber

Tchalikian, Juan Gonzales	Defendant Number Five
Thomas, Lowell	Journalist and commentator
Tourian, Bedros	Poet and Ghevont Tourian's cousin
Tourian, Ghevont	Archbishop of Armenian Apostolic Church born "Karnig Tourian" also known as "Levon Tourian" or "Leon Tourian"
Tourian, Yeghishé	Patriarch and Ghevont Tourian's uncle
Uberlacker, Charles	NYPD Patrolman, 34th precinct
Walker, Stanley	New York Herald Tribune city editor
Waters, Harold L.	Juror
Yarganian, Osgan	Defendant Number Three
Zadigian, Mihran	Defendant Number Eight
Zadikian, Garabed	Member of Holy Cross Church

PHOTO CREDITS

Unless otherwise noted, all images listed below are in the public domain.

Page 4	Ara Gureghian (Courtesy of the Gureghian Family)
Page 12	Holy Cross Church
Page 12	Archbishop Tourian
Page 15	Holy Cross Church
Page 24	Arrest of Leylegian and Sarkisian, *New York Herald-Tribune* (Dec. 25, 1933) The Queens Borough Public Library, Long Island Division, the *New York Herald-Tribune* Photograph Collection.
Page 25	Nishan Siravakian (Courtesy of George Siravakian)
Page 26	Tourian's mother
Page 34	Young Tourian
Page 46	Tourian's Tomb © 2008 Terence G. Phillips
Page 46	Tourian's vestments © 2008 Terence G. Phillips
Page 79	ARF emblem
Page 88	Front page, *New York Herald-Tribune* (Dec. 25, 1933) The Queens Borough Public Library, Long Island Division, the *New York Herald-Tribune* Photograph Collection.
Page 96	Mateos Leylegian mug shot
Page 127	Holy Cross Church floor plan
Page 132	Tourian lying in repose
Page 152–153	Defendants
Page 225	Convicted killers on a bus to Sing Sing prison
Page 226	Ara Gureghian (Courtesy of the Gureghian Family)
Page 229–230	Tehlirian Monument © 2008 Terence G. Phillips

ACKNOWLEDGMENTS

Unlike the loaf of bread in the story of the little red hen, this book was made possible only with the help of many others. For their professional services, I thank the following:

Dr. Brett Schmoll of California State University, Bakersfield, generously applied his expertise as a professor of English and history to my original manuscript. If this novel has any literary merit, it is due largely to his superb editing. **Chris Slattery** who, despite being immersed in a major career change, once again contributed his invaluable talent as cover designer. **Zand Gee** added her artistic touch and magically transformed the pages of a manuscript into the pages of this book. **Maranda May-Miller, Harris Miller** and **Sylvia Kratins** at P.E.G. Solutions patiently saw this project through to the end.

Thanks to my friends and colleagues: **Peter Laufer** first planted the crazy idea in my head that I could write a book…then insisted I do so…and (along with his wife **Sheila Swan Laufer**) graciously offered help and encouragement all along the way. Thanks for the soup, Sheila! **Mark Boyce** (along with his wife **Colleen**) gave me early assurances that I might really be a writer…but never let me stray too far from the straight and narrow path of truth.

I also had tremendous guidance before typing the first word of this book:

Albert Eisele, Editor-at-Large of *The Hill*, provided the literary equivalent of mid-course corrections at a time when I thought the manuscript was ready for final landing instructions. **Linda Braun** and the staff of the New York State Library at Albany found the original trial transcripts previously believed lost. My thanks also to **Evan Simpson** for his diligent reproduction of those documents, and to **Tara McCarthy** for sifting through the Rare Books and Special Collections at the University of Rochester to find previously unpublished documents revealing the details of Thomas Dewey's involvement in the Tourian case. Special Agent **Matthew Bertron** provided important background information about the FBI. The Bureau also made available previously classified material pursuant to a Freedom of Information Act request. NYPD Deputy Chief **Steven J. Silks** lent insight into to the Department's history and procedures.

I'm very grateful for help from many members of the Armenian community who opened their hearts and told their stories. I especially want to thank:

Ghevont "Joe" Tourian (grand nephew of the slain Archbishop) and the **Rev. Dr. George Leylegian** (grand nephew of the Archbishop's convicted assassin), both of whom offered unique insights into their families' histories; and **Dr. Dickran Kouymjian**, whose impeccable academic credentials as well as his personal connections to this story supplied essential details and credibility. **Rev. Fr. Stepanos Doudoukjian** shared his master's thesis including interviews with Armenian residents of Washington Heights and their descendants. **Rev. Fr. Shahé Altounian** and **Rev. Fr. Sarkis Petoyan** provided invaluable details about the inner workings of the Armenian Church. **Dr. Levon Boyajian** (along with his wife **Gloria** as well as his sister and brother-in-law **Anahid** and **Jirair Manoukian**) added great humanity to this story. **Meher Chekerdemian** shared his deep knowledge of the Armenian Revolutionary Federation. **Prof. James Russell** of Harvard University provided an early academic briefing. While not ethnically Armenian, his deep knowledge and interest certainly earn him honorary membership.

I'm also grateful for inspiration from these dearly departed mentors: **Herbert Baghdassarian**, who (as Armenia's top photojournalist) shared his wisdom and his friendship; **Rick Cimino**, who (along with his wife **Nikki**) taught me to look within for the truth – and to value a good laugh; **Jerome Lawrence**, who advised me to be a writer, not a "wrote" – and whose play "Inherit the Wind" taught me the value of free thinking; and **Jack Finney**, whose illustrated novel "Time and Again" showed me how to place modern characters in historical settings.

Thanks also to: **Richard Isaacs**, whose hospitality made Manhattan affordable as well as accessible; to **Jonathan Sanders** for sharing his unparalleled knowledge of New York City to make me a little less of a rube; to **George Schmitt**, my erstwhile boss who afforded me the luxury of time following our brief but profitable sojourn into the land of high technology; to **Jack**, **Diane** and **Angela McIlvain**, whose friendship is always appreciated; to **Don Howe** for reminding me to make my words relevant; and to **Robert McGlynn** for never letting me forget to tell important stories.

Thanks to everyone at **Valley Public Radio** for keeping me sane – and employed – as I finished writing this book.

Very special thanks go to my mother, **Venus** – without whom nothing else in life would be. Although this book is formally dedicated to Dad's memory, I really wrote it for you. My sister, **Genese**, always accepts me as I am. Although I'm your big brother, I'll always admire you more. You're awesome, Totzig! My godmother, **Isabelle Kabrielian**, (along with my late godfather **Albert**) provided a foundation of morality upon which life should be lived. My cousin, **Richard Gureghian**, (along with his wife **Nelly** as well as daughters **Tamar** and **Melanie**) shared precious memories of his father **Ara**.

To the **Erysian family – Bill, Siran, John and Vera,** as well as their spouses and children – my gratitude for our lifelong friendship.

My cat, **Phyllis**, reminds me to get away from the keyboard from time to time.

Lastly and most gratefully, to my muse, **Jo** – for everything!

COLOPHON

The typeface for this book is 11-point Janson Text. It was created by the 17th century Hungarian punch-cutter Nicolas Kis, although mistakenly named after Dutch printer Anton Janson. This type came to prominence during the 1930s as the face of choice for fine bookmaking.

The title font is an ultra compressed version of Helvetica. The name is derived from the Latin for Switzerland. It was created in 1957 by Swiss graphic designer Max Miedinger.

The Armenian-language font on the back cover is called "Masis," a freeware truetype created in the early 1990s by Raffi Kojian. Masis is the local name commonly used for Mt. Ararat in Armenia.

The book was printed and bound on 60-pound, Joy White, 30% recycled paper stock by Thomson-Shore, Inc., an employee-owned book manufacturing company in Dexter, Michigan.

PASS IT ON...

If you enjoyed reading **Murder at the Altar**, please tell others about it. Why not buy copies as gifts? You can order them from your local book seller or directly from the publisher. Quantity discounts are available on bulk purchases, as well as for educational purposes.

Hye Books
P.O. Box 12492
Bakersfield, CA 93389
(661) 835-1497
www.HyeBooks.com

The author is also available for public speaking and book signing.